MERRIE HASKELL

The Princess Curse

HARPER
An Imprint of HarperCollinsPublishers

Library of Congress Cataloging-in-Publication Data
Haskell, Merrie.
The princess curse / by Merrie Haskell. — 1st ed.
    p. cm.
Summary: Thirteen-year-old Reveka, an herbalist's apprentice in the Middle
Ages, attempts to break the mysterious curse on the princesses of Sylvania
and instead discovers a door to the Underworld.
ISBN 978-0-06-200813-8 (trade bdg.)
[1. Fairy tales. 2. Blessing and cursing—Fiction. 3. Princesses—Fiction.
4. Herbs—Fiction. 5. Magic—Fiction.] I. Twelve dancing princesses. English.
II. Title.
PZ8.H2563Pr 2011   2010040424
[Fic]—dc22   CIP
                                                                             AC

Typography by Andrea Vandergrift
11 12 13 14 15 LP/RRDB 10 9 8 7 6 5 4 3 2
❖
First Edition

The
Princess
Curse

For Dann and Kayla,
with much love and extreme snark

ROMANIAN WORDS THAT APPEAR IN THIS STORY:

balaur (bah-law-ow-er): a type of dragon, less human and more draconic

căpcăun (kup-kahn): a dogheaded ogre

doamnă (doh-ahm-nah): a lady, a gentlewoman

doamnule (dwahm-noh-lay): lord, sir

hultan (hool-tun): a wizard (plural: *hultani*)

Muma Pădurii (moo-mah pah-do-ree): an old "witch of the forest" fairy-tale character who enslaves and eats children

stăpână (stah-pih-nah): a term of respect, somewhere between "lady" and "mistress"; a step down from *doamnă*, but significantly stepped up from *nevastă* ("wife")

zmeu (dzmeh-you): in addition to being a type of dragon with a humanoid shape, *zmeu* is also the Romanian word for "kite" (as a kite flies like a dragon) (plural: *zmei*)

CHAPTER 1

Three days after my thirteenth birthday, Armas, the Executioner and Chief of Prisons, came for me while I ate breakfast.

"Apprentice," Armas said, his cold voice freezing the thyme pie in my throat. "Princess Consort wants you."

Cook whispered behind me, "Too many pies." I almost erped with worry. I didn't think they actually jailed people for eating too much in Sylvania, but they probably did punish new apprentices for insubordination. And I had been a tad insubordinate to my master.

I slid from my stool, feeling stiff and weak. But I held my head high and marched ahead of Armas into the courtyard while the castle kitchen burst into excited chatter behind us. My stomach knotted and tumbled harder, and I wished for a pinch of mint to settle it.

Halfway across the courtyard, I asked Armas, "Did

·1·

the Princess Consort say why—?"

"Oh, sure," Armas said. "Princess Consort tells me just everything."

I fell silent. I'd not known him to be capable of such sarcasm.

We stepped into the great hall, and I said, "I don't suppose my father . . ." But then my eyes adjusted to the dimness, and I saw Pa, waiting beside the dragon-kidnaps-a-maiden tapestry, chewing at the ends of his black mustaches.

Every step across the great hall seemed to take more effort than it should have. Pa nodded to Armas and said, "I've got her." My heart fell at his tone, and I stared at the tapestry to hide my worry. I wasn't going to be able to lie my way out of this, whatever it was. Armas, maybe, I could lie to. Armas, maybe, I could trick into mercy. But with Pa, there would be no chance to lie. Or even to stretch the truth into a pleasing shape.

I noticed a snagged thread on the tapestry maiden's pale cheek. It marred her face, though she was too frightened of the dragon to be pretty—and it wasn't just any dragon, but a fire-breathing *zmeu*, trying to kiss her.

Armas gave me into Pa's custody and went to inform the Princess Consort that I'd arrived. I stood there. Waiting. My favorite thing. I poked at the snag on the tapestry, trying to push it through to the other side of the cloth, mostly to avoid looking at Pa.

"Well, Reveka?" Pa asked. He spoke in his warning voice, the voice that had once caused thousands of men to shake in their boots but now mostly kept a lot of junior gardeners attentive to their shovels.

"I know your rule, Pa," I said, exasperated but trying to sound calm.

Like I would lie right in front of Pa.

I poked harder at the thread. It wanted to go through. It wanted to disappear.

"It's not just a rule, Reveka."

"I know. It's also a promise." I wrinkled my nose, trying not to think why I'd had to promise Pa never to lie. I twisted the snagged tapestry threads together, hoping that would make them look smaller, at least.

Pa swatted my hand away from the tapestry. "You'll unravel the whole thing, and you've no skill to put it back together." I still wouldn't face him, so he grabbed hold of my chin to make me meet his eye. "You need not be truthful for my sake, but your own. What kind of reputation do you want to have around the castle, and with the Princess Consort?"

I didn't have a chance to answer before Armas came out of the solar. He gave Pa a deep nod, then ambled away. A minor relief: Armas wasn't standing by to drag me off for a beating.

Of course, Pa had a strong arm, too.

Giving me the tight grimace that was supposed to be

his smile, Pa guided me into the Princess Consort's solar.

Princess Daciana, Prince Vasile's child bride, sat sewing in a pool of morning sunlight, a red-and-black military banner spilled across her lap. She looked so calm and regal, it was hard to remember that she'd been Princess Consort for only two years, since she had turned thirteen. It would be like me getting married this year—except the common folk don't marry so young, being more sensible than the higher folk.

Brother Cosmin stood by, looking half scarecrow, half asleep, and completely annoyed. Brother Cosmin was the herbalist of Castle Sylvian, and my master, and if anyone had a grievance against me, it was probably him. Still, I hadn't thought that he'd take my arguments about herbs so personally, as such a challenge that he'd drag me before the Princess Consort for punishment. He didn't look happy to be here, though. Maybe because it was before noon.

Pa went to stand beside Brother Cosmin, leaving me to face the Princess.

"So, Konstantin? This is your daughter?" Princess Daciana asked.

"Her name is Reveka, Highness," Pa said, while I folded my hands in my apron and examined the red and black dragons painted on the high ceiling beams. Dragons were Prince Vasile's heraldic animal, and dragons twined all over Castle Sylvian, carved into doorways, woven into carpets. They were even embroidered onto the hem of Princess Daciana's dress.

"Reveka," the Princess Consort said, holding a needle in the air between us and squinting at me through the tiny eye. "Tell me how you chose the herbs for my stepdaughters' bath this morning." She stabbed a spit-smoothed thread through the needle's eye and bent her head to continue sewing.

I stared at her. This was about the bath herbs? I was having an interview with the Princess Consort about *bath herbs*? A memory came to me from earlier this morning. When the princesses—Princess Daciana's stepdaughters, all twelve of them older than she—had entered the bath, Princess Maricara had sniffed the air and asked Marjit the Bathwoman if she'd been eating cabbage soup. I hadn't stayed to hear the answer. I hadn't thought anything of it, really. Cabbage has a strong smell, but—

Brother Cosmin frantically billowed the brown sleeves of his robe in my direction, urging me to answer.

"The cabbage was supposed to reduce the princesses' vigor," I said.

The Princess Consort frowned. Oops—I'd left off her honorific. I mumbled, "Mostnobleserenehighness," and curtsied poorly.

The Princess coughed spasmodically. I wondered if her lungs were wet. She *looked* healthy; no roses of illness bloomed in her cheeks. Too bad. I knew some impressive herbs to ease the pains of consuming sicknesses.

"How, pray tell, did concern about their vigor bring you to make my stepdaughters smell like—and I quote Princess Lacrimora—'hill cottagers at sup'?"

Oh, Easter!

"Well," I said in my best Professional Herbalist voice, "cabbage cures inflammations. It calms swellings in the liver, where the soul dwells, and the brain, where the animal feelings arise. So. Cabbage might help the princesses sleep right through the nightly effects of the curse. That way . . ." I trailed off, suddenly acutely conscious that the Princess had abandoned her banner to a crumpled pile in her lap and was regarding me curiously.

I added, "I didn't think the smell would be a problem."

The Princess Consort compressed her lips. "I'm glad to have someone working on the princesses' plight, Reveka, but you must refrain from making their bathwater smell like soup—or stew, or any sort of kitchen-made item—in the future. My stepdaughters are princesses. Tonight they must charm the Saxon delegation, for Princess Tereza is to meet her betrothed. We cannot have anyone smelling like cabbage rolls."

"Yes, Most Noble and Serene—"

"And, of course, that is simply no way to go about breaking a curse, either. Curses don't like to be broken."

She tapped her thin nose delicately. "Subtlety, Reveka. A curse should never smell you coming."

"Of course, Most Noble—"

"Now then, your punishment. You must apologize to Marjit the Bathwoman, who was so distressed by what occurred this morning."

I waited for her to continue, but she didn't. "That's all?" I blinked, surprised.

Pa shook his head at me in warning, but the Princess smiled. "That is all, Reveka. You and Brother Cosmin may go."

I was astonished. I'd had no clue what I'd done wrong when I was summoned—though that wasn't so unusual a circumstance in my lifetime—and I had expected the worst. But apologizing to Marjit was barely a punishment! Though that didn't mean that Brother Cosmin and Pa might not each have something extra in mind for me later, just to make sure I understood my transgression.

I glanced at Pa as I turned to follow Brother Cosmin out. I knew I should bolt with my collecting basket and spend the day conveniently absent while I gathered mushrooms and wild herbs. But we'd been at the castle for only a few weeks, so I didn't really know the forest. Still, it would put me out of Pa's way. The Princess Consort was holding him behind to talk, and I had time to clear out.

I was three steps ahead of Brother Cosmin when I

heard my name. Pa and the Princess were talking about me? I checked my stride and stepped slower, letting Brother Cosmin pass. And when I reached the door of the solar, I didn't follow him out into the great hall but slid behind the dragon-kidnaps-a-maiden tapestry.

I didn't hear my name again. Pa and the Princess Consort were talking about ditches and earthworks. Pa is the castle's head gardener, which makes it sound like he spends all his time with plants and trees; but gardeners are also in charge of dirt, and digging, and ditches, and earthworks, and ramparts, and everything involving dirt. Pa was known as a magician of fortification. Though it wasn't magic; it was just understanding how geometry and dirt could best be used for aiming defensive cannons and deflecting the enemy's fire.

Pa said, "The tunnel under the southern rampart collapsed again."

"I believe that means we're close," the Princess said. "Try again, Konstantin. The Hungarians *suggest* that the succession be set by autumn, and if we don't have the possibility of an heir by then, I'm sure Corvinus will march on us."

"Corvinus has problems with his own succession," Pa said. "He'd do well to turn his attention there."

"Corvinus expanded his kingdom by interfering in the affairs of other princes. Dig faster. We have *no time*."

If Pa answered that, it was with a nod or gesture, because then the Princess said, "And Reveka?"

Me?

Pa's reply was flat. "No."

No? No what?

The Princess sighed. "The cabbage incident tells me she wishes to help, Konstantin."

"Highness, I beg you: Do not confuse her childish impulse with a calling."

"This cannot be the great soldier Konstantin! I thought you seized any opportunity, and every opportunity."

"We have better—wiser—options than my impetuous daughter." I thought about taking offense at this, but then the Princess Consort dismissed Pa, and I panicked. Pa was going to catch me eavesdropping! While the tapestry hid me from the hall, he would see me standing in the gap between the cloth and the wall when he came out of the solar.

I sidled deeper into the shadows and squinched my eyes tight so he wouldn't see their gleam, and maybe also hoping, just a little bit, that I'd be invisible to him.

A hand clamped down on my arm.

So much for willing myself invisible.

CHAPTER 2

P a was very patient: He jerked me out from behind the tapestry and dragged me across the great hall, outside past the herb gardens, and through the castle gates into the plum orchard before yelling.

"Reveka!" he cried, shaking me a little. I stared at him with wide eyes, waiting for the verdict. Pa and I had been scraping along together for only a couple of years, since he'd retrieved me from the convent where Ma had left me when she died. Ofttimes, he didn't seem to know what to do with me.

I didn't know what to do with him, either, though I liked him well enough. Altogether, he beat me less than the Abbess had, and only then for breaking the eighth commandment. Lying, in Pa's view, was much worse than killing. But maybe that was because Pa was a soldier before he became a gardener, so he couldn't think too badly of killing.

"I told the Princess the truth, Pa," I said. "I didn't lie, even a little!"

"I know," he said.

I frowned. Why was he so angry with me, if he knew I hadn't broken my promise to him?

"And I'm—I'm very sorry I made the princesses smell like hill cottagers. I *am*. Very sorry."

"I'm sure you are."

"It's just—the curse. Everyone talks about the curse, and no one *does* anything. And the dowry is just sitting there, waiting." I needed that dowry, far more than the curse needed lifting.

I'd no idea how the curse had started, but the biggest problem with it was that Prince Vasile didn't have a son. If his line didn't produce a male heir before he died, the rule of the principality would be fought over by all his neighbors. Which was bad enough, but with the Turkish Empire on one doorstep and the Hungarians on the other, Sylvania would become no more than a tattered, puppet-ruled client state.

Even with three wives, the Prince had never gotten a son. The first wife had produced a couple of daughters, the Princesses Maricara and Tereza, then promptly died. The second had died before doing that much. And the third Princess Consort wasn't a mother yet after two years.

However, Prince Vasile had managed to have ten additional daughters by eight different women outside of consecrated wedlock. This shocked me when I first learned of it. I'd thought that God would not so bless women who had not received the sacrament of marriage—but Brother Cosmin said, "No, by Easter, what did those nuns teach you?" Brother Cosmin, like monks everywhere, didn't respect nuns much.

At some point, years ago, Prince Vasile had brought all his daughters to live with him at Castle Sylvian, so that he could marry them off and get grandsons to keep the principality safe. He even ennobled the illegitimate daughters, no matter how common their mothers, including Ruxandra and Rada, daughters of a tavern wench, and Otilia, who'd grown up in a mill.

But shortly after the princesses started living together in the castle, the curse came upon them. And nobody wanted to marry women, even princesses, who lived under the effects of a curse, even a silly one.

And it *was* a silly curse, wasn't it? Every morning, the princesses left their tower bedroom, exhausted, with their shoes in tatters. It was inexplicable, and it scared away all the nobles and aristocrats and royals and knights and squires—in short, everyone of gentle birth who would be even a tiny bit worthy of marrying a princess.

The curse so vexed Prince Vasile that he issued a decree:

The first man who could solve the problem of the shoes would be married to the princess of his choice, no matter what his birth, age, or rank. Even if the chosen princess was one of Vasile's royal and legitimate daughters. Even if the curse breaker was a humble cowherd.

And if the curse breaker was a woman? For her, a fabulous dowry awaited, to allow her to marry whoever she wanted. Or, I hoped, to join whichever convent she liked. It cost a lot of money to join a convent, unless one was "a highly promising candidate." I'd been raised by nuns, who had made it clear to me that I *wasn't* promising. But I *could* become rich.

"The curse is dangerous," Pa said, "and I don't want you mucking about with it."

"But Pa, it's the stupidest curse in existence! So what if the princesses are sleepy during the day and their slippers are holey in the morning? It's a curse of *shoes and naps*. It's a mystery, I'll grant you—Marjit the Bathwoman says that no one ever hears anything when they listen at the princesses' door, and that anyone who spends the night in the princesses' chamber falls right asleep and doesn't wake up."

"Marjit is correct."

"I wouldn't fall asleep," I boasted. "If you left me in there overnight, I'd figure it all out and save all the shoes."

"No, Reveka!" Pa threw up his hands. "No one cares about the shoes! That's not why people call it a curse. Did you not understand what Marjit said? They *never waken.*"

"She meant they never waken through the night and see what happens to the shoes . . . right?"

"No!" Pa closed his eyes, sucking in a deep breath before opening them again, whirling me around, and steering me toward the castle. "Come along."

Pa marched me double time between the front gate's dragon carvings and up to the western tower, which was shorter and wider than the eastern tower that served as the princesses' bedroom. Pa pushed me through a squeaky little oak door into a room.

The room was full. Row upon row of men and women, lying head-to-foot on straw pallets, spread before me. On the other side of the room, by a tiny hearth, an old woman sat in a rockered chair, netting socks. She looked up when we entered. She did not smile.

The room smelled of silence and stone—like a cathedral after the incense smoke has drifted away. It didn't smell as if dozens of people crowded into one space together.

I stared at the bodies lying on the pallets, each one abnormally still, with none of the snoring and scratching and farting normal people do when they sleep.

They fall asleep and never waken.

Pa tried to pull me back out of the room, but I shrugged away to kneel beside one of the bodies—a girl with alabaster skin and straight brown brows. I reached to touch her but paused, hesitant, noticing that I couldn't really see her chest move. "Is she alive?" I asked the old woman.

The woman set aside her netting and leaned forward. "You are the herb-husband's new apprentice, yes? As well as the gardener's daughter," she said, her voice as cracked as her face. "So you've finally come to see the dead-alive?"

I didn't know how to answer that tactfully, so I asked, "They never waken? No matter what?"

"Stick them with pins and they don't jump. Thunder and handclaps alike never disturb their dreams. Neither does fire or water awaken them."

I put aside my horror to think like an herbalist. "Have you tried rubbing their limbs with oil of rosemary? What effect has pepper blown into their nostrils?"

"I try the rosemary every week, and ground black pepper rouses them not at all." The woman looked expectant and eager, like she was curious to know what I would ask next.

Normally, I'd have been gratified to be taken seriously, but it worried me. Things were in a dreadful state indeed if people hoped for miracles from an apprentice herbalist.

I avoided her eager eyes by examining the girl more closely. She might have possessed all of thirteen years, just like me. "Do they ever . . . die on you?"

"I feed them nourishing soups," the old woman said. "Drip, drip, drip it down their throats, then massage their necks until they swallow. I swaddle them like babies and change their wrappings regularly. That is what I can manage, and it is enough for most of them. But in spite of all that, some do go around the corner alone. I never can predict which ones will go—young or old, newly fallen or asleep for years. . . ."

I shivered. The girl's sleeping face was untroubled, and her breathing so slow I could barely hear it with my ear practically pressed to her nose. She looked like a saint's corpse, dead but incorrupt. As though she would never rot. As though she would exist, always, just like this.

"How did this happen?" I whispered.

"They dared to look upon the princesses," the old woman said, "when the princesses were not wanting to be looked upon."

I didn't say anything. Neither did anyone else for a long time. Then Pa stirred behind me. "Reveka. Brother Cosmin will be wanting you."

"Yes, Pa," I said, rising to my feet. But before I followed him out the door into the living castle, I paused. "*Stăpână*," I said respectfully, "I'm sorry, I don't know your name."

"I am Adina. And this is my daughter, Alina." She gestured to the woman at the end of the row closest to her. "And that's Iulia." She pointed to the girl I'd been examining.

I asked, very politely, "*Stăpână* Adina, would it be all

· 16 ·

right if I brought some herbs to try to wake . . . them?"

"Try your best," Adina said indifferently, taking up her netting again. She didn't seem interested in me anymore, now that I had one foot out the door. I wondered how many people promised to come—and didn't.

Pa let me catch up with him outside. "Those people back there, Reveka? Those are the ones who don't disappear," he said.

"Disappear?"

"Some go into the princesses' tower and never return."

"What, are they *eating* people?"

Pa raised an eyebrow. "They leave no bones if they do. But—*now* do you see, Reva? Do you see the curse for what it is? Why you should leave it alone? Why you should not treat it as a lark, and why you should not play games with your herbs?"

"Yes, Pa, I see," I said. It wasn't a lie. I *did* see. I saw exactly why it was that I had to try even harder to break the curse of Castle Sylvian and win my dowry.

CHAPTER 3

When we had arrived at Castle Sylvian three weeks before—having walked all the way from Moldavia—I'd been disappointed to discover that the resident herb master already had an apprentice. But Brother Cosmin took me on anyway. At first I'd been pleased, but then I realized he did so because I was already well trained in herbalism by the convent, and he could lie abed longer if he had me do half his work.

The other half of his work had already settled on the shoulders of his first apprentice, Didina. When my pa had said that Brother Cosmin would be wanting me that morning, he was mistaken. It was Didina who would want me. Brother Cosmin went back to bed after the audience with the Princess Consort.

I am being truthful here, and not bad-mouthing Brother Cosmin out of dislike or something—but of his vows of chastity, obedience, and poverty, it was hard to tell which he took least seriously. He was a goodish man, a bad monk, and a middling herbalist—he thought betony was the best cure for *everything*.

"Where have you been?" Didina asked, frazzled. She was fourteen, a year older than me, though she'd been learning her art less long. "I've not seen Brother Cosmin all morning."

I hurried in, past Brother Cosmin's shelf of wondrous books (*seven* herbals, four of them press printed!), and settled down at my worktable. "Princess Daciana had a question about an ingredient in the princesses' bath herbs this morning."

"A question—why? What did you put in?"

"Wild cabbage."

She obviously didn't see the significance. "That's a terrible bath herb," she told me, and went back to powdering betony for Brother Cosmin.

I sighed. Betony is a fine plant. Some people call betony heal-all, but to me, it represents the lazy kind of healing, like the barbers who think that opening up a vein is good for every disorder, even for wounded soldiers gushing blood.

The whole of betony, from root to flower, is medicinal, and it *is* good for fevers, spasms, peeing more, peeing less, high blood, bad stomachs, worms, flatulence, excessive bleeding, and even wounds. But betony works much better paired with a second, complementary herb, and it's not suitable for *everything*, nor is it always the *best* cure.

But I was determined to behave, so I resolved not to take up the betony conversation with either Didina or Brother Cosmin again for at least a week. I owed the monk for showing up in the solar at all, even though he hadn't actually spoken in my defense—and frankly, I had worried that perhaps my diatribes against the excessive use of the plant were what had gotten me summoned by the Princess in the first place.

I worked hard the rest of the day. I took dried rose petals to the laundresses to layer in with the clean clothing. I made up hair rinse of rosemary and nettles for half the castle. I helped Didina powder wormwood to deter mice, pennyroyal to repel fleas. I made a batch of sore-leg ointment for Brother Cosmin's donkey, who was getting on in years.

When Brother Cosmin finally showed up, he directed me to make up sachets of southernwood and tansy to keep moths at bay. I gathered day's-eyes, lemon balm, and santolina for the footmen to mix with sweet rushes for the floor of the great hall, and savory, rosemary, rue, and roses for the aromatic posies the princesses carried every evening.

After this, the monk spent some time teaching us to

work with clover root and cherry bark to make a remedy for coughs.

When he stepped out for the privy, Didina said, "Brother Cosmin told me why you put the wild cabbage in the bathwater, Reveka. You'd best stay away from the princesses."

I set my jaw mutinously and continued pounding apart the threads of a clover root with my pestle.

"You don't know how many people have been lost," she continued. "It's not worth it."

"The dowry's not worth it?" I asked. "Because it *seems* worth it—not to have to marry some clod who'll make you bear too many babies, or not to live alone and have no one to care for you in your old age. . . ."

"Some clod—? What do you want a dowry for, if not to get married?"

"I want to join a convent, of course."

"Oh." Didina measured out the cherry bark she'd just powdered. "I'm sorry. I didn't realize you had a spiritual calling."

I was ashamed to admit that I didn't, so I skipped answering that. "I want to be the herbalist for an entire abbey," I told Didina. "I want to have my own herbary. My own apprentices." *To write a great herbal,* I thought, but I didn't tell her that. It seemed more like a dream than a real plan.

She squinted at the powder she had made. "That takes

a lot of money, you know. Only rich women join that kind of abbey."

"I know," I said, and pounded harder at my clover root. I'd known since I was a small child that the nuns weren't going to take me without a dowry, and I'd barely dared dream of my own herbary—a whitewashed room filled with northern sunlight and tall drying cabinets, where I reigned as mistress and none gainsaid my method for preparing pomanders. Or made too much of betony.

Before there was this dowry to try for, I'd always figured I'd have to find a husband. I didn't think it would be too hard—I wasn't entirely homely, by all accounts, and even if I were, plenty of homely women get homely husbands and make homely babies.

But then what? What about my husband? What would he be—a cabinetmaker, a blacksmith, a cobbler? The problem with marrying a craftsman is that the commerce becomes the wife's problem. And where did that fit in with my herbs? Nor could I see marrying a farming man, beholden to some estate, any more than I could see marrying a soldier—my own ma's sad life bounced that notion right out of my head.

No. The convent was the best choice for me. A place where I would have all the time I was supposed to be devoutly praying to think about herbs. I didn't really care for all the silence and singing and obedience—but my own herbary!

Brother Cosmin came back then and asked us questions about the properties of cherry bark, and we stopped talking.

In short order, I assembled the evening's posies and went to deliver them to the princesses' door.

I arrived at the same time as Florin, the youngest of the cobbler boys. The castle employed seven cobblers, total: six to make two new pairs of slippers every day for the princesses, and one to make shoes for the rest of us. Florin was the newest apprentice to his master, like me, and like me, he was the one who had to venture off to the princesses' tower. No one who could possibly avoid it went to the princesses' tower. Ever.

I looked at Florin over my fragrant tray of flowers and herbs; he looked at me over his box of slippers.

"Do you ever think that maybe if we didn't replace their posies and slippers every night, they wouldn't do whatever it is that they do?" I asked.

Florin, who was just a bit older than me but had lived at the castle since he was born, shook his head. "They tried that," he said. "They tried everything. For a week, Prince Vasile refused them any slippers. The princesses made holes in their feet instead of their shoes. It was a week of blood and blisters and hobbling about."

"Why not move them out of the castle altogether?"

"Because! Earthquakes! Wind! Terrible storms! Every time they try something, we spend a month clearing the debris and patching up the castle foundations."

"Well," I said, "maybe they shouldn't let them go to bed at night?"

Florin shook his head. "The curse is *strong*. The curse wants the princesses in the castle, in this tower, every night, no exceptions."

"Maybe separate them—"

"No." Florin rolled his eyes. "The castle's been cursed for six years. They tried everything you've thought up— twice—and eighty more things besides."

"What about—"

Florin wheeled about impatiently. "Listen. You're what, thirteen? *You* aren't going to break the curse. *Nobody* is going to break the curse, and nothing good comes to them that try. A piece of advice, apprentice to apprentice: The curse don't hurt them that don't mess with it. So you? Don't mess with it, and grow up to be a journeyman herbalist. Now. Knock." He jerked his chin toward the tower door.

I was annoyed, but I knocked. Beti, the princesses' maid, opened up to take Florin's box of shoes. Florin escaped swiftly, clearly having no intention of waiting for me.

Usually a second maid would have taken my flowers,

but tonight she was not in attendance. I tried to place the tray of flowers on top of Florin's box, but Beti grimaced. "Bring in the tray—I haven't got six hands, you know!" So I followed her into the eastern tower.

The princesses stood about in varying states of undress, preparing for the evening's meal and entertainment in their father's hall. In any other boudoir of twelve princesses, there would have been chatter and laughter. But all here was silence and strain, even though the princesses wore the most beautiful gowns of velvets, damasks, and silks—nothing at all like my sturdy woolen skirts and apron.

I set down the tray of flowers and turned to leave, but Beti asked, "Can't you stay?"

"What for?" I whispered.

"Help them with their flowers? You know all about flowers, right?"

I started to say that I didn't think they'd want me, because I wanted to go down and get my supper, but then I realized that there was no better time to investigate the curse further. What luck! And I'd almost thrown that luck away for sour soup and roasted carp!

CHAPTER 4

"Sure, I'll help the princesses with their flowers," I said. Beti flashed me her teeth in gratitude and dashed off to assist Princess Viorica with her lacings.

Several of the princesses glared at me, doubtless because of the cabbage issue. I shied from them and approached Princess Otilia with a posy, since she was the only princess who had ever bothered to learn my name. She stopped plucking fine hairs from her forehead and reached for the flowers.

"Reveka, the posies look lovely," Otilia said, burying her nose in a spray. "And they smell even better. What wonderful roses!"

"Mm, indeed, Highness." I plopped a curtsy at her, not certain if I should point out that I didn't have anything to do with growing roses, just the picking of them. "And, um, how can I help you?"

Otilia showed me how to smooth her hair back tightly and bind it with pins. We covered the knot of hair with a tall, cone-shaped cap. A veil attached to the hat with wire antennae and fluttered about her head. She told me this was called a butterfly hennin, and I could see why, with the veil spread above her head like wings.

When I stepped back to admire my work, I felt about as fine as a hill cottager, though I wore my second-best apron and my nut-dyed cowl was new. The linen of Otilia's veil practically glowed in contrast to her dark hair, and she was almost beautiful.

Otilia smiled at me. It didn't seem a happy smile, and it made her seem older than I had thought she was.

"How long have you been at the castle, Princess?" I asked, speaking softly since Lacrimora and Maricara were glaring at me periodically.

"It will be seven years this autumn. We came when I was twelve. I'm the youngest." She spoke wistfully, and her eyes were dark and moist. In a voice pitched so her sisters couldn't hear, she said, "I miss my other life. You have no idea how lucky you are, Reveka."

I frowned. I wasn't cursed, of course, but what did she know about my life? My mother had refused to follow my father once she was pregnant, because Pa was soldiering for Vlad Ţepeş then, who was not known for treating women very well, even his soldiers' women, even pregnant ones.

She had died shortly after giving birth to me, leaving me in a convent. My first eight years there were utterly miserable. The Abbess had marked me as a liar and a troublemaker from birth. All the nuns scorned me, except Sister Anica, the herbalist, who chose me to be her student. She appreciated that I was clever and a fast learner.

I never even met Pa until after he left Vlad Ţepeş's army to join the Hungarian Black Legion, when I was nine or so; he stayed in the abbey's guest hostel for a night, saw me for half an hour, and let the Abbess convince him that I was a liar on the path of sin. He didn't come to collect me until he gave up soldiering a couple of years later, at which point he dragged me away from Sister Anica to follow him around while he gardened for various nobles all over the region.

That first year I hated him. He treated me like the liar the Abbess had told him I was, and he watched me hawkishly for the slightest untruth. He made me find my own willow twigs when he switched me for lying, and I would cry as I cut the twigs, thinking of Sister Anica. It went that way until we came to our uneasy truce: I promised I would never lie to him, and he promised to trust my vow and assume I told the truth. I think we were both hard-pressed to keep our pact, but so far we'd never caught each other breaking it.

So, no I wasn't cursed. I wasn't trapped in a tower every night with my half sisters—even better, I wasn't half sister to Maricara and Lacrimora—but I felt like saying, *No, Princess Otilia, I have no idea how lucky I am. And you? Have you been switched before an entire convent for telling a harmless lie? Have you gone days with little or no food because your own soldiers set fire to the millet fields when they retreated? Have you lost nights of sleep while the infidels shelled your walls?*

But for once I restrained my impertinent tongue and whispered, "Oh, indeed, very lucky. What do you miss most about your other life, Princess?"

And here she flushed bright red, from the tips of her ears down her throat. "Oh!" she said, as though I'd stuck her with a pin. "Oh, my family, of course."

"Surely you're allowed to see your family."

"My mother, and my brother and sisters, they have come for visits before; but my father . . ." She trailed off, and I could see that this was very painful for her. The father who had raised her, who perhaps had not known he wasn't her father, given what Brother Cosmin had explained to me about the princesses' births?

"My *mother's husband*," Otilia said carefully, "owns the mill in Moara, not far from here. It's the most beautiful little village, situated right on the forks of the Bradet River. The north fork feeds our millrace; the south fork cools the blacksmith's work. We could climb into the attic and see sparks from the forge across the apple orchard. Millers always have apple orchards, because the wood is fast growing and strong enough to be made into mill gears," she said, and a large tear dropped onto her lap. "I miss the scent of applewood fires. . . ."

"Are you done hoarding the herb girl's help, Otilia?" Princess Tereza's voice cut like a knife.

"I'm done, Sister," Otilia said, voice calm as though she hadn't been in tears just a moment before. She nodded to me, and I scurried to help Tereza with her pointed slippers.

Everything after this passed in a flurry of shoes and veils, until at last the princesses were ready for dinner. They exited the eastern tower in a long line, hems held high, veils flying. It was a wonder to me that all the fine woman in the country had not died long ago, tripping over the padded, extra-long toes of their slippers, but the princesses managed well enough.

Beti sighed in relief when the last princess left, then moved listlessly about the chamber to clear up the flotsam that came from dressing twelve women.

I had a clever idea.

"You look so tired," I said to the servant. "And I never have to do much cleaning in the herbary, so I wouldn't terribly mind the sweeping up. Why don't you find your own bed and let me take care of the princesses' room tonight?"

It was that simple. Beti reminded me to put the bar on

the door when the princesses returned and I left; then she fled, before I could come to my senses.

Of course, once she was gone, I regretted the impulse. I should have let her clean three-quarters of the room and *then* offered to finish up.

I set about the tasks I had promised to do, and when the room was as tidy as I knew how to make it, I curled up on a small rug beside the fire and pretended to sleep. But really, I lay in wait. Tonight I would find out the secrets of the princesses' curse.

In pretending to fall asleep, I fell asleep in truth. The next thing I knew, Otilia was shaking my shoulder and calling my name in a whisper. "Reveka! Get up! My sisters are coming, and you must go!"

"Huhm?"

She yanked me up so hard, we both staggered. "Go. Go! If you stay here tonight . . ." She trailed off, staring at the door as though she'd heard a sound. "Go! Now!" And when I did not go, she got behind me and pushed.

I stumbled into the next room, passing the train of princesses on their way in. Princess Lacrimora came last. "Oh, Cabbage Girl? Are you coming in to spend the night?" she asked, her tone mocking.

"N-no—"

"Good," Lacrimora said, and slammed the door in my

face. From inside the tower came the clear *thunk* of a bolt being thrown home.

I dropped the bar into the slots outside the princesses' door with a clatter.

Cabbage Girl? That wasn't so bad. Nuns will not blaspheme, but they are deft with name-calling. I'd been called worse.

CHAPTER 5

When I went down to the baths the next day, I apologized to Marjit the Bathwoman for the distress I'd caused her the morning before.

Marjit rolled her pansy-brown eyes. "I'm a hill woman," she said. "I vent my spleen freely when I'm irked. It might look like distress to a more refined eye."

"Would you like any help with . . . anything?" I asked.

She snorted, and I could see that she was angry with me, even though she wasn't *distressed* by my behavior. "No. Sort your herbs and stay out of my way."

I did so, making sure Marjit could see every herb I added. She barely glanced over, being busy heating stones to throw into the bathwater and assembling her soaps and towels and oils.

The castle's luxurious underground baths were leftovers from Roman times. Chipped mosaics of pagan gods watched over Sylvian's bath-mad residents as they soaked once or even twice a day. Everyone here was cleaner than a nun, even, and nuns are *very* clean. Marjit was a busy woman.

"Thing is, I just don't understand the curse," I said, sorting out orange bergamot, rose geranium, and rue and adding them to my pile. They all smelled sharp and fresh but were also theoretically good for curse break-ing, though they hadn't worked yet in the weeks I'd used them.

"What's to understand about the curse, anyway?" Marjit asked.

"Well, who placed it, for one," I said. "What witch or Gypsy would want to do them harm?"

"There are no Gypsies in Sylvania, by law, and no witch in Sylvania would cast that hex," Marjit said. "No witch would want to. The witches in this country are only interested in wholesome magic."

I didn't think that could be true, but I wouldn't argue with Marjit about it. If I said, "You can't know all the witches in Sylvania," she'd argue that she did; if I argued that she couldn't know the secret *intentions* of all the witches in Sylvania, she'd argue that she knew those, too. Marjit knew everything.

"A witch would leave some evidence behind. You can't do magic like that"—she gestured vaguely toward the princesses' tower—"without complications. Think about just the little magics a witch does—"

"I don't know any witches," I said.

"Well, even to cure a man of loving plum brandy too much takes all sorts of implements. Water from three or more holy wells. A jar of honey. Clothing from the man, clothing from the wife. A hair from his mother . . . So many of your herbs I can't keep them all straight, but at least frankincense and basil. Oh, and a Nine-Brides Knife, too."

"What's a Nine-Brides Knife?"

"It's a knife carried by nine brides to the altar and secretly hidden in their grooms' pocket during the wedding. Do you know how hard it is to find nine women all deft enough to hide a knife on their new-minted husbands? Not easy."

"I guess not."

"No, little Reva. The curse on Castle Sylvian is not the work of a witch. A *căpcăun*, maybe," she said, naming the dogheaded ogre that liked to kidnap young women. "A *zmeu*, likely. Perhaps even a *balaur*. But not a witch."

I shivered, thinking of the creatures she'd just mentioned. Both *zmeu* and *balaur* were kinds of dragons, both always trying to marry young women. The *balaur* was frightening because it had multiple heads. But the *zmeu* was even more frightening, because it looked more human and could change shape in order to trick girls into loving and marrying it.

I worked quietly, crushing the rose geranium, before I asked, "Florin says don't bother thinking about it, since the Prince has done everything he can to break the curse, but . . . what's been tried?"

Marjit straightened from stoking her fire and wiped the sweat from her nose. "They split the princesses up," she said, sounding happily authoritative, and I realized she liked being consulted—it had a mollifying effect on her temper. "They sent them away. They even tried marrying them off, or almost. Princess Maricara got all the way to Styria to marry their Duke, but the night before their wedding, the Duke succumbed to a deep sleep that he has never woken from."

"Like the sleepers in the western tower," I said.

Marjit gave me a keen look. "Yes. He's the only sleeper who didn't end up in that tower, as a matter of fact. His mother nurses him to this day."

I frowned, wrapping crushed herbs in twists of cheese-cloth and tying them with a string. "And nothing anyone does makes a bit of difference?"

"Oh, it makes a difference, by my mother's bones!—the wind that kicks up, and the way the bowels of the castle shake, that's all different enough. The towers all got struck by lightning once!"

I tossed my herbs into the bathwater, watching the floating packets cast shadows over the mosaic faces of Neptune and his dolphins. The three tiles of Neptune's right eye were missing, making him look roguish and ungodlike.

"You're not up to more of your mischief, are you?" Marjit's heavy brows lowered, and she looked pointedly at my herbs.

"No mischief today, Marjit."

She added her hot stones to the bathwater, and herb-scented steam filled the chamber. She inhaled deeply. "Good. Smells pleasant. Nothing like soup. And well-timed. They're here."

Princess Maricara swept in first. She always led the line to remind everyone that she was the Prince's oldest legitimately born daughter. Or so Marjit said. Otilia arrived second, arm in arm with Nadia. Otilia smiled, and Nadia hesitantly did the same. The others ignored me, and I sneaked out in the chaos of the princesses struggling into their bathing shifts.

Lacrimora, the one who had called me Cabbage Girl the night before, came in as I left. I stepped aside, but she moved close to me, bending her long neck like an angry goose to whisper, "You'd do well to stay out of our tower, Apprentice." She ended the word with her teeth bared and let the last sound trail in a long hiss: *apprentissssss.*

I turned away as though I hadn't heard her, even though I should have curtsied.

In the herbary, Didina's worktable was abandoned, though a pile of asphodel flowers awaited her attention. And Brother Cosmin hadn't arrived yet. He preferred to greet the noonday sun while farting and scratching in his bed. Monks are very attached to their farts and their fleas, or so the nuns always said.

I loved having the herbary to myself. I would straighten the stacked bowls, line up the jars and flasks and terracotta pots on the shelves, arrange the drying herbs on the racks *just so*, and then sit on my stool and pretend the herbary was mine. I would mentally reorder the shelves and imagine that I stored the herbs by the best preparation methods instead of the hodgepodge ways Brother Cosmin invented. The shelf to the right of the door would be for hot infusions, the shelf to the left for cold ones. On the far wall, decoctions, tinctures, oils, ointments; on the near wall, balms, essences, extracts, syrups, lozenges, and electuaries.

But today, instead of dreaming, I went to pull down Brother Cosmin's very best book, Saint Hildegard's *Physica*, planning to compile a list of herbs good for curse breaking.

I loved reading through *Physica*; I regarded Hildegard

of Bingen as my personal saint. Hildegard founded and ran two convents, and not only had she run them exceedingly well, she had time to write songs and books, including works on medicinal simples that are read by herbalists everywhere.

But *Physica* wasn't on the shelf with the other books. I looked around the herbary and spied it on Didina's table. I fetched the book and started flipping through. There were interesting sections on reviving people that I copied to my own personal herbal, which was a fan-folded sheet of rescraped parchment filled mostly with drawings of plants that I found hard to distinguish.

Didina came in and settled down at her spot. She picked up her pestle, then noticed me. "What are you doing?"

"Copying. This is in Latin, but I think I mostly understand it." I frowned then, remembering that Didina didn't read Latin, or speak it; she could read Church Slavonic haltingly, and some Saxon. So why was *Physica* on her table? "What were you—"

"You should go collect flowers for the princesses' posies," she said.

"I have plenty of time to do that," I said. "But why were you—" I glanced down at the page I'd been copying from: *scrofula of the neck that has not ruptured—*

Didina slammed the book closed, glaring at me. But I didn't pay her any mind—my attention was grabbed by a scrap of vellum that fluttered from between the pages and slipped to the floor.

We both dived under the table after the vellum, but I got there first.

"Plantes Which Confer Vpon the Wearer Invisibilitie" was the title, written in a strange kind of Saxon.

Invisibility? I frowned and read on:

~ Gather, w. golden knife—

Didina dragged me out by my heels. I tried to stuff the vellum up my sleeve, but she saw and dug it out.

"Careful, don't rip it!" I cried.

"*You* be careful. It's *mine*!"

"Invisibility?"

"Shut up! Someone will hear you."

"Let me see it! Please?"

She paused for a moment, then made a disgusted face and threw it at me. "Fine. Look at it. Looking at it won't help you in the least."

I eagerly snatched the paper before it hit the ground and read:

Plantes Which Confer Vpon
the Wearer Invisibilitie
~ Gather, w. golden knife & in vtter silence, at mid-day or mid-night, on midsvmmer or midwinter day, the sukkory plant.

Carefvl to collect w. left hand onlie.

~ Carry w. thee a tiny horn filled with tvrnsole.

~ Wear mistletoe arovnd thy neck.

~ Collect pig's weed, to be worn as a wreath.

~ Walk with fern seed in thy pocket.

~ For six days, soak nepenthe-seed in wine; drink the wine three days rvnning whilst fasting. Afterward, thou shalt become invisible at will.

~ Wrap wolf's bane seed in a red lizard skin & carry in thy pockets.

Ideas skipped around my mind like flat stones across a pond. If I were invisible, I could watch the princesses all night. If I were invisible, I could find out what they did. If I were invisible, and provided I didn't burst out in a sneeze or something, I could discover the secrets of the curse, report back to Princess Daciana and Prince Vasile, and claim the dowry.

I stared at Didina. "Where did you get this?"

"I found it in that book when I was looking for drawings of betony to copy. It's old, you can tell, older than the book. But it's nonsense! Nothing on the list works."

"Why would someone write it all down if it were nonsense?"

"I don't know, but it is! Try something on the list— anything! There's pig's weed in the kitchen garden—Cook uses it to thicken stew."

"All right, I will," I said, marching out into the garden

to gather an apronful of pig's weed.

I twisted together a wreath in short order, perched it atop my head, and tiptoed back to the herbary.

Didina glanced up from her asphodel. Brother Cosmin also looked up. I wondered when he had arrived. They both stared right at me.

"There you are, Reveka!" Brother Cosmin said. "Have you prepared the princesses' posies yet? Princess Nadia wants day's-eyes tonight."

"I'll head out in a moment," I said, flinging the wreath into the compost bucket by the door.

"Well, don't take too long. You picked all the day's-eyes within the castle walls, and now you'll have to go into the forest."

I grunted, sitting down with my personal herbal. I flipped to a blank square and titled it "Investigation of Plantes Which Confer Invisibilitie." I wrote, "Test One: Wore a pig's weed wreath. No effect."

I shoved my herbal underneath my mortar, glaring at Didina. She said with ruthless cheeriness, "Make sure you take the left fork on the riverward path. You wouldn't want to get lost in the forest."

Chapter 6

In the three weeks since I'd been at Castle Sylvian, I'd not managed to learn my way around the Prince's hunting park at all.

This was partially because I was simply unaccustomed to wild-herb gathering. I'd grown up inside the stone walls of a convent-fortress in Transylvania, which was fortified for a reason: We were close to the Turks and always under threat of their raids.

That's just what it's like to live in the last outpost of Christianity—you don't count on having food to last all winter, and you don't take many forest walks.

We were safe here in Sylvania at the moment, or maybe I just felt safer with Transylvania and Wallachia between us and the Turks, and with Hungary at our backs. The Hungarians were a threat to Prince Vasile's sovereignty, but they were also a threat to the Turks' expansion.

But safety was a matter of perception. Prince Vasile obviously felt enough danger to have hired my father for his ditching skills.

Safety was also a matter of degree. I might not have to worry about running into a Turkish raiding party here—but there might be bears or boars or ogres among the trees. Didina had been my guide through the forest the last three times, and I wished she were coming with me now.

Nonetheless, with wicker collecting basket in hand, I marched past the Little Well, through the dragon-carved gates, down the rows of trees filled with ripening plums, and into the hunting park.

Here, the trees grew so closely together that daylight never touched the forest floor, even on the main paths. That would never do: Day's-eyes were a cheerful flower dressed in plain white petals and with a sunlike center. All sunny plants like sunshine, not forest shadows. There were wide meadows deep inside the park, but I wasn't sure *where*. Didina had said "left fork" and "riverward path," hadn't she? I knew right from left as well as anyone, but how could I know if I was on the riverward path?

The forest grew darker as I went, and the calls of cheerful, sun-loving birds faded behind me. I crept slowly along the path, clutching my basket to my side, trying to look in every direction at once. I was going to laugh at myself when I found the meadow full of day's-eyes; I was going to laugh even harder when I put them into the princesses' posies. But knowing that didn't make me feel less uneasy in this forest.

The dark path wound on and on and on. I began to despair of finding sunlight in this direction. I was just about to march back to the castle to tell Brother Cosmin that Princess Nadia was going to have to live with the disappointment of no day's-eyes when I rounded a bend and found a man standing in the forest gloom, plucking handfuls of plum blossoms from a plain kerchief and dropping them into a stream. Hundreds of blossoms, it seemed, drifted like snow to bob and float on the current.

The man himself was tall, dressed like a lord in red velvet, his black military cloak fastened with a clasp that appeared to be made from boar's tusks. In spite of the fact that he wore Vasile's colors—red and black—I didn't recognize him as one of Vasile's men.

I must have made a noise, for he whirled suddenly, dropping the kerchief and the rest of the blossoms into the stream. He drew a sword as he turned. I raised my collecting basket between us like a shield—an unexpected reflex—and took a step backward.

The man glanced at the basket with a quirked eyebrow. "You know that a wicker basket isn't much protection against a sword, don't you?"

"Yes, but it's all the protection I have," I said.

"Courage in the face of certain defeat is admirable."

"Certain defeat?" I asked. My voice wavered like a flute, showing my fear, which annoyed me.

"*If* we were adversaries," the man said, lowering his sword, "do you not think that I would defeat you?"

"Well, you do have a sword," I said pragmatically. "And in any contest that pitted your strength against mine, you would probably win. But in a contest of wits? I might hold my own." I lowered my basket and raised my chin.

"Alas, but we shan't find out the truth of that today. I find that in those sorts of contests, it takes far too long to ascertain the victor. And I have to be home by sunset."

I laughed, because I thought it was a joke; the man was younger than Pa, but clearly too old and rich to care for curfew. But he didn't laugh with me. I said, "I'm sorry I startled you, and I'm sorry that you lost your kerchief." I pointed to the stream, which still swirled a few plum blossoms on its calmer eddies—but the kerchief was long gone.

He glanced at the water. "I have no lack of kerchiefs," he said.

"Oh." He still stared at the water, and I noticed then that he was a little bit handsome in his way, with his lean cheeks and dark eyes. He wasn't wearing a huge mustache like the men of his class so often did, but rather bore a close-cropped beard along his jaw, barely more than stubble.

"What are the flowers *for*?" I blurted out—rudely, I knew, but I was dying of curiosity.

The man's dark eyes darted toward me. I didn't think he would answer. "A memory," he said at last. "And a debt."

Clear as mud. Something in his demeanor kept me from asking a further question, in spite of my curiosity ailment. "All right, but how did you get plum blossoms at this time of year?" To force blooms out of season was a skill; to delay blooming by months was another art entirely, and one I'd never heard of.

He cast me an acute look. "It's not plum blossom season?"

How could he not know what time of year it was? Even in this dark forest, the broadness of the leaves suggested high summer. I took a step backward, wondering if he was a sort of ghoul, not a man at all. These things happened. The dead did not always know where to go. . . .

My collecting basket fell out of my suddenly strengthless fingers. The man stooped forward, picked up the basket, and handed it to me, and I almost laughed with relief. No ghoul could pick up a basket *and* hand it to me.

"Are you all right?" he asked, looking into my face.

I ignored the question and asked my own. "Are you a vassal of Prince Vasile?"

"Vassal? Hardly."

"Then what are you doing in the Prince's hunting

park, Mysterious Nameless Stranger?"

"Call me Frumos," he said. "Handsome," the name meant; Frumos was also the hero of all the great tales, and further, Prince Frumos was the one who fought the *zmeu*. This fellow certainly thought a lot of himself! "What's *your* name?"

"Reveka. I'm the herbalist's apprentice at Castle Sylvian. Well, one of them. So—why are you out here in the hunting park, Prince Frumos?" And when he looked as though he might have cheerfully strangled me, I said, "Oh, you don't like being called *Prince* Frumos?"

"It might be a joke that I've heard too often," he suggested.

"Yes, but what does your Marvelous Horse have to say about it?" I asked, smirking. Prince Frumos in the stories was always taking counsel from his horse. Then again, it was a pretty smart horse, so it made sense in the stories.

"My horse tells me that you're like the old woman on the road who offers Prince Frumos two impossible choices," he said.

"How's that?" I asked, not sure if I should be offended or delighted by this comparison.

He shrugged a little, looking as if he was biting back something rude. While I didn't want to be insulted, I was terribly annoyed that he wouldn't just say what he thought of me.

I said, "I don't think it's an apt comparison. The old women who meet Prince Frumos say things like 'If you turn right, you'll walk through sorrow; if you turn left, you'll walk through sorrow as well.' I don't think that's offering impossible choices, anyway. I think that Frumos was a fool for accepting those as the only two choices. What if he went backward? What if he went straight? Maybe saying that left-right thing was the old woman's way of saying, 'Don't turn!' How did you mean this comparison?"

"I meant only good things, I assure you." He had started smiling broadly at me during my diatribe. I didn't know what to make of him at all. By now, Pa would have told me to shut up and claimed a nattering-induced headache. "I was merely commenting on the fact that we had a chance meeting on a path in the woods, like Frumos and the old woman in the story. What are *you* doing in the forest, herbalist's apprentice?"

"I am collecting day's-eyes," I said.

"Day's-eyes are a sun-loving plant," he replied, gesturing at the thick canopy of trees overhead. "You won't find them here."

"There's a meadow farther on, I think—I've been there, I just don't quite remember where it is."

"Ah, the meadow. I can guide you. It's not far." And he offered me his arm, exactly as though I were a lady and not just an herbalist's apprentice. I stepped forward and took the offered arm, but my head heated up with a blush—there's no use pretending it didn't. I couldn't explain why this man—this "handsome prince"—was being so nice to me. It was disconcerting.

We were not far from the meadow, as it happened. I'd been on the right path all along. "There," Frumos said, releasing my arm and pointing to day's-eyes bobbing and swaying on a gentle breeze. "Your meadow." He bowed, as if bequeathing it to me.

Delighted, I stepped forward into the bright sunlight, stooping down with my herb knife to cut a quick armful of flowers. I stood with the day's-eyes in my arms and turned back to thank Frumos.

But there was no one there at all; I saw only the shadows of the forest and the path back home.

CHAPTER 7

Later, after I'd returned to the herbary and made up the posies, Brother Cosmin stepped out to the kitchens for a bite of food and a dab of wine. I immediately turned to Didina to wheedle some information about Plantes Which Confer Vpon the Wearer Invisibilitie.

"If pig's weed and mistletoe *really* turned people invisible," I said, "there would be a lot more petty thefts and useful assassinations in the world."

"Pig's weed and mistletoe don't work, even woven together," Didina said.

Keeping my head bent over my task of sorting mint leaves, which were rotting in the oddly damp summer weather, I suppressed the urge to grin at Didina. She was going to talk to me about the list! I didn't even have to wheedle. "I don't suppose you've tried anything else on the list," I said.

"I've never been able to afford a golden knife, or to find a tiny horn, or to get a red lizard skin. . . ."

"What about the nepenthe seeds?"

"Drinking nepenthe wine on a three-day fast . . ."

I looked up and caught her eye. "Seems like a good way to *believe* you're invisible, without actually becoming so." We both laughed. Nepenthe was notorious for causing forgetfulness and strange behavior.

"Also a good way to stop your heart," she added.

"Or that," I said, sobering. "I thought you said the dowry wasn't worth it, but you've done all these experiments with the list. Were you just trying to scare me away?"

She set her mouth. "The dowry *isn't* worth it. It's not worth getting cursed with the sleep, anyway."

"Then . . . why bother with the list? Unless you were planning a career as a sneak thief."

She looked toward the window, where the eastern tower loomed. "You've met the woman who takes care of the sleepers," Didina said slowly. "Did you know she's my grandmother?"

"No. I'm sorry, no, I didn't know."

Didina took a deep breath, and said, "Did you also know that my mother is one of the sleepers?" Mute, I shook my head. "Ma was *their* favorite servant, and the first to fall. She wasn't trying for the dowry—the dowry hadn't even been thought up yet. She was just trying to serve the Prince, to help the princesses; she was loyal to them, and what did that get her?"

I was silent, trying to comprehend this.

Didina continued, "I want to—I *need* to—break the curse so my mother and grandmother can leave that tower."

I understood what it was like to want your mother back—hadn't I wanted that my whole life? "So, when *we* break the curse," I said, "we can split the dowry?"

She tilted her head, eyes downcast. "Reveka . . ."

"We're going to do it," I said, trying to reassure her, to help sweep some of the sadness from her eyes. "We're going to break the curse, Didina."

She didn't look up. She spoke in a low voice, as though talking to her mortar and pestle: "If you do it—if you wake up my mother—you can have *all* the dowry. You'll need it. I . . . just don't want to be an orphan anymore."

I hadn't known she was an orphan. I blurted out the obvious question: "What happened to your pa?"

"He was a soldier."

I bit my lip and nodded. I knew too well what that meant; it was all she had to say.

I left the herbary a little before sunset and went to gather some of Pa's yew.

Herbalists do not grow yew, but if assassins had gardens, they would cultivate it. Yew is a deadly poison, but it also makes a good hedge. Pa wouldn't care if I pruned his yew out of season—he was always arguing that gardens needed fewer tall plants for enemies to hide behind, not more, and would go on for hours about the dangers of overgrown hedges, and how ivy is just as good as a ladder for a soldier.

Yew branches in hand, along with some santolina from the herbary, I climbed the western tower to see Mistress Adina.

Nothing had changed. The sleepers lay still, and Adina rocked in her chair and netted her socks. "Herb-husband's apprentice!" she cried, more pleased to see me now than she had been on the day we met.

"*Stăpână*," I said, dropping the plain curtsy that indicated respect for an elder. That was an easy curtsy, and I didn't bobble like I did with the deeper gestures. But then, because I can spare only so many good manners in one day, I asked, "Why do you call Brother Cosmin 'herb-husband'?"

"Before Brother Cosmin arrived, I was the castle herb-wife," she said, stretching out her half-netted sock and checking it against a finished one. "I retired to take care of these folks here. I've nothing against Cosmin. I just think that calling him 'herb-husband' keeps him honest. He puts on airs, and uses fancy titles like 'herbalist,' because he has books."

I considered that and decided it might be safer to have no opinion on this subject, even though I took my future as a master herbalist very seriously. I would be annoyed if people referred to me as an herb-wife, someone who knew her receipts by rote instead of being able to read and write.

But I didn't want to annoy Mistress Adina, and I had great respect for her age, so I kept my mouth shut about all that.

Pa and the Abbess both would have been proud.

"Mistress Adina," I said, "have you considered yew?"

"Yew!" She rocked back in her chair, sucking one tooth thoughtfully. "What for? It's poison."

"It's been . . . it's been known to raise the dead."

She laughed. "I never heard that!"

I flushed. "I read it! In a book!" I had, though it was about a year before, in Moldavia.

And she laughed again. "Who taught you herb lore, Reveka?"

"Well, before Brother Cosmin, I learned from Sister Anica. . . ."

"Brother Cosmin aside—and I know you're lying there, because I've heard you've taught *him* more herb lore than he's taught you—Sister Anica probably never mentioned yew, did she?"

I didn't see her point, but she was correct. "No, Sister Anica didn't mention yew—except that it's a poison, as you said. What does that matter?"

"Don't believe everything you read in books," Mistress Adina said. Her needle darted in and out of the sock slowly taking shape beneath her hand.

"But—"

"Did your book tell you how to prepare the yew?"

I had to admit the truth. "No." Or if it had, I didn't remember.

"So what would you do with it?"

"Um. A tincture, to, um, drip down their throats?"

Mistress Adina shook her head. "I'm afraid not, dear. Too dangerous. Do you have anything else to try?"

"I have santolina," I said. Its scent was similar to rosemary, though folk sometimes called it cotton lavender.

"Santolina!" She set aside her needle and reached out, and I placed the packet of herbs in her hands. She opened the packet and sniffed. "What'll you do with it?"

I felt more confident with this herb. "Rub it on their foreheads and beneath their noses," I said. "Sister Anica did it for a monk who had fallen from a tree he was pruning and banged his head. He'd been sleeping for three days. . . ."

"Did it work?"

"Not then. But she'd seen it work other times. So shouldn't we try it?"

"Please do. Try." She gestured toward the man sleeping at her feet. I knelt beside him and rolled the santolina sprigs between my hands, collecting the plant's oils. I dropped the sprig and smoothed my fingers over the man's forehead, across his temples, down his cheek, beneath his nose. I massaged the pulse points on his neck and wrists, watching carefully for any signs of stirring.

Nothing.

I stood up and brushed the leaf bits and dirt off my apron. "Well!" I said, trying to sound cheery even though tears of disappointment clogged my throat. I sat down on the low stool beside Mistress Adina and made a great fuss over straightening my shoes so she wouldn't see me sniffling into my apron. "I guess I'll have to try something else."

When I looked up, Mistress Adina wasn't even watching me. She was staring out the window. I followed her gaze across the forecourt to the shadowed bulk of the eastern tower. Lights flickered in the princesses' window. Mistress Adina turned back to the room to regard the sleeping figures.

"What?" I whispered, afraid to disturb this moment, whatever it was. "What's happening?"

"Wait," Adina said.

I waited.

As one, the sleepers opened their mouths and shouted: "Don't go!"

Goose bumps rose on my scalp and scrabbled down my spine. Mistress Adina stabbed her netting needle toward the window, urging me to look: The princesses' tower was dark, the light extinguished.

"Every night," Mistress Adina said. "It happens every night when the light in the princesses' window fades away."

My throat was too dry for words to rise.

I went the next night at the same time to sit with Mistress Adina, and the next night, and almost every night thereafter while I was the herbalist's apprentice of Castle Sylvian. And every night, as the light faded from the princesses' tower, the sleepers beseeched, "Don't go!"

CHAPTER 8

The next day, I woke to find a murder of crows had descended upon Castle Sylvian. I'd heard them cawing in my sleep and thought I'd dreamed it. But there was no dreaming involved in picking a path around the lacy gold-and-white patterns of their poop splattered across the courtyard on my way to the baths.

Marjit was uncharacteristically silent while I assembled my herbs. She didn't respond to any of my efforts to jolly her. But when I made to leave, she murmured, "Stick around," her voice barely audible under the chatter of the arriving princesses.

I shrugged but stayed. Marjit had me hand her sponges and scrubbers, while the princesses and I tried to ignore each other. When Marjit had settled the princesses in the soaking pool, she pulled me into the bath antechamber, calling over her shoulder, "I'll just be attending to your toweling, dears."

I was halfway through the door to the far passageway when Marjit yanked me backward into the antechamber and slammed the passage door loudly. She held up her hand in a "Wait" gesture, then tiptoed back to listen at the door of the bathing chamber.

Eavesdropper! I stared at her with big eyes, uncertain what to say, or if I should say anything at all. Marjit, the root of the castle's grapevine, apparently gathered her information from illicit eavesdropping. People thought they were alone in the baths, but she was really on the other side of the door with her ear pressed to it.

The princesses were talking about the crows in the courtyard. "It's an omen," one of them said decisively. "The Hungarians are coming."

"At least there won't be more Saxons." This was Ruxandra's voice, sounding disgusted. Her tavern wench's accent was unmistakable. "Every single Saxon, insisting on dancing with every single one of us, for every single dance. Like we don't already get enough of *that*."

"The worst of the dancing Saxons learned his lesson," someone else—Maricara, I think—added with grim humor.

"His name is Iosif," someone else put in quietly. "And if Corvinus is coming, Iosif's the reason why, so maybe we should remember that name."

"What's Corvinus going to do?" another voice asked.

"It's the Wallachians we should worry about."

"Oh, la, Wallachians. They've no bite without the Impaler."

"Oh, la, Wallachians!" This new voice was mocking, harsh. I imagined it belonged to Lacrimora. "If your precious papa doesn't produce an heir soon, the Wallachian Prince is going to insist on being named the heir to Sylvania. And if Vasile agrees, the Hungarians will attack. And if Vasile doesn't agree, the Wallachians will attack."

"Then Papa had just better get busy with his little bride, hadn't he!"

I wanted to hear more, but Marjit flapped her hands like the wings of an excited chicken, motioning me to open and close the far antechamber door. We tromped loudly back to the bathing chamber, and when we came in, the princesses were silent, their faces as smooth as peaches.

After this, Marjit had me help with the scrubbing and sponging and hair washing. The time went quickly.

When the princesses were gone, I turned to Marjit. "What was that all about?"

Marjit shook out her towels with a snap. "One of the Saxons, Tereza's betrothed, went missing just last night. The one called Iosif."

"But why . . . what's that have to do with crows?"

"The crows are probably sent by Corvinus, the Hungarian king, to spy."

"Well, how do you know that?" I asked, astonished.

"*Corvinus* means 'crow,' doesn't it? And he's the one who supports the Saxons who live in Transylvania and fight the Turks. Which the Transylvanians are not so fond of, I might add, except for when the Turks invade." I knew this. I'd grown up with Saxon nuns in Transylvania. "The Saxons sent a delegation to us, including this Iosif, who was minor nobility of sorts, to lobby Prince Vasile for the Hungarian cause. But now Iosif is missing, the latest victim of the curse, and Corvinus is going to be angry."

"That's silly! Corvinus must know there's a curse. How can he get mad when someone gets caught up in it?"

"Corvinus doesn't actually believe the curse is real. Corvinus thinks that Prince Vasile is just imprisoning everyone who disappears, and is working dark magic on the ones who fall to the sleeping curse."

I stared at Marjit. It had never occurred to me that people would think the curse wasn't real. Or that they would think it was all part of a political machination on Vasile's part.

"The only thing that has saved Sylvania to this point," Marjit said, "is that whenever we tried to send the princesses away, storms and earthquakes rose up to chase them—and we had to bring the princesses right back to make it all stop. So Corvinus may not believe in the curse, but *everyone* in this region believes that Vasile controls a great magic. That's protected us more than anything else. They think, *If this is what he'll do to keep his daughters at home, imagine what he'd do to an invader!*"

"I see," I said, though it wasn't true; I was just barely beginning to see. "It was . . . nice of you to let me over-hear the princesses with you."

Marjit snorted, spreading out her towels to dry. "It en't kindness. I need a second witness if the princesses spill one of their secrets. I thought this morning, with Tereza's betrothed disappearing and all, we'd hear som-mat useful."

"We did! They said the dancing Saxon learned his lesson."

Marjit shook her head. "Not enough to go to the Prince about." She sighed. "Trust me."

I considered. "If we did overhear something use-ful . . ."

"We'd split the dowry, of course." She examined my face. "Why, do you have plans for the whole of it?"

"Of course," I said, blushing like I wasn't planning to use the dowry to join a convent.

"I knew it," Marjit gloated. I refrained from asking her what she thought she knew. Instead, I thanked her and left.

I scurried off to the herbary, passing Armas and Pa and

several other men loading harquebuses. Their volleys of gunfire echoed through the courtyard, scaring the crows away and awakening Brother Cosmin early, so he came to set us many tasks in the herbary long before noon.

Didina didn't come back from the midday meal. Brother Cosmin kept forgetting she wasn't in the room with us— she was much quieter than me, so perhaps it was easy to forget, especially with me there. When he called for her the third time, only to look up in puzzlement when she didn't answer, he said, "Reveka, go *find* Didina, please!"

I went, and gladly. The herbary was stuffy, with the shutters drawn to keep out the sunlight.

I was arrested right outside the door by the sight of a golden-haired boy near my age seated on the edge of the Little Well, pulling up a bucket of water.

Now, there were three wells inside Prince Vasile's walls: the main well by the kitchen, the sour well down past the stables—which gave perfectly healthful water that reeked of rotten eggs—and the Little Well near the herbary. I was told no one ever drank from the Little Well. I'd believed it had run dry long ago.

The boy, who was prettier than any boy had a right to be, with forget-me-not eyes and a rosebud mouth, scooped a wooden cup full of water from his dripping bucket. He paused, the cup held halfway to his perfect lips, and stared at me, slack-jawed.

I knew I wasn't anywhere near pretty enough to receive this kind of reaction—but neither was I ugly enough. I frowned at him—and still he stared. I felt the blood rise in my cheeks, and I grew angry. He stared like I was wearing a duck on my head. I didn't like it. It was rude.

I don't know what came over me then, other than that I was parched from working in the hot herbary and annoyed beyond belief. I marched right up to the boy, snatched the cup from his hands, and gulped down his water.

He was so astonished that his fingers didn't even fight to keep the cup. He just gawped at me. I glared back over the brim. "Close your mouth," I told him when I'd swallowed. "You'll catch flies."

I handed him the cup and turned toward the archway leading from our tiny walled garden into the rest of the castle. I glanced back at the boy: He held the wooden cup limply in his hands, his mouth open so far that his chin practically touched his chest.

The door of the herbary slammed open. I thought Brother Cosmin was coming to chastise me for lollygagging, but he didn't seem to notice me. He bolted for the Little Well, shouting at the boy. He punched the wooden cup out of the boy's hand, knocking it into the well. Then he sent the bucket and rope tumbling after.

The rope hissed away in the silence, until there came the distant splash of the bucket hitting the water.

Now it wasn't just the boy who stared with an open mouth.

"*Never* drink from that well," Brother Cosmin said, as though scolding a small child. He looked over at me; I tried to shrink around the corner, but it was too late. "Reveka! You hear this, too! Never, ever drink from here! It's contaminated."

I was going to die from drinking poisoned water! I clutched my belly, preparing for spasms. But nothing happened.

The water hadn't tasted bad. In fact, it had been very, very good. A little bit sweet but with the tang of stone and . . . almonds? And it had been oh so cold.

"Contaminated how?" I asked, afraid now of a more spiritual than physical contamination. Perhaps someone had drowned themselves in the well. Everyone knew better than to drink from a suicide well.

"It's . . . just no good," Brother Cosmin said.

"Fairies," the boy suggested.

"No, not fairies." Brother Cosmin stooped and scraped a bit of moss off one of the stones, revealing an inscription written in a language I didn't know. "Two Turkish prisoners dug this well, and when it was finished, they cursed it with this carving."

Another curse? I craned my head, even though I couldn't read Turkish. "What's it say?"

"Are you sure they were Turks and not fairies?" the boy asked.

"Who are you?" Brother Cosmin snapped.

"I'm Mihas," the boy said. "I came to the castle just yesterday to sell a cow, and they gave me work in the gardens."

"Get back to your work, Mihas." Brother Cosmin turned to me. "And you, Reveka: Go find Didina!"

Mihas slouched after me out of the courtyard. "He didn't have to throw the bucket down the well," he said. "That was Master Konstantin's bucket. He's going to be angry."

"Yes, well, don't lie to him about it, whatever you do. Master Konstantin can't abide liars."

"Why would I lie, when that monk is the one who threw it into the well?"

I half shrugged. When I was very young, I might have made up a story about forgetting the bucket, to put off getting beaten for losing it. Of course, when I was a little older and the Abbess eagerly noticed my every transgression, I would have lied and said I never borrowed the bucket in the first place, or whatever I thought I could get away with to avoid trouble. Later, once my reputation was firmly established with the Abbess, I could have told the truth entirely about a monk throwing the pail down the well, and no one would have believed me—and I would have had to go a week without wearing a shift between my wool clothes and my skin, fast for three days on bread and water, and recite extra psalms for the dead, as well as endure a beating. I could almost feel the sting of alder sticks smacking my thighs.

I came back to the present with a shiver. Mihas was staring at me, mouth open.

"What? Why are you staring?"

He licked his overpink lips. "I hope the fairies didn't curse you," he said earnestly.

The boy was an idiot. Brother Cosmin had told him that there was a Turkish curse on the well, and he still thought it was fairies. I couldn't believe Pa had hired him.

I turned on my heel and went looking for Didina.

CHAPTER 9

After checking the kitchens and the privy, I went to look for Didina in the western tower, where her mother slept and her grandmother watched.

I climbed the tower, assessing the whole time whether I felt sick from drinking at the Little Well, but . . . nothing came of it. I had a small ill feeling in my midsection, but that was because I was a little bit afraid of why Didina hadn't come to work in the herbary that afternoon.

When I opened the door to the tower, my worst fears were realized. Didina huddled in Mistress Adina's arms, crying.

My throat went dry. "Is it . . . is it your mother?"

Adina looked up over Didina's scarf-covered head, eyes sad and red. "Yes. My daughter is—slipping away."

I sat down hard on a stool and stared in shock at my fellow apprentice.

"I'm sorry," I whispered. I couldn't even imagine what

I would do if Pa were lying cursed before me—could imagine even less what I would do if he were dying. We hadn't gotten along perfectly—he was too quick to believe the worst about me—but he was all I had, and he'd done more for me than many fathers might.

"There has to be something you can do, Grandma," Didina pleaded.

Adina looked helplessly at the girl. We all knew there was nothing anyone could do. I had talked it over with Adina. When any of the sleepers started to fade, in a matter of weeks they wasted down to skin and bones and simply . . . died.

Since it was better than sitting there, crying, Adina got us up and moving, to help her with the caretaking of the cursed sleepers. We washed their bodies, we fed them, we moved their limbs. We checked for sores and lice and fleas.

I moved in dumb silence, berating myself for my self-ishness, swearing to do better. I'd jumped headlong into the puzzle of curse breaking, so pleased about the dowry and the opportunities it represented that I hadn't bothered to discover the truth of what the curse really *meant*.

"I'm sorry," I said again, staring at Didina's calm, strong hands combing out her mother's hair.

"Sorry for what?" she asked. "You didn't do this to her. To any of them. It was all set in motion long before you arrived."

I gave Didina a regretful smile. "If my ma weren't dead, but just asleep, I'd steal the sun and stars to try and wake her."

"If you knew how," Didina said coldly, and I realized it sounded like I blamed her for just not trying hard enough.

"No—no, that's not what I meant. I meant . . . thank you for being so kind to me, Didina."

The cold anger melted from her face, leaving behind a puzzled expression. "How do you mean? I've not . . . I've not been particularly kind to you, Reveka."

"Not *particularly*, no. But wouldn't I just want to slap silly any girl who thought the dowry was more important than my mother, even for a moment?"

Didina's expression thawed further. "Reveka, you actually tried to wake the sleepers. I"—she clasped her hands over her heart—"I thank you that you tried."

I nodded. "And I thank you still, for not slapping me silly."

I stayed with them until the sleepers made their nightly cry, then took Didina down to the herbary loft, where we slept. I gave her valerian tea to help her rest while I stayed up for some hours combing through *Physica* in hopes that Saint Hildegard had performed a miracle and left the clues to a cure within the pages of her herbal.

When finally I slept, I dreamed.

Sunlight fell on my shoulders as I followed a road through wide, striped fields. The road rose slowly into the mountains—never steep, though. My feet carried me without effort. There was something at the top I had to see, something I had to know about.

I climbed to the crumbling gate of a large palace hewn from a type of shining rock that I didn't recognize. The whole edifice was a ruin, and the only truly intact piece was a doorless archway. Carved into the keystone was a sleeping human face, troubled in its repose.

I started forward to examine the face, and its stone eyes opened. "Ruin is everywhere," the mouth said. "A reminder that eternity exists."

My heart pounding in my ears woke me.

I rose early, unable to sleep after the dream and not wishing to disturb Didina's slumber. I lit a candle and studied the list of Plantes Which Confer Vpon the Wearer Invisibilitie.

I copied the whole list to a tiny scrap of vellum, rolled it tightly, and tucked it behind my ear, underneath my cowl. Maybe if I carried it near my brain, it would make more sense. And if I studied it in leisure moments, that might help, too.

At dawn, I went out to the herb garden, coating my bare feet with chilly dew, to smell the scents of earliness.

In the convent, I would have been roused for Lauds at dawn to pray, but I hadn't seen this hour since Pa came for me. I'd expected to have to keep the night watches for prayer again when I was apprenticed to a monk, but Brother Cosmin's lax monkishness didn't demand prayer even the night before an important saint's feast.

I had gathered great armfuls of mint and tansy and was headed to the baths when I caught a flash of red and black in the shadows near the Little Well. It was Frumos—the strange man from the woods.

He was less handsome than I remembered, and he was younger than I remembered, too.

"The herbalist's apprentice," Frumos said slowly. "Remind me of your name?"

I tried not to mind that he'd forgotten me, even though I remembered every detail of him, from the ugly tusks on his cloak clasp to the way his eyes smiled more than his mouth.

I said, "If you can't remember my name, then I won't remind you."

He cocked his head. "I didn't think you were old enough to be so coy."

I shrugged and scrutinized him. His clothing was exactly the same as it had been in the woods. What did that mean? Did he not have another suit of clothes? Owning only one set of fancy clothing seemed like the sort of thing an impostor would do, but who was Frumos imposing on?

"What are you doing here?" I asked, thinking that the only reason I knew for random men to show up at Castle Sylvian was if they were going to try to break the curse.

"I came to see if the Hungarians had arrived yet."

I pointed to the crows clustered on the eaves. They had returned in the night and now shuffled and eyed us with annoyance. "Just those ones. Do they count? Everyone says Corvinus sent them."

Frumos eyed the birds. "Not Corvinus himself, of course," he said. "But someone close to him."

"What?" I asked, startled. "What does that mean?"

"I mean, he has a . . . magician of sorts, a *hultan* on his side, who controls the crows and uses them as spies."

I shivered. *Hultani* were great wizards, powerful enough to harness a *zmeu* dragon and ride it.

I wanted to ask Frumos how he knew that, about the *hultan* and the crows, but he was staring at the Little Well, tracing his fingers over the carving where Brother Cosmin had scraped away the moss. "Well," I said, reluctantly hefting my basket of herbs, "I have work to do." I bobbed about half a curtsy less than what a lord was due, turned, and marched out of the courtyard.

There was laughter in the voice that followed me. "Have a good day. Reveka."

I didn't turn around, even when he said my name. I don't think I even broke my stride. But I did wish him luck breaking the curse—not because I wanted him to steal my dowry, but because I didn't want him to end up in the tower asleep, or simply gone, like all the others.

CHAPTER 10

Marjit thought I was early enough that I should have a bath before the princesses arrived. She never could forgo an opportunity to scrub someone.

I let her soap me and put me into the hot bath, but I stewed only a moment; it was really too warm at this time of year. The green-blue dolphin mosaic at the bottom of the cool plunge looked trapped beneath glass, and I shattered the smooth surface with a yelp. The sudden change in temperature made my skin prickle, but it cleared the dream and the conversation with Frumos from my mind.

Marjit held out a big towel for me. "A bath every two days!" she said with mock wonder. "I don't know, Reveka. You might just become a sybarite. Weren't you raised in a convent?"

Marjit's teasing was always the price of getting such a good bath. So I just grinned and toweled myself. But my grin faded when Princess Otilia entered the bathing room. I froze. We'd lost track of time, and the princesses were here!

Princess Otilia looked as surprised to see me as I was to see her—but Marjit's expression was cool as fresh butter. "Oh, Mar—Marjit, I came early," Otilia stuttered. "I thought you'd be alone."

I tried to curtsy, but the towel gaped, and it was not my most graceful moment ever. I backed away and put my clothes on while pretending to be invisible.

"Did you . . ." Otilia hesitated, looking from me to Marjit. She seemed to decide I wasn't a threat. "Did you have something for me?" she asked the bathwoman.

Marjit raised her eyebrows. "Nothing but a nice bath, Your Highness," she said.

"Oh, well, I'll come back for that," Otilia said hastily, and retreated up the passageway.

I dressed with speed, biting my tongue to keep from asking what all *that* was about. Not out of any respect for Otilia's or Marjit's privacy, mind you; but there are no secrets in a tiled room, and I didn't want Otilia to overhear me on her way out.

I silently raised my eyebrows at Marjit.

Marjit waited until Otilia was probably out of earshot. "That one has never really taken to being a princess," she said.

I shrugged. "Who really could? They wear ridiculous hats, and overlong shoes, and dresses that collect all manner of dirt along the hem."

Marjit snorted. "I don't think you've thought the matter through."

I ignored that and started preparing the bath herbs—hollyhock and mallow today—while waiting for Marjit to give me the gossip. She didn't, though. How disappointing! I'd been told there were three things you could rely on at Castle Sylvian: sunrise, sunset, and Marjit's gossip.

Frumos was nowhere to be seen on my way back to the herbary, but I did spy Mihas trimming back the yew hedges. I'd rather have found Frumos, but on the other hand, I didn't need more mysteries today.

Didina and I worked steadily all morning, not saying much to each other. I attributed the silence to her sadness for her mother, but I wondered if something else was going on. She kept chewing mint. To settle her stomach?

At midday, she asked Brother Cosmin if she could go sit with her mother, and he granted her request. I worked twice as hard in her absence so she didn't have to feel she was making a hardship for us.

I went to deliver my posies to the princesses, and ran into the Mihas boy again in the narrow courtyard outside their tower. Now he was trimming ivy from the tower walls. I tried to scoot past without acknowledging him, but he called my name and then stood there, staring at me with his mouth open. I grimaced at him, with what could be taken as either fierceness or regret, and scurried into the tower as though I didn't have time for pleasantries. He was gone when I came back out.

I headed to the kitchens, plagued with a growing knot in my stomach that just didn't seem to want to go away.

Didina never showed up to supper. I rushed through Cook's fine dish of trout in garlic sauce and went to the western tower, hoping to find Didina visiting with her grandmother.

But for the sleepers, Adina was alone, netting socks furiously as though winter were coming and no one had boots. She waved me in to sit with her, but I begged off.

I double-checked the herbary, but Didina hadn't returned.

My stomach clenched with fear. I knew what was worrying me, what had been worrying me all afternoon.

I pelted through the castle's courtyards, crossing shadows that grew longer by the moment. I ran into the princesses' maids leaving their tower but didn't pause to talk to them. I slid to a stop inside the tower bedroom.

Didina was standing in the middle of the room, searching high and low. Looking for a hiding place.

"What are you doing?" I cried.

She whirled around, clutching her chest. "By the cross! I thought— Reveka, what are you doing here?"

"What am I doing here? *What are you doing here?*"

"Shhhh!" She looked frantically around. "Come on, now, you need to leave. The princesses must be on their way back, and I must hide!"

Footsteps sounded outside the door. Didina squeaked and shoved me under a bed. "Didina!" I whispered furiously while she slid behind a cluster of gowns hanging from pegs on the wall.

"Shhhhh!"

I held still, trying not to breathe. I heard footsteps, words. "This will be an *utter* disaster," someone said in a low voice. From the refined accent, I thought it must be either Princess Maricara or Princess Tereza.

"I can't believe the effrontery," another voice answered. "They send an emissary who is really no more than a *merchant*, and he wants to put us in iron shoes?"

"And when our feet are bleeding raw, what will happen then?" another voice chimed in.

"Papa will never agree to it."

"Papa will agree to it until he sees it has no effect. Then he'll have the irons struck off. And then he'll apologize— just like the last three times his meddling made us bleed."

"Ooooh, but what if I fall out of my boat?" The voice belonged to the princess wearing blue slippers. "I'll sink directly to the bottom of the river, and that'll be the end of us all! I can't dance on the river bottom!"

"We will do what we have to do." I recognized Lacrimora. "We will wear whatever shoes *Papa* demands, and we will dance the dances that our lord demands, and there's an end of it. Try not to fall out of your boats either way."

"Lacrimora is entirely right," Blue Slippers said.

"Lacrimora is always right," Princess Maricara answered snidely.

"We should just confess," a smaller, quieter voice said. I thought it was Otilia. "We should just tell Prince Vasile everything."

"And *what*? Papa will buy us out of our bargain?" Maricara again.

"Not my bargain," a dark voice muttered.

"Girls. Hush. It's time," Princess Maricara announced.

At once, everyone fell silent, and footsteps moved to every corner of the room. "This bed's clear," Blue Slippers called.

"And this one," Maricara said.

I began to panic. They were only three beds away from me.

I heard the solid thumps of a heavy object hitting fabric. "The tapestries are clear," Lacrimora said.

"My bed's clear," two princesses chorused.

"The dresses are—" Lacrimora began, and something thumped.

But in addition to the thump, there was a cry.

"Got one," Lacrimora said softly.

Footsteps thundered as half a dozen princesses ran across the room. Then came the sounds of a struggle, and Didina screamed.

"Who is *that*?" Maricara asked.

"It's . . . it's the herbalist's apprentice," Otilia said, sounding near tears.

"But that's not Cabbage Girl," Maricara said. Did they *all* call me that?

"There are two apprentices," Lacrimora told her. "This is the other one. What did you hear, Apprentice?"

"N-nothing," Didina said.

"I don't believe you," Princess Maricara said.

"She was *right there*," Princess Blue Slippers said. "Not even under a bed."

"She heard enough," Princess Tereza said. "Lacrimora, fetch the wine."

"No!" Otilia cried, but no one listened to her.

I bit my thumbs, forcing myself to stay still and silent. There was no way I could fight all twelve princesses—or even eleven, assuming Otilia might be on our side. There were two farm-girl princesses whose names I didn't even know but who each alone could beat me up.

"Plug her nose," Blue Slippers said, and there came a horrible gagging sound and the plash of liquid hitting the floor. I moaned into my hands, but no one heard me over Didina's gulping and gasping.

"She'll sleep," Lacrimora said with grim satisfaction.

"Hurry up! We're going to be late!" Blue Slippers said, and with an ungentle thud, they let Didina fall to the floor.

The noise of stone grinding on stone, louder than any millstones, filled the chamber.

"Come on, get up, dear," Otilia said. "I'll help you to my bed." Didina murmured something unintelligible to her. "I know. I know. Shhh . . . but it's better this way. You don't want to become like us. You don't want to lose your soul."

"Otilia!" Lacrimora's voice was vicious. *"Leave her."*

"I'm so sorry, Didina," Otilia whispered. "Sleep well. . . ."

"Otilia!" Lacrimora spoke again. Otilia's footsteps faded, stone ground against stone again, and the light disappeared from the room. I imagined I could hear, all the way across the castle, the words of the sleepers: "Don't go!"

"Gone," Didina muttered. "All gone." Her speech was slurred. "Don't go. . . ."

I waited about two seconds more before crawling out from under the bed. "Wake up," I said sharply to Didina, and began pawing through my herb bag to find a stimulant.

"What did the wine taste like?"

"Oversweet, but bitter. Awful. There was . . ." She trailed off.

I slapped her cheek, bringing her awake again. "Nepenthe!" she said. "For certain. Perhaps narcissus. Something stale and dark, like dirt. Or mold. Or heartbreak . . . if that has . . . flavor. . . ."

"Didina!" I cried. I turned her on her side, sliding her half off the bed, and stuck my fingers down her throat. She vomited widely onto my shoes and the floor. I had to turn my head away to avoid vomiting myself.

I slid her back onto the bed and went through my herb pouch again. I had nothing to counteract such powerful sleep agents, nothing at all. But back in the herbary—

I ran to the door, but it had been barred from the other side, like it was every night. I kicked and screamed at the door, but no one came.

I ran back to Didina, tried to rouse her.

But she was asleep.

CHAPTER 11

I did not immediately have the presence of mind to investigate the poison the princesses had used, but after I'd sat vigil over Didina's peacefully sleeping body for a time, it occurred to me to do so.

I uncorked the wine jug they'd left on the table and sniffed it carefully. Didina had already identified nepenthe and narcissus. I wondered what would happen to me if I licked just a drop from the bottle's lip: Would I fall immediately into the same magical sleep as Didina?

I had to risk it. They'd poured a lot of this down Didina's throat before it took effect. I wet my finger and dabbed it on my tongue. Immediately, I could taste sticklewort, possibly thorn apple. There was also a flavor like peaches . . . or maybe almonds . . . maybe cherry bark. But it was overpowered by the taste of mold and death. Didina had noticed it, too. Graveyard dirt? That seemed an appropriate additive for a witches' brew. I knew of no counteragent.

The tip of my tongue went numb. I spat repeatedly and scrubbed out my mouth with my sleeve and a handful of mint from my herb pouch.

Rather than risk discovery and my own inconvenient poisoning, I slipped underneath a bed as far away from Didina's vomit as I could get. The hour was late, and though I was terrified of discovery and mournful over my friend, I fell asleep.

I dreamed. I shouldn't have; I never was much of a dreamer. Certainly, I had nightmares when I was small, usually about Muma Pădurii boiling me up in soup because liars taste so good, but that's standard fare for anyone who's heard too many Mother of the Forest tales.

In this dream, I stood on the far shore of a dark lake, looking up at a shadowed castle on a mountaintop. People were all around me, but none of them could see or hear me. And I knew, in the way you know things in dreams, that I was invisible because of my magic hat.

I jerked awake, certain that I'd heard the princesses' voices. But there was nothing and no one. The room was silent.

I did not sleep again. I lay in misery and terror until the room lightened, and birds sang outside, and stones ground against stones.

I had a good enough vantage point to see that a hole opened in the floor when this noise came. The air filled with the voices of quarreling princesses.

Otilia crawled out of the hole and went immediately to Didina. She said dully, "Surpassingly good job, Lacrimora. Your skill with the potion improves every year."

"You know it's not my choice," Lacrimora hissed.

"Disgusting. She's covered in vomit," Ruxandra said.

"Show a little remorse! A little compassion!" Otilia cried. "If you lose those things, you may as well just *marry him*."

Silence, then—at least, no more speech. Bars and bolts thunked open, hinges creaked. Footsteps retreated, footsteps approached. I barely breathed.

The princesses were gone, leaving only their maids in the empty room. "Go and fetch Mistress Adina," Beti said to her comrades. "This poor lamb needs to be put to bed in the other tower."

The maids departed—one to fetch Adina, one to fetch water and a scrub brush—leaving me alone at last. I crawled out, cast a sad, scared look at Didina, and fled straight to the Princess Consort.

I had to wait a long time in the hallway next to the dragon-kidnaps-a-maiden tapestry while a servant explained to the Princess Consort that the troublesome herbalist's apprentice was begging for an audience. I noticed that the snag on the maiden's cheek was gone, repaired by expert fingers. Now there was nothing to distract the viewer from the menacing *zmeu* looming over the maiden, his long red fingers reaching out to caress her, his spiny cheeks glistening with ichor.

I wondered how she hadn't figured out he was a *zmeu* before, maybe at their wedding ceremony. In the stories, you always know who the *zmeu* is; the storytellers always say he's charming and friendly and looks like an ordinary man, but they also drop hints so broad that you can't help but think the girl is stupid for not knowing.

The servant came out, looking frazzled. "Go on, then," she snapped. "Princess Daciana has little time, so make good use of it!"

The Princess Consort was pacing anxiously before I even told her what I'd seen the night before. And once I'd finished, she looked ready to scream.

"A hole in the floor!" Princess Daciana said, hitting fist to palm. "We're so near! We knew they were leaving the tower at night, but they weren't flying out on broomsticks or transforming themselves into birds or bats . . . so it had to be underground. It had to be a tunnel. That's why we hired your father, to break into the princesses' tunnel. Only *our* tunnels keep collapsing."

"Most Noble and Ser—"

"Call me 'Your Highness,' or simply '*Doamnă.*'"

"Your Highness," I said, uncomfortable with *doamnă*, since it just meant "lady" and the Princess Consort was more than a lady. "My father has forbidden me to meddle with the curse, on account of what has happened to the others who have tried."

"Understandable," Princess Daciana said. "Of course, it is not meddling with the curse proper to try yew or santolina on the sleepers. . . ."

My eyes might have bugged out of my head with surprise at that—very attractive, I'm sure—but I couldn't help it. "Who—how—why do you know this?" I asked.

"This is my castle, is it not? I have the running of it. A proper chatelaine knows everything that goes on in her domain."

"Then—you know that Didina's mother, she's slipping away? She'll die in a matter of weeks if—"

The Princess interrupted. "Yes, of course, and the Duke of Styria, too."

"Pardon?"

"Princess Maricara was once betrothed to the Duke of Styria. He succumbed to the sleep the night before their wedding. My spies tell me he is slipping away as well."

The Princess had spies? I was impressed. I wanted spies.

She went on: "Should he round the corner alone . . ." She shook her head. "We will be at war. The Hungarians arranged that marriage between Maricara and the Duke, and they take it as a personal affront that it hasn't worked out. The Hungarians have been looking for an excuse to roll over us, the better to harry Moldavia's borders, I suppose."

To "roll over us"? Wouldn't Pa's defenses hold them up even a day? My stomach flopped.

I'd lived in a country that had been "rolled over" before. The Turks had raided into Transylvania several times a year for my whole life. I dreaded war. Pa would take up soldiering again, probably, and then, in addition to the threat of bloody battles, there'd be the fear and the famine. . . .

I wasn't sure how I was supposed to answer the Princess, but I thought signaling comprehension was a good idea. "Oh. I hadn't heard."

"No. You shouldn't have. Don't spread it around. We do not need to worry people unduly, and . . ." She darted an uneasy look at the solar door, like she was expecting someone unwelcome to come through it. "The Duke of Styria hasn't died *yet*, so carry on, Reveka," she said, sitting down and waving me a dismissal.

"Carry on?" I said. "Carry on with what?"

"With your experiments to awaken the sleepers, of course. Waking the Duke is our first priority."

"What? No! You don't understand. I found a list." I

didn't quite know how to explain myself, so I stripped off my cowl and pulled the little scroll from behind my ear. "It's a list of 'plants which confer upon the wearer invisibility.' And we've been experimenting with them, Didina and I, though with no success thus far. But I can't actually try everything listed here. We—I don't have the resources."

The Princess leaned forward in her chair, trying to read the vellum scrap I held. I handed it to her without a qualm, since I'd memorized the words by now.

"Which of these things have you tried?"

I told her how Didina had been working on the list, and how I'd tried pig's weed my own self.

"It may very well be another fool's errand, trying to figure out this list," the Princess said. "What was your plan, if you managed to discover a method for becoming invisible?"

"The same as anyone's, Princess. Hide and watch. Only with a more refined method of hiding."

"I see." She waved the list languidly for a moment, then said, "Let me keep this for a bit, so I can supply you with the items you are missing. Then I want you to begin your experiments anew. And come tell me right away if you discover anything. But whatever you do, keep trying to waken the sleepers. We have, perhaps, two weeks before the Duke of Styria dies and war becomes inevitable."

That was a sobering deadline, even though I was elated at the prospect of the Princess Consort's help. I agreed to the Princess's plan, and she dismissed me.

Outside the solar, I ducked behind the *zmeu* tapestry—and trembled.

I steadied myself with a pinch of sage under my tongue, but I'd need a calming tea to really make a difference. I dropped my head back against the wall, willing myself not to cry.

Didina's ma and the Duke of Styria were both dying, and Didina herself was asleep in the western tower, and someday she'd start slipping away, too. And if war came to Sylvania—would Pa keep me here, or would he send me away? Without me, what would happen to Didina? Adina couldn't wake her, and no one else even knew how start trying.

I had to work fast. And secretly. Pa was going to be righteously angry with me if he found out I was involved in *any* of this.

CHAPTER 12

I wanted to go to Adina, but I couldn't face her yet. I went to the herbary instead, and found Brother Cosmin uncharacteristically busy.

"There's an emissary from the Hungarian King just arrived, late last night," Brother Cosmin said. "We have no time to waste." He pointed to a list of about a thousand tasks that he'd written out for me.

"Didina—" I began, and started to sniffle.

"I know," he said, shaking his head, his mouth a narrow white slit where he pressed his lips tight. He jabbed his finger at the task list. "We have work to do."

I couldn't believe him—to think only of work at a time like this! And this was Brother Cosmin, who barely ever thought about work at all. My tears dried up. I slammed over to my table and looked for something to pulverize.

Brother Cosmin didn't speak, not even when Pa burst

through the door and grabbed me up in a tight hug.

Fortunately for me, Pa hugged the breath out of my lungs before I could speak, because it took me a moment to realize he had no idea that I'd been in the princesses' tower the night before. He was just reacting to Didina's situation. He didn't suspect my involvement.

I figured this out because he wasn't shouting at me.

Pa left again in short order, and Brother Cosmin still didn't say anything—just pointed at the next item on the list when I finished something. He had me bundle countless stems of santolina and rue into fumigants for the castle fires, and boil rosemary with orange peel for the Prince's after-dinner wash water. Only when I assembled the posies did he speak.

"One of the gardeners will take those to the tower for us," he said, placing the box of flowers outside the door. "I don't want to go up there. I suspect you don't, either."

I supposed I didn't.

The gardener who showed up in due course was none other than Mihas, the boy I'd accidentally saved from drinking from the Little Well. He stood holding the flower box, gawking at me until I was uncomfortable. To my surprise, Brother Cosmin ordered him to attend to his business. "Ridiculous boy can't keep his mouth closed," my master muttered. "Is he setting up housekeeping for moths?" This made me snort. At least I wasn't the only one who'd noticed Mihas's mouth problem.

Brother Cosmin went off to supper. I wasn't hungry, so I brought *Physica* over to my table, looking through it to see if the saint had anything useful to say about lizards. In her opinion, they weren't very poisonous, and they had no use in medicine. There was, of course, nothing about invisibility in the entry on lizards. Or in the entry on mistletoe. Or the one on pig's weed. I checked.

I wondered, not for the first time, who had placed "Plantes Which Confer Vpon the Wearer Invisibilitie" inside this book, and where they'd gotten their information—useless, pointless list that it had turned out to be.

And yet, here I was, still working at it. Still trying to solve the puzzle.

I flipped through *Physica*, looking for something about nepenthe, when quite unexpectedly I ran across a bit about yew. "The smoke of burning yew wood," Hildegard wrote, "when inhaled, dissolves bad humors so gently that there is no crisis in the body of the patient."

I thought about the yew I hadn't known what to do with in Mistress Adina's tower. It hadn't occurred to me to burn it.

When I came in the door with an armful of yew, Adina said, "I'm glad the princesses didn't get you, too."

"I, er . . ."

"The Princess Consort told me."

"The Princess *Consort* told you?"

Adina shrugged. "I've mentioned, I think, that I was the herb-wife to this castle before this nonsense began. I've been looking for a cure since you started losing your milk teeth." She sighed, settling back into her chair. "A cure for the sleep, that is. I don't give a fig for the other parts of the curse. Even if it does mean all the handsome young men disappear."

"Huh?"

Mistress Adina spread a hand out, gesturing over the bodies of the men, women, and children in the tower. "You see them, yes? The girls, the women of every age. Older men. A few boys. But of the youths—well. No judgment on Sfetnic and his friends here"—she nudged Sfetnic's body with her toe—"but they have faces that would scare away Christmas. Their handsomer friends disappeared and have never returned, awake or sleeping."

Adina picked up her netting, fretting with the edge of an unfinished stocking. "They don't show it, but they must feel bad about this. They must. They're human girls, so they have to."

I didn't agree that the princesses felt bad, except Otilia. But I didn't say anything. I asked, "What do the princesses *say* when this happens? When someone disappears or . . ."

"Oh, they say they were fast asleep and have no notion of what happened. Princess Maricara always speaks for them, her face smooth as settled cream. I don't believe a word of it, though!" Adina's netting was crumpled now in one fist, and she beat the arm of her chair.

I changed the direction of the conversation quickly over to the yew I'd brought, and I told her what Saint Hildegard said about it in her book.

"Try it," Adina said, but she didn't seem excited.

Yew smoke, in spite of Saint Hildegard's recommendation, did nothing for the sleepers. I was sorely disappointed, but Adina was unsurprised. I hung my head out the window until the green smoke cleared and wondered what herbalism was *for* if it couldn't wake the sleepers.

"If there was a natural cause, I'd have found the natural cure by now," Adina said.

"That might be true," I admitted. "But it doesn't make this less disappointing."

"Disappointment, ha," Adina said. "Why don't you come here and learn how to net? You'll never want for socks with a handy skill like netting."

I was a failure as an herbalist, I thought. Why not learn something practical for a change?

I settled down next to Adina and let her show me her needle-binding method for making socks. It was slow going, and my sock was so lumpy and ugly that I couldn't imagine anyone actually wearing it, not even with the most beautiful leg wraps to cover it up.

"You were there with my Dina," Mistress Adina said at last. "Tell me, then, what happened."

I did. I told her everything I could remember. We both cried a little bit, but I went on, all the way to my investigation of the potion and its dregs. "There was something else in there, something I couldn't identify, something a bit like peaches, a bit like almonds."

Adina put a finger to her wrinkled lips, thinking. "Peach pits, the inner seed of them, are almost exactly like bitter almonds, in shape, in size, and even taste."

"But bitter almond is poison. Wouldn't everyone here be dead if that were in the potion?"

"Peach seeds are different. You have to eat so many of them that it's barely worth knowing as a poison. There are grannies in the hills who use them to make seed cookies. But don't send a pig to forage through a peach orchard, or it'll keel right over in a day."

I took note of that, in case anyone ever gave me a pig.

I said, "Well, it could have been either bitter almond or peach seed, but that doesn't exactly help us."

"No, it doesn't." Adina looked over the sleeping bodies spread before her and went back to her netting.

We netted together in silence, waiting.

Darkness fell. The light faded in the princesses' tower. "Don't go!" the sleepers implored, and returned to silence.

I got up, curtsied politely to the *stăpână*, and slumped off to the kitchens to grab a few thyme pies before sleep.

Cook's superlative crusts aside, I was partial to thyme pies because I felt I had an especial right to them: I tended and harvested and dried all of the castle's thyme. Cook gave me two pies when I showed up, letting me sit in a quiet corner of the kitchen while he finished kneading his bread dough and gossiped with his undercooks.

I wasn't really paying attention—I had more important things to think about than who went strolling down to the orchard with whom—until Armas came in. He didn't see me sitting in the corner. Marjit entered just a few seconds later and tried to hand him a small square of parchment. "From our mutual friend," she murmured.

He stared at the square like it was a packet of poison. "I don't want it."

Marjit glanced around, saw Cook staring at her, saw me in the corner, and quickly tucked the square into her sleeve. "That's going to cause some disappointment in certain quarters," she said.

"She knows my terms." He strode from the kitchen without acknowledging anyone else.

"Lovers' quarrel?" Cook asked, winking at Marjit.

"Hardly," Marjit answered.

"Didn't mean *you* and Armas. I know sommat you don't think I know."

Marjit looked haughty. "I doubt that very much, Becer."

Cook grinned. "I discovered just the other day, Armas's pa was the blacksmith in a village wherein a certain princess was born in a mill," he gloated. "So much for secrets, Bathwoman!"

Marjit's expression changed in a flash from consternation to easy teasing. She laughed. "You're wrong about that, my friend! There's no way a princess would let a blacksmith's son court her." For a moment, I believed her carefree attitude, but then I remembered what Otilia had told me about her home village when I'd helped with her hair, a few days before. She'd mentioned she could see the sparks from the blacksmith's forge from her attic, and spoken with a certain longing. . . . Marjit was *such* a liar.

"There's no way Prince Vasile would like it, sure," Cook said. "But a man like our Chief of Prisons, he's resourceful."

Marjit told Cook to leave the gossipmongering in expert hands and turned to me. I shrank back into the corner. "I hear you have a suitor, Reveka." She spoke loudly. I could see Cook and all his assistants listening intently.

I started and blushed—for a moment I thought she meant Frumos, though how he could count as a suitor I did not know, nor could I figure how she knew about him.

"A suitor?" I asked with false coolness. I wasn't afraid to stretch the truth to Marjit, now I knew she was a liar, bigger and bolder than I'd ever been.

"You're of an age to think about courting soon," she said. "And a girl likes to understand her prospects, maybe practice a thing or two." This brought laughter and some nudging from the undercooks.

"What are you talking about, Marjit?" I asked.

"Your pa's new assistant! The cowherd from the hills. He always makes sure to watch for you when you take your flowers to the princesses."

I blinked. "Who?"

"The really handsome boy, Mihas!" Marjit exclaimed.

Mihas! The boy at the Little Well? Him? The under-cooks were laughing harder now and casting me sly looks. Cook was making mouths at me. I was getting angry.

Marjit went on. "He's too young for me, of course. But he's not too young for you!"

"No, but he could be too stupid," I said.

Silence descended in the kitchen. I heard the shuffle of sandals from beyond the threshold, and then Mihas entered the room. I'd not been able to see out the door from the corner, so I had no notion if he'd been standing there, listening—but the way everyone acted, I thought he must have been. And they'd all known it.

I stood abruptly and left the kitchens. A chorus of cat-calls and guffaws followed me out.

Mihas also followed me.

"What?" I shouted, and then felt immediately cha-grined when he flinched and nearly dropped the pie he held in his other hand.

"I just come to see if you felt sick from drinking from the well."

"I feel fine," I said, praying he hadn't overheard me call him stupid.

"Oh," Mihas said. His jaw dropped open, and I thought I was going to be treated to another long view of the interior of his mouth—when he lifted his pie and took a big bite. He stared at me, chewing. Just like a cow chewing its cud.

"Is there something else you wanted?" I asked.

"I don't have to replace the bucket that monk threw down the well," Mihas said after a moment.

"That's good," I said. Maybe I did wish that he'd overheard me call him stupid. Marjit was right that he was handsome, but his cowlike qualities made me feel ashamed for admiring his looks. He didn't need to know that, though, and feel bad. It's not like he could help having spent all that time around cows, picking up their habits.

"Good night," I said finally.

"I hope you don't fall ill from the water," he said.

"Hm," I said. Not "Thank you," not "Go away!" Just "Hm." My face grew hot. "Good night," I repeated, and scurried off to the herbary and slammed the door behind me.

CHAPTER 13

I dreamed again.

I stood on a mountaintop at night. The only light came from a few faint stars that disappeared if I looked directly at them.

A man stood beside me in the dream darkness. "All my lands," he said, "now bow to you."

I shivered, and the figure beside me flung his cloak over my shoulders and wrapped an arm around me so that we stood side to side, letting his warmth and the cloak's suffuse my body.

I woke feeling both comforted and uneasy. Throughout the next day, at odd moments while I was concentrating on other things, like copying passages from *Physica* or measuring out toadflax, I could feel the warmth and the pressure of the cloak. But as soon as I thought about the feeling, it disappeared.

Strange, I thought that morning, that I should dream so intensely. I'd dreamed the night before last, too, I remembered, and at first I thought the dreaming was a product of the poison wine I'd touched to my tongue—the faintest taste of what the sleepers in the tower must experience. But when I next tripped over Mihas the Stupid Cowherd, I remembered that I'd started dreaming after I'd stolen his cup and drunk from the forbidden well.

The Princess Consort was true to her word and sent to me a tiny horn and a red lizard skin.

I set to work right away, and in two days, the page where I'd begun recording my experiments in my herbal now read like this:

Investigation of Plantes Which Confer Invisibilitie

ⱷ Test One: Wore a pig's weed wreath. No effect. Later, tried around neck, and as a girdle. No effect. Also, twined with mistletoe. As per Didina's previous experiment, no effect.

ⱷ Test Two: Placed turnsole (heliotrope) from the garden inside tiny horn, no effect. Reported to Princess; she will send away for Egyptian heliotrope. Better quality may yield better results.

ⱷ Test Three: Mistletoe: no effect, and fell out of tree while retrieving it.

œœ **TEST FOUR:** Began soaking nepenthe seeds.

œœ **TEST FIVE:** Lizard skin and wolf's bane, no effect on first effort. Will try different configuration.

œœ **TEST SIX:** Cannot find fern seeds.

In the following days, I tried everything that I could think of, ten different ways, except for the succory, which had to be collected at Midsummer or Midwinter, and the nepenthe wine, which was still soaking. And I didn't try the fern seeds either. I spent half a day shaking fern leaves out over a white cloth, getting nothing but some brown pollen for my efforts. I finally buried my pride and asked Brother Cosmin how to collect fern seeds.

He snorted. "Good luck. Fern seeds are invisible. Which is why they confer invisibility, I suppose. . . ."

I cannot guess how the expression on my face looked at that moment, but fortunately, Brother Cosmin had his nose buried in a preparation for Prince Vasile's aged mother. "In—visibility?" I asked, almost choking in the middle of the word.

Brother Cosmin shrugged. "So the stories say. They also say you can collect fern seeds only on Saint John's Eve—your birthday, no?—and only by placing twelve pewter plates beneath the fern. The seed will fall through eleven plates, but will be stopped by the twelfth." He stopped peering at his measurement of powdered cat's wort and dumped it into a bowl with flour, water, lard, and vandal root, then looked at me. "That is, if fairies don't snatch the seed from the air as it falls."

I must have looked dubious, because Brother Cosmin opened up one of his herbals and found the passage for me. I read it carefully and sighed, frustrated. If it was in a book, it must be true. . . .

There were just no breaks for invisibility seekers, I guessed. I added to the Test Six entry: "Abandoning fern seeds, as they are invisible."

It looked like the nepenthe seeds would soon be my only hope.

My work in the herbary suffered without Didina to compete with. I found myself powdering herbs that only needed to be crushed, or overlooking bits of mold on the herbs in the drying racks. I often fell into daydreams over what it would be like to be invisible, or reveries pondering the secondary issues of invisibility. I thought about chewing strong mints so that neither stinking breath nor heavy breathing would give me away. But too much mint might give me away just as easily—

"Reveka," Brother Cosmin said, thumping the table in front of me. "Reveka!"

Startled, I glanced up.

"I've asked you three times to go out and transplant

the rue," Brother Cosmin said.

"Oh. Sorry." I got down off my stool and wandered distractedly into the garden, still thinking furiously about how to be invisible scentwise, as well as to sight. I knelt down in the dirt and dug eight small holes to put the rue transplants into—and was well into the ninth hole when I realized someone was calling my name.

It was Otilia, appearing distressed. She glanced around and ran over to me, grabbing my wrists. Astonished, I just stood there. She pressed a knotted handkerchief into my hands.

"These are for the girl," she said.

"The girl," I repeated.

"The other apprentice, the one who . . . who fell asleep."

I was frozen into silence by this absurd claim. Didina *fell asleep*, did she? Just like the apple "fell" into Eve's hand. *No one* helped either of them along?

When I made no move, Otilia worked at the knot of the handkerchief to reveal a handful of stones, white-clear, tiny, imperfect. Uncut diamonds?

"Her parents can sell these for a lot of money," Otilia said. There were twelve diamonds. I stared at them with wide eyes. "They can take her away, try to cure her elsewhere."

I cupped the stones, weighing them against each other.

They were light, not heavy as I'd expected gemstones to be. "Didina is an orphan," I said. Otilia's face fell, and she reached to take the gems back. "But her grandmother might find a use for them," I added. *Might.* Adina could take just *one* diamond and be able to seek the best physicians to try to cure her family.

You could leave tomorrow with all but one of those diamonds in your pocket, a sneaky and mean little voice said inside of me. Almost immediately, my face grew hot for even thinking that.

"Definitely, give them to your friend's grandmother!" Otilia was nodding enthusiastically, happy that someone would care for Didina.

Any convent in the world would take you with eleven of those—make you herbalist, if you wanted, make you abbess, if you wanted that instead, the voice went on. Truly, Didina and all the sleepers needed only one diamond. My fingers curled around the stones. Unbidden, a vision rose before me of whitewashed walls hung with drying racks and shelves arranged just so. Could I really be so close to realizing my dream?

In the distance, a voice called Otilia's name. My vision slipped away as I flinched, recognizing Lacrimora. Otilia flinched, too.

Otilia slapped frantically at my fistful of diamonds. "Hide them!" she whispered. I stooped down and dropped them into one of the holes I'd dug for the rue, and scooped a little dirt over them loosely just as Lacrimora came into the small garden courtyard.

Otilia's eyes were panicked and pleading. I couldn't understand why—was she not allowed to talk to me, if she wanted? She glanced back at Lacrimora with dread.

"Oh! I'm terrible at thinking up lies on the spot— they never let me talk to anyone when—" Otilia gripped my hand. "Reveka, don't tell her anything! She absolutely must not learn that I took the diamonds!" She kicked out of her shoes, gathered her skirts, and ran, fleet as a deer. Her silken bulb-nosed slippers remained in the dirt before me.

Lacrimora came up, panting and glaring. "Cabbage Girl! What did Otilia want?"

"Nothing," I said, stalling for time to think.

"She clearly had a reason to talk to you—and she clearly didn't want me to know about it," Lacrimora said. She pointed to the shoes in the dirt.

I didn't hesitate. Pa was never going to know, and the situation was urgent. And fortunately—as unfair as it was that the Abbess had so often accused me of lying—the truth was, I was a remarkably *good* liar. I had become so just to stay ahead of the Abbess's constant accusations.

"Of course she doesn't want you to know it," I said, making my voice sound angry. "It's none of your business who she—" I clapped my hand over my mouth, as though I'd said too much.

Lacrimora's eyebrows arched. "Who she *what?*" Lacrimora asked.

"Nothing," I said. "No one." Then I looked toward the castle gates, where Armas stood talking to a guardsman, as was his wont.

"Armas?" she asked.

I tried to look defeated, though mostly I just made sure I *didn't* look at the hole where I'd buried the diamonds. I said, "I didn't say Armas!" in a loud, annoyed voice.

"Why would Otilia come to talk to *you* about Armas?" she asked.

I lifted my chin. "Maybe I'm friends with Armas! You don't know!"

Lacrimora's mouth relaxed. I'd eased her mind, somehow. But even as her expression changed, her eyes narrowed. "Address me properly, Apprentice," she said.

For a moment, I thought about disobeying her, but I decided that would take the distraction too far. My goal had been to let Otilia get away, not to get into trouble myself. I curtsied. "Yes, Your Highness," I said, doing my best approximation of meekness.

Now her eyes *really* narrowed. I knew that look. The Abbess had gotten it whenever she thought I was faking good behavior. Lacrimora drew herself up taller and took a step closer. She wasn't much bigger than me, but I still shrank back a little. "You've been in the wrong place at the wrong time twice now, Cabbage Girl," she said. "I hope for your sake there won't be a third."

Was that a threat? Was she actually threatening me? After what she'd done to Didina? I pulled my shoulders straight and set my jaw. "I do what I have to do," I said, dropping the acts of both Otilia's defiant confidante and the meek peasant. I made to move past Lacrimora, to go into the herbary.

Her hand shot out and gripped my wrist. "Stop stirring the pot, Reveka. Let it boil down to nothing, and you won't get burned." She almost sounded kindly, for all that she was holding me between her evil pincers.

I tried to jerk my hand back, but she was stronger than she looked. Then I remembered that she was royalty, and if she wanted to slap me, she could. She could have Armas come and haul me off to prison if she wanted. I tried to cast my eyes down, I tried to be the docile commoner, but the words burst out of me.

"How can it boil down to nothing, with you all stealing the people of the castle like vampires in the night?"

Lacrimora threw my hand back at me like it was a serpent. "What are you saying?" she asked in a frozen voice.

"How many young men have gone missing? How many people, men and women, lie trapped in sleeping death in the western tower? Is that part of your *nothing*?"

Lacrimora recoiled. "You have no idea what you're talking about, Cabbage Girl. Get out of my sight."

Pa's voice cut across the confrontation. "Don't worry, Princess. You'll never have to see her again."

We both whipped around to see Pa bearing down on us like Greuceanu coming after the dragons that kidnapped the sun and moon—there was no mercy in him. Lacrimora caught her breath, drew herself up to her full height, and said, "I trust that is true, Gardener." She nodded austerely to him and swept away.

Pa grabbed me by my upper arm and propelled me in the opposite direction of Lacrimora, into the herbary.

CHAPTER 14

Brother Cosmin looked up when we came in, but Pa paid him no attention, spinning me around to face his icy wrath.

"Young Mihas will take your flowers to the princesses in the evenings. You're to be done with your herbs for Marjit before the princesses arrive in the morning. Do you understand, Reveka?" Pa shook me until I nodded. He looked at Brother Cosmin. "Do *you* understand, Brother?" And Brother Cosmin nodded, too, though he was also scratching himself under his robe and looking out the window and muttering about betony.

"Pa . . ." I began.

"No, Reveka," he said, his voice deadly. "No. You will not argue. You will not plead. And you will certainly not lie. That's it. The princesses will not see you; they will not know you are in the castle. You will be invisible to them—"

I couldn't help jerking my head back in surprise at the word *invisible*. Pa didn't notice, didn't care. That's when I caught Brother Cosmin sliding out the door, avoiding every pleading glance I sent him.

"You are the ghost that makes up their flowers and scents their baths. Now tell me, Reveka. Do you under-stand?"

"Pa, I—" But I stopped talking and shrank back as he loomed over me, eyebrows knit together frighteningly.

"Do you understand?" he barked, and I understood better than I ever had what he had been like as a soldier and a leader of men, and why my mother had been so eager to leave him to his wars when she got pregnant with me. He was scary right now, in a way he'd never been even during the worst of my punishments.

I wanted to lie then, and I might have, if I hadn't been so afraid of him. "Yes, Pa," I whispered. "I understand."

"Good," he said. "And in case you *don't* understand . . . I am this close to sending you away. For your own good. Do you understand *that*?"

My heart froze for a long moment, then thudded back into motion. Send me away—from him? Send me away from . . . the castle? *Perfect timing,* the sneaky voice said. *You have the diamonds. You can join a convent. Any convent you like! Pick one far from Sylvania, far from the Turks.*

If I left now, with the diamonds in my hand, could I live with myself? I probably wouldn't get caught in my thievery.

I could leave with no one the wiser about how I'd achieved my heart's desire. It was the perfect opportunity: Otilia would never betray her own secrets to expose mine.

And Pa? Would Pa track me to the convent and demand to know how I'd paid the dowry to join? What lie would I tell him about how I got there? It wouldn't be hard to break a promise, if I'd already stolen eleven diamonds.

You're going to have to break your promise anyway, said a new voice in my head. It wasn't the nasty, greedy voice. This was the normal, practical tone of my everyday thoughts. *Whatever you do from now on to break the curse, you're going to have to lie to Pa.*

And that's when I knew I couldn't leave Sylvania. I couldn't leave Didina and the sleepers, not when I might be able to break the curse—not when I might be their only hope.

I squared my shoulders, bracing myself for the shame I would feel in lying and breaking my vow to Pa, and for the harsh blow of losing the convent and my own herbary— when they were for the first time within reach.

"I do understand," I said to Pa. That much was true. I had no lack of understanding. "I understand everything."

I just left out the part where I'd obey.

After Pa left, I peeked through the window to see him corner Brother Cosmin, no doubt to set the poor man to watching my every move like a hawk. I sighed.

Brother Cosmin came back and put me to work pulverizing celery seed with powdered rue, nutmegs, cloves, and saxifrage, for Prince Vasile's gout. Every time I tried to make up a reason to leave and collect the diamonds buried in the garden, Brother Cosmin made me stay and quizzed me on the properties of celery.

Admittedly, I had not known that much about celery prior to that day, but by late afternoon, I knew that celery juice was good for watery eyes, and that when cooked, celery makes healthy humors—but no one should eat it raw.

Or perhaps it was the other way around. I was too distracted, my thoughts careening between Didina, Lacrimora, and breaking curses.

And the diamonds buried in the garden, too. Adina was going to burst apart crying when she saw them.

Brother Cosmin said, "So celery is cold and dry?" and I nodded. "Wrong! Celery is *hot* and *green* in nature."

I repeated "hot and green" and went on with the celery seed, glancing furtively at my personal herbal, trying to reread the notes I'd written about the lizard skin.

"Well, Reveka?" Brother Cosmin said.

"Hot and green," I said obediently.

"That wasn't even the question! You're useless today. Go to bed. Without your supper!" And he pointed at the ladder to my loft above the herbary.

I climbed up and waited for Brother Cosmin to leave so I could get out to the garden. But the day was hot and drowsy, and before I knew it, I had fallen asleep.

I woke to evening twilight and to blessed silence below me. I strolled out into the herb garden, looked around— including up at all the castle windows—to make sure no one was watching me, then went to dig up the diamonds for Adina.

I easily found the eight holes I'd dug earlier. But instead of the ninth hole, where I'd dumped the diamonds, I found only a small, tightly clustered patch of very strange-looking weeds. Weeds that shimmered white, almost like glass, and instead of the usual false leaves that sprout first from most seeds, these plants were small and tightly curled . . . like fern heads.

It hit me then, like the bolt from a *hultan*'s thunder-cloud: the diamonds were gone. The diamonds had never *been* diamonds. These ferns had grown from them. Otilia hadn't given me diamonds at all, but fern seeds! Magical ones that grew just a few hours after planting.

How stupid had Otilia been, to believe that fern seeds were diamonds?

How stupid had *I* been, an herbalist who didn't recognize seeds when she saw them?

I cursed and stomped about, working myself into a

right frenzy. I'd missed the only chance I was probably ever going to get to test fern seeds! I'd never seen seeds like those before. Well, I'd never seen ferns like these before either.

I went back to bed, hungry, disappointed, angry. I curled around all the hollow feelings in my midsection and forced myself to sleep, until the Little Well's unfortunate gift of dreams filled my mind once more.

When I woke the next morning, I was on my side, facing Didina's empty pallet. I lay still for a long moment, thinking about all the things on the Plantes Which Confer Invisibilitie list, and how each item seemed so easy, and how each one had managed to fail so pathetically.

Something about the whole Plantes list was off. Wrong, somehow. I didn't know much about magic, but wasn't it a complicated business, as complicated as herbalism? You shouldn't be able to create a magic as powerful as invisibility by simply plaiting a wreath and tossing it on your head, should you? No more than you could make an effective salve by throwing comfrey into a pot and letting it sit for three weeks. There's more to herbalism than the right ingredients: There is also method. The same must be true for magic as well.

It came down to this: I needed a witch.

The problem was that the only person who had ever mentioned witches to me in any sort of authoritative manner was Marjit the Bathwoman.

After the bathing chambers cleared out from the servants' jolly baths, I stole down to visit Marjit.

I didn't mean to sneak, but I moved too quietly, and the lady squawked like a crow with pulled tail feathers when I came up behind her. "Why are you trying to frighten old Marjit?" She asked it jokingly. Even if she wasn't in the prime of her life, she felt young. She'd said so many times.

"First," I said, "let's establish that I have a secret. And I need you to keep this a secret. All right?"

Her lips twitched, and she laughed. "I would have thought that anyone who brought a secret to me wanted its truth trumpeted around the land!"

"No! No, it's important to keep this a secret. Because if my father finds out, he's going to send me away. And if the princesses find out, they'll probably . . ." I trailed off, wondering how to end that supposition. *Poison me?* "I came to you because I need a witch, and I thought maybe you knew one."

The laughter left Marjit's eyes. "This is a lucky day for you," she said. "For *I* am a witch."

CHAPTER 15

In the end, it was the very fact that she'd been able to keep her witchcraft a secret that made me trust Marjit. I told her everything about the list.

Right away, she saw a number of things that I'd done wrong in trying the herbs on the list of Plantes Which Confer Vpon the Wearer Invisibilitie. "You've no *intentions*. You've not called on any Holies. There's nothing to spark the magic. Invisibility en't a simple quality of these plants, it's a sleeping quality that must be drawn out, with a rhyme or holy water or sommat similar."

I understood this. It was like how burdock works best on burns if you say a prayer for frost first. At the same time, I didn't like it, because it wasn't very clear or precise. None of this was written down on the list, and Marjit seemed very blithe about waving her hands, chanting a few words, and expecting it all to work.

"And I bet your ferns will work without the seeds," she added.

"How?"

"Go out and cut some of them. Not all! You'll want to nurse them along and try to harvest the seeds if this fails. What you cut, fashion into a wreath—or no, a cap. That'll stay on your head better. You know how to net? You've spent all that time with Adina—she's got to have taught you."

"I'm bad at netting, but . . ."

"You'll be good enough. You'll make up your cap, I think with a prayer to the Big Lady—"

"The Big Lady?"

"Hush, don't you worry about that." She stared off into the middle distance, muttering slightly under her breath, before saying, "You'll need a special needle."

"A Nine-Brides Needle?" I asked. It was a stupid joke, but she took me seriously.

"No, though that's a good thought, because of the stealth. No. I don't have one on hand, and—well, I don't know of nine weddings happening anytime soon. Sommat else. I'll have to think on it." She counted something on her fingers. "Come back in twelve days. The dark of the moon is the perfect time to do a ritual of invisibility."

"No. It can't wait that long! By then . . ." By then, Didina's mother, and maybe the Duke of Styria, too, would be dead, or past the point of no return. "Look, the moon is waning. Isn't that good enough?"

Marjit started to shake her head, then sighed. "I can't guarantee anything, mind you," she said. "Come tomorrow night at midnight. Have your ferns ready. And be prepared for a long night."

I nodded. "Can you keep this a secret, Marjit?"

Marjit appeared to think about this. "Well, I suppose. . . ."

"Marjit!" I begged. I thought she was teasing, but I couldn't risk anything.

"Of course I can keep a secret," she said, and leaned down to kiss my cheek.

It wasn't until later that I realized that wasn't the promise I'd wanted.

Pa came with me to help Adina with the sleepers the next day, I think because he felt bad about being so harsh to me. Adina smiled at him and asked him for news of the castle.

"I've no good tidings, I'm afraid," Pa said. "I was at the morning summoning—do you know of this ritual, Reveka? Every morning after they bathe, the princesses are brought before the Prince, to answer for the holes in their shoes. Princess Maricara always steps forward and says that they do not know, because they are asleep when the holes are made."

I rolled my eyes. "Can't Prince Vasile tell they're lying?"

· 122 ·

Pa said, "It takes a liar to spot a lie." He pinched open Sfetnic's mouth, dropped in a spoonful of broth, then massaged the boy's throat. I waited for Pa to give me a significant glance, to make this a lesson about truth for me, but he didn't. He just added, "Prince Vasile is terribly honest."

"Honest for a prince," Adina amended. "He's not honest for a normal man."

Pa continued with his news. "Usually, the Prince invites the princesses to sit down for a cup of spiced wine and some bread, but this morning, he let another man speak—an emissary from the King of Hungary, who has been sent to investigate the disappearance of a Transylvanian Saxon named Iosif—but really, he seems to be here to wring concessions out of our Prince about his heir—or lack thereof." Pa frowned, staring down at Sfetnic's peaceful face. "The Hungarians want Vasile to agree to become a count, beholden to King Corvinus, like the rulers in Marmatia."

I frowned. "I thought that the Hungarians wanted to invade us."

"The invasion would be solely to make Sylvania into this sort of vassal state. But they wouldn't mind just bullying Prince Vasile into handing over his principality instead."

"Would Prince Vasile do that, instead of letting the country get invaded?"

Pa grunted. "Doesn't matter if Vasile would or wouldn't.

King Stefan in Moldavia won't let that happen. Sylvania has been a good buffer for his country against Hungary, just as Moldavia has been a good buffer for us against Poland and the Turks. There'd be a war either way."

I shivered, thinking of holes blown into the side of the castle, of cannonballs shooting through Brother Cosmin's herbary or into this room among the helpless sleepers.

"Anyway," Pa continued, "all week, this emissary has been pressing Vasile for the release of the Saxon, Iosif, who Princess Tereza was set to marry. Iosif disappeared a week or so ago; the rest of his delegation hurried away from here, and I'm sure they didn't go home to Transylvania but ran straight into King Corvinus's arms."

"But Prince Vasile can't release Iosif. He disappeared!"

"The emissary doesn't believe in the curse—because Corvinus doesn't believe in the curse. They think everyone missing or sleeping in here is a political enemy of Vasile."

"Even Didina?" I asked, my voice rising with anger.

Pa shrugged. "How do we know what they really believe? Perhaps it is more convenient to deny the curse and think that Vasile is the villain. To believe that all of this is a political ploy to avoid allying with Hungary."

Pa crossed Sfetnic's hands over his chest and moved on to the next sleeper. "The emissary has been pressing for an old idea, I think because he's been told to call Vasile's bluff and get the Prince to confess that the curse isn't real. He's been wanting the princesses to be fitted with iron shoes. And today Prince Vasile agreed," Pa said.

"What?" Adina and I chorused.

"He had to. The emissary has Prince Vasile trapped. If Prince Vasile doesn't agree to it, he's all but admitting the curse isn't real. If the root of the problem is that the slippers have holes in them every morning, make slippers that won't wear through—I think that's his logic."

I stared at Pa, appalled. "Surely it's just a threat."

"It's not. Armas and a dozen of his men came into the room at that moment, and after them came the blacksmiths. Armas's men seized the princesses, and the blacksmiths riveted the shoes on right there in the hall, like so many prisoners being shackled."

I thought of the conversation Cook and Marjit had had in the kitchen and couldn't believe it. Armas loved Otilia, I thought!

"And then Prince Vasile said to the emissary, 'Go back to your King and tell him iron shoes can't break a curse.' And then"—Pa's fingers tightened so hard around the cup of broth he was holding that I wondered if he would crack the wood—"the emissary said, 'Maybe iron shoes could break the curse if you'd heated them as hot as the rivets before you put them on.' And one of the princesses fainted."

"Which one?" I asked, fascinated and horrified all at once.

"I don't know her. Not Lacrimora, not the two legitimate ones. Not Otilia, either."

Adina burst out, "How could he do that to his own girls?"

Pa shook his head. "It was that or war," he said, though he didn't sound convinced. "Armas and his men, once they were out of sight of the emissary, picked up the princesses and carried them to their tower."

"Not good enough," I muttered. "Not nearly good enough."

I didn't quite know if I meant that in terms of Armas's behavior or in terms of the princesses being punished.

Perhaps both.

On the way out of the western tower, Pa stopped me with a hand on my arm.

"I know," he said.

"You know what?"

"That the Princess Consort has you investigating ways to turn people invisible, for spying on the princesses."

I blinked, examining him closely. He didn't seem angry.

Then I really heard what he had said. *Ways to turn* people *invisible.*

Not *me. People.*

"She told you about the list, and how I've been testing the things on it?" I asked, cautious not to reveal that my plan all along had been to be the invisible spy.

He nodded. "She told me to assist you if I could."

"Well," I said, thinking. "I have a strange nepenthe-seed concoction that comes ready tonight, which I'm not sure how to test."

"Test it on me," he said. I frowned at him. Didina had been right to be dubious about the effectiveness of the potion. I didn't want to test it on him any more than I wanted to test on me. But Pa's size did mean it was less likely that I'd overdose him.

"What's the risk, exactly?" he asked when I seemed reluctant.

"Hallucinations, catalepsy, death . . ."

"Brother Cosmin lets you use herbs that can kill people? You haven't been his apprentice for even two months!"

I stared at Pa. "You can kill someone with most anything if you try hard enough. Or, more likely, when you *don't* try hard enough."

"You are not reassuring me, Reveka."

"Pa, I studied herbs at the convent. I've been learning for *ages*. And herbs that don't have a drastic effect on the body aren't much use. Controlling the dosage is the true art of herbalism."

"Can you manage not to kill me?"

"Certainly," I lied. It was a tiny lie. I was pretty certain, and Pa had never admired hesitancy. "When?"

"Why not tonight? You said the potion was ready."

True! But so were my plans with Marjit.

"You'll need to fast for the potion to be effective," I hedged.

"I haven't eaten since before noon."

"Well . . ." I tried to think how long that would leave me with Marjit.

Pa was starting to get that frowny face that meant he thought I was lying. So I smiled, and said, "Sure. Tonight."

CHAPTER 16

P a looked reluctant when I peeled back the layered cheesecloth from the bowl to expose the sodden mess of nepenthe seeds, but he drank a cup of the wine down to the dregs anyway.

The nepenthe wine had no immediate effect, and we sat together in silence while I leafed through *Physica* and Pa pared his fingernails. The noise of the paring stopped after a bit. I didn't look up, thinking that he'd simply gotten his nails to their preferred length, but when I finally glanced at Pa, I was surprised to find him staring into the distance with his knife paused halfway across one nail.

"Pa?" I asked, and he looked toward me as though startled. His pupils were tiny.

"Reveka," he said very loudly. He clapped his hand over his mouth, dropped it, and said my name at a more normal volume. "Reveka." He smiled broadly at me then, a smile so relaxed and friendly and un–Pa-like that I would not have recognized him as my father if I'd met him on the street.

"Are you all right?"

He giggled. My Pa, dour soldier, *giggled.*

"Fiiiiiiiiiine," he told me. "Can you see me? Am I invisible yet?"

"No, not yet," I said.

Pa stood up and strode across the room and back, then settled down beside me on Brother Cosmin's stool. He stared at me for a long moment. "You know," he said, "I don't think I'd know you for your mother's daughter, if we were strangers. Fortunately, I know you for *my* daughter: that chin"—and he jabbed my chin—"that cowlick of hair just there . . ." He poked at my forehead. "Just like my mother's and my brothers'. But not a touch of your mother in you. I can barely remember what she looked like, except she didn't look like you."

She was prettier than me; that I knew. Enough nuns had told me so. And taller. I thought you were supposed to get to be prettier and taller than your mother, but this must be a fable they tell to girls so that we keep trying to grow up.

Pa giggled again, so hard that he lowered his head to the herbary table. His shoulders shook. "I said 'fortunately,'" he said.

"What?"

"I said, when I talked about you looking like me . . .

I said, 'fortunately.' It can't be fortunate for you, though."

"Pa," I said firmly, "let's leave the discussion of my looks alone."

"Yes." He stood and paced the room a few times again, then climbed onto the table and lay across the open copy of *Physica*. There was no rescuing the book, but as long as he didn't squirm, it probably wasn't in danger.

"Pa, maybe you should—"

"Am I invisible yet?"

"No."

He turned his head to look at me, his cheek resting against the page I'd been reading. "You're a good child, Reveka," he said. "I don't tell you this, because the Abbess said that praise inflates your pride, but you *are* good. You don't even lie as much as she said you did."

I bit my lip, scowling. He didn't notice this. He was rolling his head back and forth across Hildegard's words and looking dreamy. "And she's just so beautiful."

"Who? The Abbess?"

"Not the Abbess," he said. "The Princess—"

A scraping noise came from outside. Pa bolted upright, swiveling his head like an owl's to stare at the casement. "I heard that!" he cried, and ran over to open the shutters. Before I quite knew how it had happened—or even noticed who was standing on the other side of the casement—Pa hauled Mihas the Cowherd in through the window by his collar.

The boy didn't even struggle. He'd gone limp in Pa's grip, like a cat grabbed by the scruff. His mouth hung open like he wanted to mew.

"Why were you listening? What were you trying to hear? Do you work for the Hungarians?" Pa was shouting into the cowherd's face.

"Pa, no! Pa! Shush!" Pa's roars subsided into shouted whispers. I wondered if anyone would come to investigate the commotion, but then, every man drank too much plum brandy now and again and started a row with his family. Or with the herbalist. Right?

"Cowherd!" I shook my head at Mihas. "Tell him you aren't a spy, Cowherd." Of *course* he said nothing. "Pa, you know he's not a spy!"

"I'll sit on him until he tells us who he's spying for. Or wait—is he here to steal? Does he want the golden cup?"

"Oh, Pa," I cried. "Stop it! Let the boy go!" Pa'd been a bit mad before, but this was utter nonsense.

As suddenly as he had grabbed Mihas, Pa released him. "I don't feel so good," he told me, plopping onto my stool so heavily that the wood creaked.

"I can see that." I sighed. I turned to the cowherd. "Go *away*, Mihas. No one wants you here!"

He stared at me with giant eyes turned violet in the candlelight.

"She said *go*," Pa said, lurching to his feet. Mihas

scrambled backward, I think trying to reach the door, but instead bashing into a low shelf of flasks. A rain of rose-scented oil fell over his head. I groaned. Rose oil was so expensive.

"Pa, sit *down.*" I stomped on his foot, and he sat on his bum like a two-year-old.

Mihas scrubbed at his face and spat, trying to get the oil out of his eyes and mouth. I stepped forward to help him, but he staggered away from me, toward the door again—and this time stepped into the compost bucket. "Augh!" he shrieked, trying to shake the bucket off his foot, but it was firmly wedged. He stumped away, faster than I would have thought possible with one foot disabled and his eyes full of rose oil.

"Mihas!" I called, but there was no getting him to wait. I was about to run after him and offer my aid when I heard Pa retching violently behind me.

"Oh, Easter," I muttered, and went to help Pa.

When he had evacuated the contents of his stomach all over the herbary floor, I said, "I think we can call this effort a failure."

"Agreed," Pa said, and calmly leaned over to erp again. Ew.

I cleaned the herbary quickly and left Pa snoring on my table. Outside, I looked around but found no signs of

Mihas. I went to the ferns growing among the rue and cut three-quarters of the fronds. The night previous, they had been short and tightly curled; tonight they were in full leaf.

I met Marjit beneath the never-blinking eyes of the Little Well's carved dragons. She hauled a fresh bucket of well water and set it down.

"Brother Cosmin said we mustn't drink that," I said.

"Heavens, no! It used to be a holy well, they say, though at some point it gained a reputation for turning people into werewolves."

Uh-oh.

"But," Marjit continued, "it's merely that the well is blessed by a capricious fairy, and it was just safer for everyone to avoid drinking from it."

She spoke like this was a well-known fact. My lips itched a little.

"Are you sure? Brother Cosmin said that it was cursed by Turkish prisoners." I pointed at the inscription.

Marjit snorted, sprinkling dirt into the bucket of water. "Brother Cosmin thinks he knows more than the rest of us. It's a holy well, trust me."

"Could drinking from it give dreams?"

"Dreams, art, dancing, beauty, luck, kindness—it could grant any of those things. Or it could cause toads to drop from your mouth when you speak lies. It's risky.

Don't drink from it. Now. Put your ferns in there." She gestured at the bucket.

When I was slow to move, she grabbed my hands and plunked the ferns into the water, then waved her hands over the bucket and muttered in the church language. I could make out only a few words, mostly numbers. My eyes glazed.

"I'm calling on the Big Lady now," Marjit told me. "And to Athena, the goddess, who stole the Lord of Hell's own cap of invisibility and gave it to Perseus. I figure her for your best patron. Not so much Hades, given what you've said."

"All right," I said. Pagan nonsense, I supposed, calling on dead gods instead of ever-living saints, but I still suppressed a shiver. At least it wasn't the Devil. I closed my eyes and muttered a prayer for intercession to Saint Hildegard.

Marjit's droning continued. At length, her waving and words grew to a climax, and she drew out the last word in a moan and pulled her hands slowly apart. In the palm of her left hand was a netting needle—a big one, white like bone, with a large eye.

"A Thrice-Mothered Needle," she said. "Bathed in a mother's tears, a mother's blood, and a mother's milk. The eye is big enough for a fern stem to pass through." She handed it to me. "Get to work."

The sky was graying, and I was only half finished with the simple cap I'd planned. A rooster called in the distance, waking the crows along the rooftops, who cawed morning insults to one another. At least, I always thought caws sounded like insults. Perhaps caws are actually love poems to other crows.

"When are they going to leave?" I said, stabbing almost blindly with my needle, my eyes crossed from the night of netting by the tiny light of a dark lantern.

"I imagine when Corvinus gives up on our country," Marjit said. "That is the lumpiest hat I've ever seen."

I smoothed the cap. I was still clumsy at netting, and I hadn't known how to handle the fern fronds at first without snapping them.

"No harm in the extra time to finish?" I asked. "It's daylight."

"If you're done before next moonset, there's no more harm than there is in old Marjit." She patted her chest.

I smiled, but my liver wasn't in it. I rolled up the cap in my apron and tucked it under my arm. "Good night, Marjit."

"Hmph. The least you could've done was cut me some fresh bath herbs. Sleep well, Apprentice."

I slept hard through the early hours, and I woke bleary-eyed at midmorning when Brother Cosmin stumbled into the herbary and called for me. He was only half awake himself.

I poked my head over the edge of the loft. "Would you like a tisane, Brother Cosmin?" I asked solicitously. He agreed, and I slid down the ladder and set about warming a nice tisane for each of us. I made mine with pearl barley for wakefulness. In his, I mixed a strong dose of valerian for sleep, and covered the bitterness with three kinds of mint.

He drank, and I wondered if it was too much. He was older than he seemed. Perhaps his heart couldn't take it. I promised myself that if he woke hale and strong, I would never slip secret sedatives to old men again.

As soon as he nodded to sleep over his mortar and pestle, I whipped out the cap and started netting, keeping my apron at the ready to throw over the top of my work if I heard the door squeak.

An hour passed, then two. The ferns dried out and started to break, and I had to soak the whole mess in water again.

When I had knotted the last stitches, I held the cap doubtfully for a moment before placing it on my head. It was a misshapen mess, worse than the socks I'd made, but I blamed the material as much as my lack of skill. Nonetheless, it fitted my head, and stayed on, and didn't disintegrate, for all that it appeared fragile and strange.

I looked at my hands. They were as my hands always

were, though perhaps a bit more blue than normal. In fact, the whole world appeared a little bluer.

"Did it work?"

Brother Cosmin snorted awake at the sound of my voice. "Hello? Reveka? Now, where did that shirking girl go off to this time?" He looked all around him.

And he didn't see me.

He didn't see me.

CHAPTER 17

That night, I huddled in a corner of the princesses' tower, well out of everyone's way, invisibility cap perched atop my head, and watched.

The princesses took their evening meal in their room, in light of their injuries. They passed the time with moaning, while shoving sheepskins and moleskins and battings into their shoes to ease their pain. I thought it was too bad for them that they would try to poison me if they found me, since I knew a really excellent recipe for meadowsweet tea that would help their feet.

"I'd curse *him* if I knew how," Princess Maricara said, after dismissing the servants.

"You say that every day," another princess said. "I wish you'd just figure it out and stop carping about it."

"Sisters," a third princess intervened, "peace! We have important issues to discuss. We need to bring Iosif back. Bring him back and give him to the Hungarian emissary.

Then the shoes can come off, and—"

"And just how do you propose we do that?" Maricara snapped.

The rest of the princesses shook their heads. "There's no way," Otilia said. "Even I can see that."

"There's one way," Tereza said. "And that's if one of us accepts the proposal."

Stone silence greeted this suggestion, until Ruxandra, one of the tavern maid's daughters, said, "Fine. *You* accept it."

This led to an outbreak of squabbling that Lacrimora shushed. "No. Absolutely not. No one is accepting anything."

"I . . . I could—" Otilia began.

"No," Lacrimora said. "We have come too far in this together to accept losing one of us now. And—Otilia, you love another! Even if there are those among us who don't care for your immortal soul, surely they can see how wrong it would be."

"On the contrary, we are princesses," Tereza said with overweening dignity. "Princesses do not marry for love, like peasants or minor nobility. They marry for wealth and peace, for the good of their countries. Honestly, what could be for the better good of our country?"

"I think we're back to *you* accepting the proposal," Princess Viorica said.

"I think we're back to reminding each other about what losing your immortal soul actually means!" Lacrimora said. "We may only be sisters by half, but we do owe this consideration to one another."

Tereza bowed her head. "Yes. Of course, Lacrimora is right."

"Besides, Iosif is a pawn in Hungary's game. They don't actually care if they get him back," Lacrimora said.

There were a few grumbles, but everyone agreed.

Lacrimora, gazing out the window at the sky, said, "It's time."

Viorica and a few of the others went around the room, peering under beds and poking behind curtains. I held my breath when Princess Suzana stopped, one hand raised, and put a finger to her lips. She jerked her head at one of the beds. Everyone nodded. But there was no call to action, no swarming on the hidden person, like there had been the night they'd caught Didina, even though it was clear they had found someone else in the room.

Maricara and Suzana limped over to step on opposite corners of the hearth. With a grinding of stone on stone, the floor opened to reveal stairs leading down.

Maricara led the way, a tiny dark lantern in hand.

The others followed her. Just as I was about to tag along at the end of the procession, Mihas slid from beneath a bed and sneaked down after them—far too close on Lacrimora's heels, I thought, for someone who didn't have an invisibility cap! I goggled at him, unable to determine why he was here and what he thought he was doing—but

I didn't have a chance to goggle long. The stone floor started to close up again. I dashed down the steps after the procession, and the stones drew together behind me with a tired rumble.

I was standing in darkness only faintly broken by Maricara's narrow lantern beam ahead.

In front of me, Mihas trod on the back of Lacrimora's trailing gown. She cried out.

"What's wrong?" Otilia asked.

"Um, nothing," Lacrimora said. "I put my hand on something slimy." Indeed, the wall to my right held a faint sheen reflecting the light from the dark lantern ahead— water, and also slime. She motioned Otilia ahead, and the procession continued.

Idiot cowherd, I called Mihas under my breath. He was going to get himself killed. Or whatever it was that happened down here.

The descent seemed to take forever, with the princesses hobbling on pained feet. Most of them were only capable of walking down one step at a time, like a small child who is first learning how to use stairs. I took care to hang back, well away from Mihas, and Mihas seemed to have gotten the sense to stay well away from Lacrimora's hem, at least.

Eventually, the stairs gave way to . . . snow.

I hesitated on the last stone step, my foot poised in midair. The snow glowed slightly, even where it covered winter-sleeping trees ahead. The door in the floor I'd expected, and the stairs leading down, and the dark passageway . . . but I'd never anticipated a whole world beneath the surface of our world, a world with trees and . . . snow. "Saint Hildegard's garden," I swore in amazement.

My hand flew to my mouth, covering it too late. None of the princesses glanced back, but Mihas looked over his shoulder. His glance passed right through me, though, and while he hesitated a long moment, he followed Lacrimora.

I dropped my foot to the ground. The snow crunched lightly, and the chill spread slowly. Snow in July. It was impossible, wasn't it?

I trotted after the princesses, catching up with Mihas as he entered a copse of trees whose trunks were tarnished silver. Icicles like faceted glass dripped from laden branches. Wonderingly, I reached out to touch a branch: Were these living trees?

The small branch broke as soon as I touched it, and it plopped into the snow. The brittle snap of the twig rang out in the silent wood like a harquebus shot. Mihas jumped behind a tree trunk, while I froze in place. A few princesses peered back toward me, saw nothing, and went on; only Otilia stopped dead on the path. My stomach seized with apprehension. But she didn't look around.

Lacrimora nudged her sister in the back. "Move along. They're waiting."

Otilia moved on, and Lacrimora followed. Mihas

eventually broke from the cover of his tree and went after them.

The silver twig shone dully in the snow. I scooped it up and tucked it into my herb pouch, resolving not to touch anything else. I hurried after the group.

The forest lightened with each step. At first I thought the snow was glowing brighter, or perhaps my eyes were adjusting, but truly the sky was lightening, and we were walking into dawn.

The snow grew patchy here, giving way to piles of autumn leaves of bright pinks and purples and golds such as I had never seen, not among summer flowers or even royal silks.

And the sun—*a* sun, anyway, narrow and dark as though we were viewing the normal sun through the blue veil of the Virgin in a stained glass window—rose, sending slender shafts of light through the trees. The trees changed from tarnished silver to greening copper. My fingers itched to touch and investigate these plants. I dared not touch any more branches but did spy bits of deadfall. I collected a verdigris twig from the ground, rolling it between my fingers. I sniffed it, and it smelled like metal. I put that twig in my pouch, too.

The sun rose quickly—so quickly that it seemed like a dream. With every footstep, the strange sun gained a degree in height, and only when I stopped to collect the twig did I realize that the sunrise was in direct correlation to our progress through the forest. When I stopped walking, the sun stopped rising. I paused many times, trying to make sense of this phenomenon, until I lagged far behind the princesses and had to sprint to catch up. They had no care for any of this. They were well used to it, I guessed. Did Mihas notice? I couldn't tell. He didn't seem as intrigued by the forest as I was.

The sun became of secondary concern to me as autumn forest became summer forest. The darkened sun was at noon height now, and the tree trunks were spotty brass. Leaves of dull emeralds hung silently on still trees. It felt most strange, to be in a forest without animals, without wind, without water. The dark light was oppressive, casting strange, deep shadows everywhere.

The forest path wandered through a field of shimmering white ferns, like the ones my cap was made of. The princesses' long skirts slithered against these plants, spilling diamond seeds to the ground. Here, the path was a glittering scar of brown earth worn into the forest floor. I longed to kneel and bury my fingers in the soil to assess its qualities for growing herbs, maybe even to dab a bit of the dirt on the tip of my tongue like Sister Anica had taught me. But it wasn't even proper soil. It looked like crushed garnets, and it made me uneasy.

The whole forest, in fact, made me uneasy: something

about the unreal shine to everything, while fascinating at first, felt unnatural in the end.

I did stoop to pick up a fallen brass twig, however, which I also tucked into my pouch.

Then summer forest gave way to spring. The sun was setting here—or was it rising? We had walked backward through the seasons, so perhaps we were also walking backward through the course of a day. I couldn't say. Long rays of dull red light shot through bronze trees. Ruby and emerald buds dotted the branches, and the forest floor was speckled with patches of young grass and amethyst starflowers. The effect was pleasing, until I looked more closely: The buds bore blight at their centers, and the grass was pale and withering. I collected a bronze twig here.

We came out of the trees onto the banks of an enormous lake, where starless night reigned once again. The blazing light of ten thousand candles danced across dark water, shining from a golden pavilion standing on a hill. Sweet music drifted to us, and twelve little boats waited on the shore, each with a lantern hanging from a tall hook at the stern. Beside each boat stood an oarsman wearing red livery—each oarsman more handsome than the last. Each man held out a hand to a princess, who took the hand and turned to wait for her sisters.

"My lords," Lacrimora said, the last to arrive, "we have a follower." She turned and swept her arm out wide, to point straight at Mihas, half hidden behind a bronze tree and frozen in fear.

Like dogs on a hunt, the oarsmen raised their heads toward Mihas and attacked as one.

CHAPTER 18

Mihas stood no chance. The oarsmen brought him down, bound him swiftly, and threw him into one of the boats.

"The gardener's boy?" Princess Nadia asked, standing idly by.

Lacrimora shrugged. "Might be," she said, and bent to fiddle with the bandages in her iron shoe.

I was so horrified by this whole scene, stiff and staring, that I missed jumping into Otilia's boat with her. Her red-liveried rower had already pushed away from the bank by the time I regained my senses.

Lacrimora, on the other hand, still wasn't ready. I scuttled up behind her and stepped into the boat nearly simultaneously with her. The boat rocked and swayed wildly with my inept boarding. Lacrimora cried out and sat down heavily on the middle seat. I cringed in the bow.

"Careful," her oarsman said in a strong Saxon accent. "We almost capsized."

"It's these wretched shoes," she said.

"No one else had any problem with them."

She scowled. "Thanks for pointing that out, Iosif."

Iosif. Iosif, the missing Saxon!

Iosif pulled away from shore with a grunt. "Oof. The boat is very heavy today!"

"It's the shoes," Lacrimora said, sharply this time.

"I don't think they were this heavy last night."

"It's the shoes," she growled.

Iosif shook his head. "It'll be a wonder if you can lift your feet to dance, then."

"I'll dance as beautifully as ever, fear not." She said it so icily, I thought for sure Iosif would shut up then, but he didn't.

"Oof!" He rowed with his full strength, only barely outpacing the boat that contained a princess, an oarsman, and Mihas. "Your shoes don't explain why we're falling behind!"

"No, only you can explain that, lazybones," Lacrimora said.

Iosif sighed. I felt sorry for him.

The two overloaded boats struggled to the far shore. Ours pulled in just ahead of Mihas's. The other princesses and their oarsmen had long since arrived and now were wending their way up to the pavilion. An immense dark figure waited on the shore. The silhouette of the waiting figure resolved into a bestial, hoofed creature with tall, spiked wings. I froze with one hand clapped over my mouth so I would not cry out in wonder and terror.

The boat slid into a slip, and the dark figure leaned down. Its narrow, tusked face came much too close to me as it plucked Lacrimora from the boat as easily as if she were a child, holding her gently in its talons; its hot breath skated across my face, leaving behind the scent of bitter almonds and smoke. I could not control the shudder that ran through me.

A *zmeu*. A dragon, a demon, a hoarder of treasures, a kidnapper of young maidens.

"Lord Dragos," Lacrimora gasped. I'd never seen her discomposed before. I understood her terror perfectly. I was petrified. My stomach was clenched hard in a knot of fear at the very center of me.

"You're still wearing the iron shoes," the *zmeu* observed in a low, rumbling voice. "Your father's wisdom surpasses itself." It—he, really—was dressed in a split black cloak that did nothing to hide goatish legs clad in short trousers. He wore a king's ransom in golden bracelets on his wrists. His cloak was fastened with a clasp altogether too reminiscent of his own curved, vicious teeth. I bit my fingers to keep myself silent. If he discovered me—if he found me!

All my childish nightmares of Muma Pădurii paled into insignificance next to the scents and sounds of a live *zmeu*.

"My father's wisdom is to plug the hole in his bleeding pocketbook," Lacrimora was saying. Though perched in Lord Dragos's red arms, she had regained her composure and was cooler than rain. I envied her courage. "Iron shoes are proving infinitely more durable than our previous calfskin and satin."

Lord Dragos snorted a fine, ashy smoke from his nostrils. "Are your iron shoes as durable as my hooves?" he asked. He stamped a hoofed foot on the stones beneath his feet, drawing sparks, and the sound raced, sharp and hollow, out over the lake. An echo shot back from behind the pavilion, as though there were a stone wall beyond it. I squinted and became aware of two kinds of darkness, one being empty, the other being rather solid. A mountain?

Lacrimora smiled and said nothing. It was not a friendly smile, but Lacrimora's smiles never were.

"Who is our new guest?" the dragon asked.

For one panicked moment, I thought he meant *me*, and I nearly screamed. But for the fist that I now had practically stuffed into my mouth, I probably would have. But the *zmeu* was looking at Nadia's boat, the one containing Mihas. A small cadre of red-liveried men trotted down from the pavilion and dragged him away as soon as his boat reached the shore.

"Just another young idiot," Lacrimora said, raising a shoulder in a shrug, and that was the tally of Mihas, right there.

Even though it didn't differ all that much from my assessment of him, her casual dismissal made me angry, and for half a second, I forgot to be afraid.

The *zmeu* carried Princess Lacrimora up the path after Mihas, while Iosif crawled out of the boat and dragged it farther ashore, grunting as he pulled the boat with my weight in it. Then he followed Lacrimora and the *zmeu* toward the pavilion.

Stay in the boat, I told myself, watching them walk up to the pavilion. *I'll just stay in the boat. I won't go anywhere near that creature.*

But in spite of that wise warning, I climbed out of the boat.

Fine, stretch your legs, I told myself. *Just don't follow them.*

But of course, I followed them.

You are without question your own worst enemy, I scolded myself, even as I tiptoed after them.

From a distance, the structure was merely lovely; up close, it was fantastical. The supports of the pavilion were trees of gold, and the roof was the interwoven golden canopy of their leaves. A pearly cicada flew past to land on a tree trunk, where it rubbed its legs together to produce the sweet tones of a lute. All the music was made by tiny jeweled creatures, by lizards and locusts and small birds.

And the light came not from candles but from a myriad of wasps with small, glowing bums. Pretty enough, if you like that sort of thing, but it gave me an itchy feeling to see all those waggling antennae. I decided not to look too closely at them anymore.

A series of raised platforms surrounded a large central floor of gleaming golden wood. One of the daises held a banquet table; another, a small, tented bower; a third, a number of silk-swathed chairs. At the edge of the banquet dais, Lord Dragos set Lacrimora on her feet and offered her his enormous hand. She grasped his smallest finger and allowed him to lead her up to the table, where her sisters were sitting. Poor Mihas was tied to a small chair at one end.

Dragos helped Lacrimora hobble to her seat. "I'll remind myself not to worry about the shoes. Because if your father interferes too much, if even one of you is incapable of dancing . . ."

"Fear not, my lord. We are all as capable of dancing as ever we were. No forfeits will be made tonight."

"How lovely," Lord Dragos murmured, his voice shaded with more layers of meaning than I could even guess at, and pushed in her chair.

I approached the banquet table. Each princess sat between two men in red, and behind each diner, a footman stood at attention.

The food spread before the princesses and their companions was glorious—and incongruous. Ripe red apples were mounded next to luscious grapes and stacks of bright oranges, lemons, and limes. Plums, currants, and strawberries nestled together with wintergreen berries, bilberries, and pears. I'd never seen an orange in summer before, let alone summer strawberries side by side with autumn apples, and my hands twitched to reach out and verify that this fruit was indeed fruit, and not more oddities like silver or copper trees. How did all this get here? Where did it come from?

The fruit wasn't even the main part of the meal; there were fine, crusty breads and ripe cheeses, cakes and sweets, eggs and pickles, pies and roasts. The scent of it was overwhelming, and though I hadn't been unbearably hungry in years, the sheer bounty of the feast was staggering, and terribly, terribly alluring.

And I grew angry, looking at this pile of food spread before the princesses.

How was this . . . a curse?

I was torn. I wanted to climb up and stomp through the food, smashing it to bits before any of it passed the princesses' lips, as it doubtless had been passing their lips nightly. I also had a strong desire to rush in and steal a pocketful of cheeses and fruits for myself. But for once, rationality reigned and I stayed far back from the table, refusing either temptation. And refusing, also, the temptation to leave the pavilion, row myself back to the far shore, and climb to the surface world to tell Prince Vasile that the curse had everything to do with a *zmeu*.

Girding myself with a deep, calming breath, I forced myself to wait and see what they would do to Mihas.

Lord Dragos seated himself at the head of the table. His great wooden chair creaked and moaned beneath his weight. I crept closer, looking for a place to watch from that was out of the way. I thought about crawling under the table, but I couldn't see my way through the forest of chair legs and people legs, and instead I drew close to lurk behind the horned lord's chair, since he didn't have a footman and there was no danger of a collision. I stood near him, so close that I once more smelled his scent of bitter almonds and fire.

"So, Princess Maricara," Lord Dragos said, motioning to the footmen to serve the food spread out on the pavilion table. "This new one doesn't look like much of a fighter. And I do not think he will be courtly enough for you girls."

"We can always use another strong oarsman," Princess Maricara said. She bit the tip of her finger delicately and giggled. Lord Dragos chuckled, a deep sound that made me think of giant drums sounding in the distance.

If it was a joke, it was not a joke I got, but the

princesses tittered appreciatively—all but Lacrimora and Otilia. None of the men in red livery gave any indication that they'd heard the words exchanged between Lord Dragos and Maricara.

Curious.

I thought about sneaking up behind Maricara and stabbing her heel lightly with my herb knife for joking so merrily about poor, stupid Mihas, but in the end I decided that saving Mihas's life might be more important than saving his honor.

"So, you claim him?" Lord Dragos asked, sipping from a golden goblet.

"We claim him," Princess Otilia said.

At the *zmeu*'s nod, two of the footmen placed food before Mihas and untied one of his wrists so he could eat. He looked confused, but since everyone else was eating, he took up a bit of bread and cheese and chewed it carefully.

There had been tension among the princesses, and even with Lord Dragos, which I had not really perceived until it drained out of them once Mihas had chewed and swallowed his first bite. He ate more, and more still, greedily chomping down fruits and breads and chicken legs like he hadn't had a meal in weeks.

The other diners ate very little, as though it were a token meal. This made a sort of sense: The princesses had eaten in their room just a few short hours ago, maybe less. It was hard to tell time in the Underworld's darkness, and the changing seasons and times of day in the forest had confused me. I had no clear idea how long it had been since the stone floor had closed behind us.

When Mihas was sated, Lord Dragos stood up, stretching to his full height and flexing his wings before folding them neatly against his back again. He gestured, and two footmen came forward and led Mihas away. The cowherd seemed docile, and duller than usual, with his face glistening with chicken grease.

"With that duty taken care of, let us begin," Lord Dragos said. "Princess Maricara, you are the eldest. Will you marry me, or will you dance?"

CHAPTER 19

I couldn't help the gasp of horror that escaped me, but no one reacted to it. Except, perhaps, Lord Dragos's ears twitched. However, the *zmeu*'s big webbed ears often twitched, expanding and contracting, as expressive as a human face, and nothing else happened.

"I will dance," Princess Maricara said, and reluctantly put her hand in his. He helped her to her feet and led her to the center of the pavilion. All of Maricara's sisters and all of Lord Dragos's men ringed the dance floor, watching. I crept closer to watch, too.

Lord Dragos snapped his taloned fingers, and the musical animals around the pavilion popped to attention and began to play the loveliest, strangest music.

Lord Dragos and Princess Maricara whirled around the pavilion together. I wondered if Princess Maricara enjoyed this, if she liked being the center of attention, but once the music wound to a halt, dying back to nothing more than the ordinary chirping of crickets and calls of tree frogs, I knew she had not enjoyed a moment of it: She fainted in his arms. Bright blood seeped through the batting she'd tucked around her feet, making it look for all the world like her iron shoes were lined with red silk.

Lord Dragos pulled the Princess upright, patting her face gently. Her eyes fluttered open.

"Perhaps you should rest," Lord Dragos said. I didn't know how to interpret his words. Were they kind? Were they usual? Was he practicing mercy or was he annoyed at her weakness?

So this, then, was the curse. This was how the princesses wore the holes into their shoes every night. This was the secret the princesses protected with poison and with lies: They came to the Underworld nightly to feast and dance with a demon, because it was that or marry him.

No wonder Lacrimora was convinced their immortal souls were in peril. Consorting with demons, even unwillingly, was a sin.

One of the oarsmen helped Maricara hobble to a red silk chair the exact color of her blood—also the color of Lord Dragos's skin. She sat upright, pinch lipped, her pride a shield.

But my sympathy was fleeting. In another life, in that world above this one that I almost didn't believe in anymore, I'd spent too much time with the sleepers to feel bad for her.

Lord Dragos approached the next princess and bowed.

"And you, Viorica? Will you marry me? Or will you dance?"

"Dance," Viorica said at once, and took his hand. The music swelled forth again from the throats and limbs of a hundred small creatures in the trees.

This dance went much like the other, though the tune differed. And when the dance ended, Viorica lifted a foot and examined it, poking at the bloody batting. "No holes," she said neutrally. "In my shoes, I mean," she added.

I admired her coolness, if nothing else.

An oarsman guided her to a red silk chair beside Princess Maricara. Both princesses sat stoically, hands folded over their knees, frowning as Princess Tereza was offered the choice: marriage or dancing.

It was a ritual, a call–and–response. And there was no question in anyone's mind what the outcome would be. No one would choose marriage to the *zmeu*.

What would happen to the one who finally agreed to marry him? What happened to your soul if you chose to become a demon's bride? I shivered.

I noticed Mihas across the room, now clean and dressed in red livery like the other men. He watched the dancing with a blank expression.

I slid to the pavilion's edge, skirting the crowd to reach him. Mihas stood by a pillar, hands folded behind his back.

I crouched behind the pillar and hissed, "What are you doing here, Cowherd?"

Mihas shook his head slowly, like an old cat being wakened. "Who—?"

I hesitated, wondering if I was about to make a huge mistake, but I plunged onward. "It's Reveka."

He peered behind the pillar, but of course, he could see nothing.

"Stop looking about—you'll give me away!"

"Reveka . . ." Now he examined the pillar and the vines twisted around it. He came face-to-face with one very large cicada, which had taken a break from the music making and no longer produced the piercing sounds of a bladder pipe, thank goodness.

"Reveka, have you become an insect?" he asked.

I rolled my eyes. "Yes. I followed the princesses here, and they caught me and turned me into a cicada."

"Oh no!" He clutched his throat.

Seriously? He believed that? I hastened to say, "But do not fret; I'll be fine. I am concerned about you. Why are you here? What happened?"

He bent over so he could speak in a quieter voice, which of course made him more conspicuous. "After— after everything in the herbary, I had to prove myself to—to—I knew I needed to prove myself," he said. I covered my mouth to keep from yelling at him. "I decided I would break the curse. So I sneaked into the princesses' tower, hid under the bed, and followed them . . . but they found me." He closed his eyes and shuddered. "You haven't eaten anything here, have you, Reveka?"

"No."

"Don't. Don't eat anything from here. Ever. No matter how hungry you are. It's what traps you here. That's what they told me. I ate, and now I'm here . . . forever."

"But the princesses ate—"

"They're trapped here, too. They have a deal with Lord Dragos, though, that they may come and go nightly, as long as they agree to consider marriage to him. And as long as they dance."

The music had stopped, and another bleeding princess was guided to a chair. Mihas, idiot that he was, didn't notice. He kept talking.

"I don't know if *he* turned you into a bug or if you did it yourself or what, but even as an insect, you must not eat—or drink, either, no, don't ever drink the wine, and the water—"

Lord Dragos was watching Mihas from across the room. I wanted to tell Mihas to be quiet, but at that moment, the cicada took wing and flew away. That shut Mihas up, maybe better than me shushing him. He straightened, watching the cicada, clearly of half a mind to follow until he saw he'd gained Lord Dragos's attention.

Without taking his eyes off Mihas, Lord Dragos went to the next princess and gave her the choice of marrying or dancing. She danced, of course.

Suddenly despairing, I turned my back on the bright pavilion and made my way down to the lakeshore. I crept into Lacrimora's boat and huddled in the bow, waiting.

I didn't have to wait long before the princesses returned to the boats, each carried by her oarsman. Lord Dragos came last, holding Princess Lacrimora in his arms. He deposited her in the boat with a strange sort of tenderness, whispering an apology in her ear. I examined him, considering. What sort of creature, dragon-demon or otherwise, apologizes for dancing a woman's feet bloody? Why not just let them go if he regretted it so much?

Iosif shoved off with a grunt. He rowed slowly behind the others, glaring at Lacrimora the whole while, as though it were possible that she with her slender frame had actually managed to gain a whole person's weight in the course of one day.

When we finally reached the other shore, I disembarked as quietly and gracefully as possible, which honestly wasn't very quietly or very gracefully. Still, Iosif didn't notice, and Lacrimora said nothing. I made sure to walk far behind the princesses as they limped slowly through the forests.

What was going to happen, exactly, when Prince Vasile learned that the curse on his daughters was a strange bargain with a *zmeu*? If I told Prince Vasile and the Princess Consort what was going on down here, would that really put an end to all of this? *Could* it? Just discovering what the princesses were *doing* wasn't actually enough, not in the face of the awesome powers of a *zmeu*.

I had to find out how to end this, how to free the princesses from the *zmeu*. Then they could stop poisoning people; then they could go out into the world and make important marriages that would bring peace and security to Sylvania; then they could produce those heirs for Prince Vasile.

Then they could wake the sleepers.

I stared at the plants in the strange forest and wondered if one of them was the secret of the deathlike sleep. My fingers itched to take a sample of every growing thing, just in case, but the fear of being trapped in the Underworld spurred me onward.

This made me think of Mihas, of course. Poor Mihas— I could pity him now, had to pity him now. I couldn't leave him to this darkness alone.

And then there was the matter of Iosif the Saxon. He was surly, no question, but being Lacrimora's oarsman would make anyone surly. More to the point, though: If

Iosif was the linchpin in Hungary's machinations against Sylvania, wouldn't it take the wind out of their sails if Iosif showed up and told them that the curse was real?

Before I quite knew it, I had decided that I had to return to the Underworld again. My first priority was to free Iosif and Mihas; my second was to learn how to break the curse.

In the winter forest, I drew closer to the princesses, determined not to be left behind. They murmured about the chill of the snow freezing the iron surrounding their feet.

"Feels bloody wonderful," Ruxandra said.

"They're going to hurt even worse when they warm up again," Viorica said.

I grimaced. That was certainly true.

I trailed up the stairs after Princess Lacrimora and hid in my corner by the chimney until the outer bolts were thrown and the princesses filed off to the baths. I raced invisibly ahead of them to the gardens to cut huge swaths of hollyhock, stuffed my cap into my apron, and brought my late herbs to the bathing chamber just as Marjit was about to put the princesses into the hot water.

I said not a word to them, didn't look at them. Just like a proper peasant, who knew nothing at all of royal secrets.

CHAPTER 20

I stopped in the kitchens for a bit of food and learned that the Prince and his Consort had ridden out to hunt at a distant estate and wouldn't be back for days. *That answers that question,* I thought, biting into a thick piece of bread. I didn't even need to argue with myself about going to the Princess Consort and telling her what I'd seen, and her absence gave me time to rescue Mihas and Iosif.

I grabbed a few extra pocket-sized loaves for that night's trip. It had been hard looking at all the food in the Underworld and being unable to eat it. I felt very clever for thinking to bring something of my own.

Back in the herbary, I discovered that Brother Cosmin had reverted to his old ways, for he was nowhere to be found. I seized upon this opportunity to reclaim some of the sleep I'd missed the night before. It was an odd luxury, to sleep with the sun on my face. I could see why Brother Cosmin often reveled in it.

I slept so deeply that when I woke and found my invisibility cap missing, I had no notion of how it had been taken.

"Reveka!" Brother Cosmin called again. It was his first call that had awakened me. "Are you up there?"

"Yes," I hollered back, frantically shaking out my blanket and hoping the cap would roll out. Then I shook out my clothes, lifted my pallet, and—

"Reveka, are you ill?"

Who could have stolen my cap? Who would have? Who even knew about it? When I found out who'd stolen it, I'd wipe his mother's grave with my dirty socks!

Marjit. Marjit was the only one who had known.

"I'm a little ill," I said, climbing down from the loft. I did feel like I was going to erp everywhere.

"You're shivering," Brother Cosmin pointed out. And I was. Vibrating with anger, actually.

"Yes—I'm going to the baths," I said, and was out the door. Let him assume I was going to the soaking pool to warm up.

I pelted toward the baths but was brought up short when I noticed the man sitting in the shadows by the Little Well. A man wearing a black military cloak over red velvet. Today, he did not wear the cloak pinned jauntily back over one shoulder; rather, the hood draped low over his face.

Frumos. There was no mistaking the clasp on his cloak.

There was also no mistaking the fact that Lord Dragos had worn one identical to it last night, a clasp made of animal bones. When I'd first seen Frumos in the woods, I'd thought they were boars' tusks, but now I'd seen a *zmeu* and knew that they were a *zmeu*'s face spikes.

Perhaps this really *was* Prince Frumos, hero, slayer of *zmei*. How else did you get a *zmeu*-spike cloak clasp?

Frumos stirred, lifting a small, wet bucket to his mouth, and drank. In that moment, I remembered the taste of the water, and my mouth filled with saliva. I wanted to drink from the well again; I wanted it more than anything I'd ever wanted—even my urgency over my invisibility cap had faded into the background of my thoughts. I lurched forward, hands reaching for the bucket.

My feet scraped on the stones, and Frumos spun to face me. We stared at each other for a long moment, until he said, "Reveka," in a tone of recognition, and relaxed.

"Prince Frumos," I said, and dipped a curtsy.

"How goes the life of the herbalist's apprentice?"

I stared at him. There was no explaining my life. None at all. So I just said, "It goes." I stared at the bucket in his hands. My mouth watered. "May I have a drink?"

He looked at the bucket, then back to me. "This well is . . ."

"Contaminated," I said. "I know. Marjit the Bathwoman says it's the work of a fairy. But I drank from it once before, and it had no ill effect on me."

He considered me. "No, there'd be no ill effect on you. You're young. And innocent. Well-intentioned and fair."

I confess that I blushed at this. I was unused to compliments. But I was a bit angry as well. I was hardly an innocent: I was too familiar with lying for that. So I laughed and made a joke of it. "Oh, certainly. I'm a lovely helpless maiden, ripe for kidnapping by any *zmeu* who wanders by." I stared at the bucket, practically licking my lips thinking about the stony-sweet taste of the water.

I only looked at his face when he didn't respond right away. He wore a deep frown. "Go ahead and drink," he said roughly when I met his eyes. He held out the bucket, and I put it to my lips. The water was as cold and as glorious as I remembered, but the tang of stone was even stronger.

I drained the bucket and put it down, then wondered if we had drunk from the same spot. *If we did, it would be like we kissed,* I thought, and knew it was a stupid thought even as I had it.

"You haven't asked me why I am here," he said.

"I assumed you came to break the curse. That's why young men come to this castle, isn't it?" I asked, thinking of Mihas.

He blinked. "The curse?"

"The curse on the princesses, the one that causes them to wear through their slippers every night. That curse?"

"Oh, *that* curse. I cannot break that curse," he said.

"But you're Prince Frumos," I said. *The one who fights the* zmeu.

"It's not my real name."

I tried to hide my sudden and acute disappointment with a laugh. "I suspected as much. No one is named 'Prince Handsome' anyway. And when we met, you said, 'Call me Frumos,' but you didn't say that Frumos is your name."

"True," he said, nodding, still watching me carefully. His regard grew difficult to bear. I felt like he could see through my clothes and skin, into my liver. He said, "You have still not asked me why I'm here."

I said bitterly, "I'm the herbalist's apprentice. Matters of state aren't any of my business."

"You're assuming I'm here on a matter of state?"

"When one prince visits another prince, is it not always a matter of state? Unless . . . you aren't a prince, as well as not being named Frumos."

"I'm a prince," he said. "Or I was, once. Anyway, let us call this a shadow visit. Your prince doesn't know I'm here."

"Well, how could he?" I said. "He and the Princess Consort have gone to the hunting lodge of one of their vassals."

"Ah. Well, I'm here on another matter entirely. I had

a . . . an unexpected visitor to my lands last night, who I tracked to this castle. I wanted to know who he was, and why he was visiting." He watched me with sharp, dark eyes.

I stared right back, just the way you're not supposed to stare at royalty. Neither of us said anything.

He was nowhere near as handsome as Pa and had nothing at all on beautiful, stupid Mihas, but there was something striking about him nonetheless, in the leanness of his face and the sharpness of his features. He didn't look like much of a soldier, being a bit skinny for it, but he carried the air of a general. He looked like a strategist, or a thinker, and he had that same something about him that Pa had: He looked like he could command men. And maybe women, too.

"It's time I went." He nodded to the bucket. "I would not drink from that well a third time, were I you."

I felt my mouth set in an obstinate line. "And why not?"

"There's no fairy in that well. It is something else entirely. And I would very much like you to continue living your proper life, Reveka, well-intentioned and fair."

As confusing as I found him, I was rather delighted to be called fair. I'd never confess to anyone that my head swam because of a simple compliment, but I had to admit it to myself.

I thought he would leave then. It seemed like the fitting

thing: You received a compliment from a mysterious and handsome prince, and that was the end. But he stayed still, stayed watching me.

"We've reached stalemate, I see," he said at last.

"I don't understand."

He pursed his lips. "Maybe not stalemate," he murmured. "Maybe it's check."

I frowned.

He heaved a sigh. "I will be honest," he said, as though it pained him a great deal. I sympathized with that. "I won't leave if you are looking at me."

That startled me. I blinked.

"Yes, like that. Only . . . blink longer."

"I can't blink longer. My eyes would actually be closed if I blinked longer."

"Fine, then close your eyes." His exasperation was amusing, to him as well as me. We smiled at each other.

"I don't understand," I said, still smiling, but I closed my eyes nonetheless.

And when I opened them, he was gone.

CHAPTER 21

I cursed, then cursed again.

There was only one way that someone could disappear like that, and that was if he had my invisibility cap!

But how could Frumos have stolen it? How could he have even known it existed? Marjit was the only one who knew!

I stormed down into the baths to find Marjit alone, scrubbing wall tiles in the soaking pool.

"I know you're working for Frumos!" I shouted. My voice magnified in the tiled room.

Marjit screamed, turned, and winged her scrub brush at me. The hard wooden handle thunked into me at my hairline, above my right eye.

"Ow!" I cried, and fell to my knees clutching my head.

"Oh!" Marjit exclaimed, clambering through the soaking pool toward me. "Child, I thought you were a vanguard for the Turks! I'm sorry, I didn't realize it was you." She knelt and peeled my fingers away from my forehead, examining the spot where she'd conked me. "Didn't break the skin, but you'll have quite a goose egg."

"Marjit!" I was still angry, but now I sounded whiny as I rebuked her through my tears. "How could you tell Frumos? How could you let him steal my cap?"

"Who's Frumos?" Marjit asked, soaking a towel in the cold plunge and wringing it out. She folded the towel and placed it on my sore head.

"Frumos!" I cried. "You know, *Frumos.*" Frustrated, I remembered I didn't know his real name.

"No, Reveka, I'm afraid I don't," she said. "Now lie back. You've had quite a blow."

"Marjit, someone stole my cap, and the only other person who knew it existed was you!" I struggled against her, refusing to let her push me backward.

She stopped trying to get me to lie down and gave me an impatient look. "Really, Reveka. If I wanted an invisibility cap, I could have just repeated the spell on the fern fronds you didn't use."

If my head hadn't hurt so much, I would have smacked it.

I groaned. "Oh, I'm so stupid," I muttered.

Marjit shook her head. "You're plenty clever. Just, sometimes, a little too clever."

"Marjit, if I apologized for what I thought about you, would you help me make a second cap?"

"Does that mean the cap worked?" Marjit asked, astonished.

I nodded miserably.

"Would a second cap make up for throwing a scrub brush at your head?"

I nodded again.

"Yes, we can work on it tonight."

"Today! It has to be today!"

Marjit frowned. "I don't know how the spell will work, in the day." She considered. "Maybe if . . ." She shook her head.

"We can try, right? I don't have a choice."

Reluctantly, she agreed. I brought her ferns and a bucket of Little Well water, and we did the ritual in the baths. At least we were underground, I thought. No natural light could penetrate here. That was like the Underworld. That had to help.

But the baths were used often, and once the ritual was over and only the netting remained, Marjit sent me away. I sneaked back to my loft.

The first cap had given me enough practice that the netting of the second went markedly faster. It also helped that I used a large, looping stitch, since I hadn't enough fern fronds to do a tight cap like the first one. It probably wouldn't wear as well, or last as long. If it worked at all.

Stupid thief, ruining everything.

Brother Cosmin solicitously made me a posset for my

illness and left me alone through the day. The clink of flasks and pots, the roar of his fire as he brewed extracts, the steady pounding of his mortar and pestle, all soothed me and set the rhythm of my netting.

I jumped when the door banged open and Pa's voice asked, "Have you seen Mihas? He hasn't been around all day."

"No, I haven't seen *your* apprentice," Brother Cosmin answered.

"Wait—where's Reveka? Did she go off with him?"

"Go off with him?" Brother Cosmin repeated, sounding surprised.

Pa's voice was grim. "He's got something of a crush on her."

I buried my face in my hands. Why did Pa know this?

"Why would you think that means she'd go off with him?" Brother Cosmin asked.

A good question, Brother Cosmin! Why would Pa think that I'd be interested in a cowherd's stupid crush and take up a dalliance with the boy—to the point of neglecting my work and letting Mihas neglect his? Now, granted, I *was* neglecting my work, and Mihas *was* one of the reasons, but this was *life or death*, not a crush.

"I don't think you need to worry about that," Brother Cosmin said. "She's about as interested in Mihas as she is in my donkey. Which is to say she might stoop to giving him mashed juniper berries for his colic, but that's about all the notice she pays either of them."

I never realized Brother Cosmin understood me so well. Though I had to say I liked his donkey *better* than I liked Mihas, even though Old Magar tended to bite.

"She spends most of her time dreaming about her nunnery, in fact," Brother Cosmin added. "I don't know if she's ever noticed any man about the castle."

Well, I argued in my head, *I notice men.* I just wasn't particularly impressed by any of them. Except for—

No. I wasn't going to think about him. And he wasn't "about the castle," no matter where his shadow diplomacy had brought him today.

"Let me know if you see her," Pa said.

Brother Cosmin said mildly, "Well, she's upstairs in the loft, dealing with a slight ague and probably listening to every ridiculous word you're speaking."

There was a silence from below, which I interpreted as mortified. I stuffed my half-finished cap under my apron, pinned the netting needle to my sleeve, and waited.

Pa's head poked up over the edge of the loft.

"Sorry," he said grumpily.

I shrugged.

"Do you need anything?"

I shook my head.

"Hope you feel better soon," he said, and disappeared.

I flopped back on my pallet and wondered why it was we had fathers, anyway.

It was on toward sunset when I finished the cap. I tested the cap's invisibility on Brother Cosmin, and it passed. I hurried to the eastern tower to hide—and wait.

That night, on the slow journey behind the princesses, I decided not to ride in Lacrimora's boat. But as we approached the shore, she yawned and stretched hugely, casting her arms wide behind her. She said nothing as she made contact with my stomach. I was hard-pressed not to squeak in surprise as she grabbed the fabric of my chemise and tugged me toward her boat.

She knew. She *knew*.

Unfortunately, I couldn't speak to her. I wordlessly stowed away in Iosif's boat. Iosif rowed even more slowly than the night before, glaring at Lacrimora the whole time, which I would have found funny if I hadn't been wondering what Lacrimora was planning.

Long before we reached the other shore, I could make out the silhouette of Lord Dragos.

"Two nights in a row he's been waiting," Lacrimora murmured.

"You've been late both nights," Iosif said.

I expected Lord Dragos to speak, to make some sardonic comment as he had the night before about the iron shoes, to pluck one of the princesses from her boat and carry her. But he just waited while the princesses disembarked, then offered his arm to Nadia on the march to the pavilion.

Tonight, there was an empty chair pulled up to the heaping table of food, and instead of sitting down at the head of the table, Lord Dragos went to stand behind the chair. The princesses wore puzzled expressions as they watched him pile a golden plate high with grapes and cakes and place it before the empty seat. The grapes on the plate glowed red like blisters filled with blood.

The princesses sat. Mihas was there, attending Princess Viorica. Everyone watched Dragos; no one paid any attention to the banquet.

"Before we begin our evening . . ." Dragos said, and his long, flexible fingers groped the air over the empty chair for a long moment, then made a plucking motion. Pa appeared, gagged and tied to the chair. In Lord Dragos's fist was my first fern cap, which he flung disdainfully onto the table.

I cried out then, but so did half the princesses, and the sound of my voice was masked. The liveried men appeared unmoved, except for Mihas, whose jaw dropped open—predictably.

"That's Konstantin, the gardener!" Princess Stefania said.

"Little Reveka's father!" Rada added.

Lord Dragos scrutinized the princesses. "And the lover of one of you, I surmise," he said.

"Hardly," Tereza sniffed. "He's the gardener. Oh, I'll grant you, he's quite swift at digging a ditch, but that sort of thing doesn't really catch my eye."

"He's quite well-looking, I thought," Lord Dragos said. "You could do worse." He gestured at himself.

"I claim him," Lacrimora croaked into the silence that followed.

"I didn't ask if you claimed him," Lord Dragos said. "Those rules don't apply to him. This gardener entered my dominion by some back way. He has a cap of invisibility. He swam my lake, and I found him inside my pavilion. He did not come following you, so your protection cannot apply.

"Further, he has intruded on this land once before. Last night, he watched you all dance. You, sir," he said to Pa, "are a trespasser."

I almost cried out that this was untrue! I was the one who had visited the night before! The only thing that stopped me was the memory of Prince Frumos at the well, saying that he had tracked a visitor from his lands to Castle Sylvian last night. My mouth froze in an O of horror.

The pieces clicked into place: the clasp, the names, the strange comments. Prince Frumos, the fabled champion of young maidens, the storied enemy of the *zmeu*, actually a *zmeu* himself? It was a horrible joke.

Just the sort of joke that a demon might enjoy, I thought.

"Kill him if you want," Tereza said. "You're right—none of us has anything to do with his being here. Only wait until we've returned to the surface for the night. I'm afraid you won't get very good dancing from the weaker-stomached girls if you drink his blood in front of us."

"He's worthy of your service!" Lacrimora interrupted. She sat limply in her chair, the color drained from her face. She shook her head slightly, over and over. I don't know that she was even aware of the motion.

I glanced at Pa, who stared at Lacrimora. Also shaking his head. Equally despairing.

It hit me like a thunderbolt. A very, very, very big, awful, stupid thunderbolt, the kind that makes a person extremely angry.

When had my father fallen in love with Lacrimora?

And she with him?

Lord Dragos had been watching the princesses, absorbing all their reactions. Now he extended one extremely long, sharp claw, as strong and sturdy as a dagger, and slowly moved it toward Pa's throat. I was about to cry out—

"I remind you of Tereza's warning, my lord," Lacrimora croaked. "We won't be much for dancing if he dies in front of us."

Lord Dragos checked his motion. I wished—oh, how

I wished—that I could read the *zmeu*'s expression. I tried to impose my memory of Prince Frumos's lean face over the dragon's toothy jaws, but it was impossible. Not even the eyes were alike. Surely if Prince Frumos and Lord Dragos were one, their eyes would be the same?

"There is one way you could forestall his death," Lord Dragos pointed out.

Lacrimora bit her lip. "Would you—would you let him go if I married you?"

Uproar followed this. Pa yelled angry, misshapen words against his gag, and Otilia leaped from her chair and clapped a hand over Lacrimora's mouth. The rest of the princesses all spoke at once. Even the footmen looked surprised. I used the uproar as cover to sneak over to Pa, pulling my herb knife as I went, intending to cut his bonds and give him a fighting chance against the *zmeu*.

"She don't mean it, Lord Dragos," Princess Rada hollered, her tavern wench's screech cutting across the commotion.

"Absolutely, she means it!" Princess Maricara shouted back.

"You would say that, you highborn snot! You've been trying to make us pay for your foolishness for six years!"

It was as if they knew I needed the distraction. I would have thought it was all on purpose, except that Otilia's struggles with Lacrimora looked very real. Then Rada

· 182 ·

leaned over and punched Maricara in the nose. As blood poured across Prince Vasile's eldest daughter's lips, I spoke softly into my father's ear—"It's me, Pa"—and sliced through the bonds at his wrists.

"No, Reveka!" Pa's voice was low and urgent, pitched well under the noise of the commotion around us. Only, it came out "Doh, Bubefa!" through his gag. I thought about swatting his head for saying my name—but I had already made the fatal error. Pa's bonds fell to the floor. And there was no hiding that.

"Interesting," Lord Dragos said, and stared right at me. "It appears that I have a second visitor." And he reached over and plucked the invisibility cap off my head.

The fighting and arguing stopped as soon as I appeared.

It must have been an interesting tableau, me poised over my father with a knife, Lord Dragos holding a cap above my head.

I curtsied to the *zmeu*, suddenly sure of myself, suddenly certain of what I had to do then, to save us all.

"Lord Dragos," I said. "You may let everyone else go free. I will marry you."

CHAPTER 22

"I accept your proposal," Lord Dragos said, and the finality of his words was like a thunderclap.

The strangest details revealed themselves to me in that moment, as if the time between heartbeats had grown to encompass days of wakefulness. I'd not untied Pa's feet, which was probably the only thing that kept him from imprudently launching himself at the *zmeu*, though he struggled to move. Lacrimora finally broke free from Otilia and climbed to her feet. Princess Maricara held her streaming nose, while Tereza and Viorica kept Princess Rada from inflicting further damage. Mihas's expression veered between anguish and puzzlement.

Lord Dragos put an oddly gentle hand on Pa's chest to keep him from trying to untie the rest of his bonds. I looked down to see the first invisibility cap lying on the table.

I scooped the cap into my herb pouch, knowing that no one saw me do it.

Then my pulse sped up and time resumed its normal pace, and all was chaos and confusion again.

"You are released from your oaths," Dragos said to the princesses. "You're free. Go. Now!"

"The—the men—" Princess Otilia said.

"Take them," Dragos said. "Take all of them. You'll have to waken them. They're dull as ditchwater right now." He looked at me. "Come to me, Reveka."

A sudden sob of fright welled up within me, but I choked it back. I would not go to this new life weeping. Nor would I let Pa's last memory of me be of a terrified, crying girl. I lifted my chin with bravery I did not feel, blinked through the tears, and smiled at Pa as I took a step toward the *zmeu*.

Lord Dragos held out a long-fingered hand, and somehow, I forced myself to grasp it. He pulled me into an embrace so warm that I felt as if the fires of a glassblower's furnace had engulfed me. I heard the snap of his wings catching the air, and with his arms tight around me, he lifted me upward and away. We swooped from the pavilion and into the darkness, leaving behind the cries of the princesses and my father.

My stomach plummeted and rose, then completely flipped, and I almost lost its contents all over the *zmeu's* chest. *Don't,* I ordered myself. *Just don't feel this, and you'll be fine.* This tactic worked well enough to keep my innards in.

Lord Dragos's breath blew heavily in my ear, and his

arms were too tight around me. His wings stroked steadily, and I couldn't decide if I wished I could see or if I was glad for the darkness. But wait—I *could* see. The glow of the pavilion had fallen behind us, but I could distinguish over the *zmeu's* shoulder, between his wings, the dazzling lights on the water. Twelve shadows marred the perfection of the pavilion's reflection: the boats were crossing the lake.

They were leaving. Just like they were supposed to.

"Go," I breathed, a sort of prayer to Lacrimora. I imagined her entering the western tower and waking the sleepers, now that the curse was broken. Didina, awake! Her mother, saved! I thought of Mistress Adina's face wreathed in joyous smile wrinkles, and I smiled just a little, too.

Then I wondered if Pa was in one of the boats or not.

My smile faded, and I found I was clenching my fists. *He'd better be.*

We landed in darkness, in a place that smelled of minerals and water and clay. "We're here," Dragos said, releasing me but for a guiding hand on my shoulder as we moved forward. "I'm afraid that since I've just let all of my servants go, there is no one to light our way. But I have a knack for darkness." He spoke wryly.

"Why did you tell me your name was Frumos?" I asked.

His step faltered and he sucked in a breath, but then he

was pushing me forward again. "As you yourself pointed out, I never said it was my name," he said, his voice grown considerably softer. "So. You knew when you agreed to marry me?"

"Not much before that, but yes."

He was silent a long moment and then spoke harshly: "If you were hoping that the other is my true form and this one the facade, then you made a poor decision."

I was glad that darkness hid my face. It wasn't that I'd thought Frumos was the true form and Dragos the false one; but I'd hoped that there was enough truth in Frumos to make Dragos bearable.

I breathed deep and tried to summon bravery. "Where are we going?" I asked, instead of the fourteen thousand other questions that occurred to me.

"To find candles. This place is too dark for your eyes yet." He guided me on, and I walked trustingly, not hesitating as my feet continued to pat along on flagstones. I supposed that if he really wanted to run me into an oubliette, he would, and it didn't matter much if I toed my way into it or walked confidently over the edge.

"So you're the . . ." I paused, uncertain of how to phrase my question. "What exactly have I betrothed myself to?"

"'What?'" he asked flatly.

I made an impatient gesture, hoping he could see it. "You're a lord. Of. A really dark realm."

It *is* the Underworld. Southeast of us is Elysium; ₁west, Tartarus. This is Thonos, which is the name of the realm, the name of this mountain, and the name of my castle. And when you are its Queen, I will be your King."

Not merely a lord, but a king? "If you had told the princesses that one of them could become a queen, Maricara would have married you on the first day you asked," I said. "Even if this is Hell." I shivered. "Is this Hell?"

"No, Hell is a lake of fire," he said. "This is but a region of the Underworld, and a haven and a waypoint for souls that die. Some go to Hell from here. Some go to Heaven. And some stay. Ah! Here we are."

He took his hand off my shoulder, and for one too-long moment, I was alone in darkness. Too alone. Where was up? Where was down? Back? Forth? The darkness seemed to press in on me, curling around my ribs, constricting my breath.

A hissing pop and a flare of light came from my left. I turned to watch a thin stream of fire leak from Dragos's mouth and ignite a series of candles. The warm scent of melting beeswax filled the air.

He placed candles all around a wide stone hall, which was sparsely furnished with a long dining table to one side and a few armchairs arranged before an empty fireplace at the other end.

The light grew as Lord Dragos lit more candles. I stared

at Lord Dragos's hands, their thick black claws, his
dine skin. I shuddered and looked around for sor
to hide. Under the table was bad. Under the table l
reach me easily.

But there wasn't anywhere else to hide from him and
his demon hands and face.

"That's enough light," I croaked.

He turned to me. I looked at him. A curl of smoke
escaped one of his nostrils.

"Please?" I asked. "Please. I won't ask again. Probably
I won't. No promises. A promise like that would be a lie.
But could you be Frumos for a bit?"

I wished I could read his expression. He lifted one
shoulder in a shrug. "I don't have that sort of power over
my form," he said. "I'm sorry."

I took a breath, involuntarily shuddering. "There are
at least a dozen stories of maidens who married hidden
monsters and never knew it. I envy them."

"Would you rather live such a lie?"

I had to look away. "I'd rather the lie if we are to be
married," I said to the flagstones.

Silence. I dared not look at him until I heard him snort.
"You're a bit young for marriage, Reveka, aren't you?"

I should have been relieved at this indication that
I might not be marrying him immediately. Instead, I
was instantly irate. "But girls my age marry all the time.

Among the nobles, anyway. Peasants and guildsmen, sensibly, marry later."

"Certainly, girls your age do marry, all the time," he agreed. "But a girl as young as you lives as a daughter of the family, as a sister to her husband, until the couple prove their maturity to their parents. Consummation . . . waits. For many years, sometimes."

I'd never heard that about the ruling classes, but suddenly, it made sense why Princess Daciana wasn't a mother yet.

"You're telling me you went to all this trouble to get a bride, and you want to wait a few more years before getting your heirs?"

"I will have no heir of my body here," Dragos said, and for an instant, his voice—well, perhaps more his accent—sounded like Frumos's. If I closed my eyes, could I imagine that he was the slender young man who'd pretended not to know my name? "It is only a bride I require, a queen for my land. And I'm very grateful that you've sacrificed yourself by marrying me. For yes, I am a dragon, a *zmeu*, and that's as bad as anything. But you must have had plans. You must have wanted . . . a family? Children?"

"We won't have *any* children?" For this, I was mostly grateful. I couldn't imagine bearing little red-skinned, horned babies. But I also felt the pang of a loss I did not even fully comprehend. I had never intended to marry, but how could I gain a husband and lose all prospect of children in a single day? In a single hour?

"I am a lord of the Underworld. This is a domain of darkness and death. No life begins down here." He spoke so sadly, my ire fled, and with it my sense of gratitude and loss. Mostly, I just felt pity. And that emotion seemed to be a doorway for the darkness.

"All life begins in the dark, though," I said, looking at the candles. They did very little to hold the darkness at bay. "All seeds sleep in the dirt." The words felt hollow. I could feel the darkness pressing on me. I tottered on my feet, losing my balance a little.

Dragos was there in an instant, hoisting me onto a chair by the cold fireplace. A flash, and he ignited the fire. "Stay a moment—I will fetch you some food and water. You will be all right, with the fire and the candles?"

I nodded and buried my head in my hands, wondering how I was going to live here, and that's when the darkness came striding in like it owned my soul, robbing me of my breath. For a long, horrible moment, I could only remember the lies I'd told, the half-truths I'd kept, and the fear of punishment in this life and the next that lying brought. I moaned—and then, the darkness was gone.

I breathed. It was like lead ingots had been removed

from my chest. That . . . thing, it wasn't just darkness. That was . . . *Darkness*.

A few moments later, there was the scuff of a footstep, and I sat bolt upright, terrified, my hands clamped down on the arms of my chair. Lord Dragos didn't have footsteps, he had . . . hoofbeats. This was someone else, and there wasn't supposed to be anyone else. "Who's there?" I cried, and nearly jumped out of my skin when Mihas stepped into the light.

CHAPTER 23

"Reveka," Mihas whispered, lurching to kneel before me. "I have a message from your father!"

"What?" I leaped to my feet, capsizing the cowherd. He lay on the floor, looking confused.

"Before I came back up the mountain, your father and the mean princess, Lacrimora, said I was to look to your welfare—"

"Did they order you to come back here?"

"No. I offered to come."

"What? Why?"

Mihas looked confused.

"You idiot! I came here to free *you*!"

His mouth gaped open. He gestured around. "You did this for me?"

"For all of you! For my pa, of course, mostly, but for all of you trapped idiots, too. And for the sleepers in the tower—Lacrimora will wake them now." Tears of fury sprang to my eyes.

He got slowly to his feet. "Your father's message—he says, 'Hold fast. Eat nothing. Drink no wine, or beer, or the water of Lethe. Do these things, and you can leave the Underworld again.' He will come for you. He will rescue you."

"The others, they all drank the wine and ate the food, and Lord Dragos released *them* from their bonds—"

"I asked this same question," he said. I felt markedly stupider for thinking like Mihas. "Princess Lacrimora said Dragos would never release you if you ate here, because you agreed to be the consort of the Underworld. But your father shushed her and said— Oh." Mihas looked sad. "He said not to tell you that."

I ignored this. "So am I just supposed to starve?" The Darkness was pressing at me again, trying to steal my breath. I tried to ignore it.

"I will bring you food and drink from the World Above as I can," Mihas said. "I'll be your footman. If I set a plate of food elegantly before you, you can be sure that it is safe. If I fumble with it, then it is not safe."

Amazing. Perhaps he wasn't a total idiot after all.

"Now, the water you can drink, as long as you are careful never to drink from the river Lethe."

Lethe—I'd heard of that. In the Greek myths, it was

the river of forgetting, which souls had to drink from in order to leave behind their lives on earth. "All right. No food, no wine, no Lethe. I understand. I assume it's all right to use the toilet facilities, however?"

Mihas looked confused, then vaguely appalled. "I didn't ask!" he wailed.

"It was a joke, Mihas."

His brows drew together. "How can you make light of this?"

"How can I not?" I peered into a water pitcher standing alluringly on the table. I hadn't been hungry or thirsty until Mihas had told me I was on a restricted diet. "Did my father give you any further message for me? 'Don't eat. Don't drink anything but water, and then not if it's from Lethe.' But nothing else?" No 'Thank you'? No apology for stealing my invisibility cap?

"I . . . I don't think so," Mihas said, sounding confused.

"Never mind." I poked my nose into the pitcher and inhaled. It smelled like springwater. "What's the water of Lethe like?"

Mihas appeared to consider. "Like water," he said. I groaned and put the pitcher back down.

I didn't hear Dragos enter, but I felt the room fill with his presence. I turned to find him glaring at Mihas.

"Why didn't you go with the others?" he asked the boy.

"I vowed to serve you," Mihas said.

Dragos snorted, looking carefully from Mihas to me. "And I released you from your vows. You should have taken the chance while you could. You will not be released a second time."

"I came to serve," Mihas said. "May I show your guest to her room?"

"She is my betrothed and your future queen," Dragos said. "Not a guest. *She* will tell you what she wants."

"I could rest," I said feebly.

"Very well." Dragos extended his hand to me, and for lack of anything wise to do, I let my fingers touch his. He bent nearly in half to press his dragon lips—which were not really lips at all, but simply the coldness of his tusks where they poked from his mouth—to my hand. I tried not to shudder.

He stepped back. "I must see if I can find servants for you," he said. "Mihas here will not be enough. Sleep well, Reveka." And his hand and his tusks and the whole of him were gone in a swirl of red wings and black cloak.

I stared after him for too long a moment, until Mihas coughed, evincing more discretion than I had ever suspected he possessed. He held out his arm in a courtly manner, and I took it, as if it were the most normal thing in the world for an herbalist's apprentice to play queen to a cowherd's footman.

Mihas took a brace of candles and led me down two hallways to a bedroom. Bedchamber and hallways alike were stone, stone, and more stone. There was no softness anywhere, no carpets or tapestries. The bed even lacked curtains, which it direly needed, for I was beginning to feel the stone-damp in my bones. There was at least a mattress filled with something softer than straw, covered by a bearskin—head still attached.

I dropped to one of the chairs, which was of course stone. Like miniature thrones, all of them, and every single one needed a cushion. I pressed my palms against my eyes, keeping the tears away just barely by remembering that Mihas was in the room with me.

I was, for the first time, glad of his company.

While my head had been buried, he'd made a fire in the hearth. "This will take the chill off the room. I must go to serve my lord now."

"Our lord," I said, but not very loudly, more trying out the words than anything.

Mihas heard me anyway. "Our lord," he repeated.

After Mihas left, the Darkness pushed in close around me. I was having a hard time breathing. I closed my eyes, selecting a darkness of my own choosing . . . though my presence here, that was my choice, too, wasn't it? I'd saved Pa, ended the curse—tried to save Mihas, not that the stupid cowherd would stay saved. . . .

The wave of palpable Darkness rolled back just enough for me to crawl into bed, so crawl into bed I did, though I made sure to turn the bear's head as far away from mine as possible. I didn't want to spend the night feeling like it was going to eat my face. Or kiss me.

I thought about crying but just went to sleep instead. I didn't sleep terribly long, and I certainly didn't sleep well. I dreamed of earthquakes, and falling buildings, far too vividly.

CHAPTER 24

When I woke, the fire had warmed the room to a tolerable temperature. So that was something. But the Darkness dimmed the light of the fire and pressed me into the bed. I lay feeling paralyzed by the weight of endless night. It took me a long moment before I could convince my limbs to move. Wondering if I was awake or dreaming, I tried to say, "Get up! Your eyes are open! You're awake! Move!"

But even my effort to speak was strangled by the Darkness, and I could only grunt.

Hearing my own voice freed me, though, and I was able to wiggle my fingers, and from there to sit up.

I crawled stiffly out of bed and went to crouch by the fire. I stayed there for what felt like a long time, until I wondered if anyone was ever going to remember me. Probably not. Lord Dragos had indicated that the enchanted footmen were the only servants he'd employed, and if Mihas was now doing the work of thirty men, it was unlikely anyone was going to come in and solicitously ask if I needed a chamber pot. Or a fresh change of clothes. Or a bath.

I shivered. I doubted proper bathing facilities existed in the Underworld. And if they did, a "proper bathing facility" probably meant a cold bath with sandpaper towels.

And yet, the pavilion below had been well-appointed and delightful to the senses. And warm enough. Couldn't this castle be made as comfortable?

Well, I was used to shifting for myself. I jammed my feet into my shoes, supremely grateful for my thick woolen socks. If I were dressed like a princess, I'd probably freeze to death here. On a hopeful hunch, I dug under my bed and found a chamber pot, and used it.

I wondered if I was allowed to leave my room at will. I tried the door, and it opened.

"Of course," I said airily. "You're the future queen. And where would you go, anyway?"

I grabbed up a candle and lit it from the hearth. It was not difficult to find my way to the hall from the night before. A fire crackled there now, and a wolfskin rug had been added to the floor, along with a few rather hairy cushions. "How delightful," I muttered, lifting one of the cushions to my stone chair and settling down on it.

The Darkness pressed on me, pressed on my eyes. In spite of fires and candles, the shadows crawled ever closer.

I heard hooves on the stones of the hall and braced myself.

"Did you sleep?" Lord Dragos asked, entering the room.

"A little."

"It's morning in the World Above."

I frowned. "Already? Perhaps I slept longer than I thought."

"Time does not run reliably on the same track below as it does above," he said.

I should have expected time to be different. There are stories about people who dance with fairies for a night and in the morning find a hundred years have passed and everyone they loved is dead of old age. But . . .

The Darkness crept closer, seeped into my pores, wrapped itself around my waist like a bodice.

I moaned, and the Darkness broke over me like a wave. The walls swayed around me, and I found myself slumped in my chair, limbs stretched out as I attempted to bear the weight of the Darkness. I lay still for a long moment after it released me and moved on.

No wonder people drank Lethe. It would be a sweet relief, after moments like that.

When I could breathe and see again, Dragos was watching me gravely. He extended a silver goblet. "I'm sorry. Drink this."

"I don't want it," I said, feeling ragged. I levered myself up to sit on my hands, so they wouldn't betray me by taking the cup. "And what are you sorry about?"

"I forgot what it was like when I first came here. I apologize. I should have remembered. . . ."

His eyes were still not Prince Frumos's eyes. Not that it mattered. I didn't trust Prince Frumos any more than I trusted Lord Dragos. Or King Dragos. Or whatever he was calling himself. Only, there was something sad and honest in his expression now.

I looked at the goblet. "When you first came here? Haven't you always been here?"

He lowered the cup and stared into it. "I am as newborn to this world as you are, in the grand scheme of things. Drink," he said. "It will make things easier. It is the same water that you drank from the Little Well in Castle Sylvian. The fact that you once drank that water is probably all that's kept you from going completely under by now."

I frowned. "I don't understand. You told me not to drink from the Little Well a third time."

"That was when you were for the World Above, when you were to live and die there. Down here . . . The Underworld is for the dead. Mortals who come here have a particularly hard time adjusting. You will be susceptible to the influences of the—well, let's call it the air.

"My servants, of whom Mihas is the only remaining representative, were given the waters of Lethe to help them forget the world they came from, so they would not mourn what they had lost and to decrease their confusion. Some call it the Water of Death. But myself, I drink Alethe, which is the opposite of Lethe in every way and is what we call the Water of Life."

"What did the princesses drink?"

"Alethe as well," Dragos said. "Because they needed to remember their life in the World Above in order to return to it at the end of every night."

I frowned.

"In any case, the Little Well in Castle Sylvian draws from the river Alethe, and you have already tasted it. If you drink more of it, things will only be easier for you in this world."

I cocked my head. "So you will allow me to remember my life above? Even if I mourn what I've lost? Even if I grow confused?"

"This water will keep the confusion at bay. The Darkness already presses on you, yes? And soon it will cloud your mind. You will go mad if you don't drink either Alethe's waters or Lethe's. The choice is yours: remembering or forgetting. But you must drink something." Dragos held the cup out to me again. "And if you mourn, it is only proper."

I reached for the cup, but I still hesitated.

"What if this is Lethe?" I whispered. "What if you are lying?"

"I do not lie," he said, fingering the brooch on his cloak.

"Never? Not to spare someone's feelings or even to save your own life?"

Dragos took the cup out of my hand and drank deeply, then handed it back to me. "There. Proof."

"But you're a *zmeu*. It proves nothing. I am human."

He sighed, exasperated but not angry. I raised the cup, and it did smell like the water of the Little Well. But I didn't drink. I remembered the last time I'd had the opportunity to drink after him and had thought, like a foolish child, that if we drank from the same spot, it would be like kissing. How stupid I'd been! I'd been thinking about kissing a *zmeu*.

"I swear, it will do you no harm," he said.

"Because I am young?" I said. "That's what you said when I drank from the Little Well. You said I was young, and innocent. And . . . well-intentioned and fair. Oh! You lied there. I'm not fair at all. I'm quite dark, and have never been pretty."

"As to that, by *fair* I meant fair-minded. Just and true, in your convictions and assertions."

Well, farts of Easter. I'd rather enjoyed the memory of

being called fair, even though I'd known it was untrue. Now I didn't even have the memory of a false compliment to enjoy.

I took a sip.

The water was sweet and stony, and my stomach welcomed it.

Immediately, the Darkness took a step backward. Another sip, and I could breathe without constriction. I drained the goblet. I fell back into my chair, eyes closed, breathing heavily.

When I opened my eyes again, Dragos was sitting quietly, wings folded neatly around the back of his armless chair.

"I have found servants for you," he said, as though we had been having an entirely different conversation. "They will be difficult to communicate with at first, as they are eidolons—ghosts—the souls of pagans who died long ago. The lands above have been Christian since Roman times, when the language was very different, and since Christian souls move on, it is only the ancient pagan souls who stay here."

"Pagan souls," I repeated. I remembered a conversation I'd overheard among the princesses. They'd been talking about accepting a proposal—Lord Dragos's proposal, I understood now—and Lacrimora had said, no, no, they'd come too far to give up then, for any one of them to to surrender their immortal soul. . . .

Was I giving up my soul? My chance at an afterlife? As the bride of a lord of the Underworld, how could I possibly still hope to go to Heaven?

Dragos hadn't noticed my reverie and was continuing. "Mihas will be one of your footmen; he has asked to be, and I see no reason to refuse him. But you must also have handmaidens. This has been a bachelor residence for too long. I'm afraid we've forgotten to supply many amenities. Is there anything you'd like? To be more comfortable? Clean clothes, obviously."

"Clothes, yes, and warm ones."

"Of course."

"And I need to know where to empty my chamber pot."

I couldn't tell if he looked confused or horrified. He was awfully aristocratic, even for a dragon-demon, so probably he found the thought of emptying one's own chamber pot as mystifying and terrible as I found his cheek spines and red skin.

Or possibly, *zmei* didn't poop.

"Yes, well, I'm sure that when you have a handmaiden, she will take care of that. . . . Until then . . . Mihas, perhaps . . ."

"Well, what about bathing facilities?"

"That I can do."

"And . . . rugs for my bedchamber floor, curtains for

the bed, perhaps a blanket or two that doesn't have a face attached? And perhaps . . ." I hesitated.

"Ask, and if it's in my power to grant, you shall have it."

"An herbary?" I asked in a small voice.

Dragos's cheek spines lowered. "Perhaps it could be arranged, but I don't see why you'd want one," Dragos said gently, as if trying not to hurt my feelings. "There's no call for herb lore down here. The mortals you may encounter are already long dead, and the immortals do not sicken. They have no need of healing here, in the land of the dead."

This, more than any other thing I'd yet contemplated about the choice I'd made—more than the potential loss of my immortal soul—was too much of a blow. No true marriage and no children with Dragos? All to the good. But the prospect of no herbary—of *nothing*, nothing at all to look forward to, nothing at all to comfort me?

Silence stretched between us. "I'm sorry," Dragos said at last. "I'll have Mihas bring you food."

He left, and in short order, Mihas arrived.

"Reveka, are you all right?" the cowherd asked. He carried a tray of bread and fruit, and my stomach flopped with urgent desire for it.

"Can I eat any of that?" I whispered.

Mihas set the tray down hard on the table. A few grapes rolled off the plate, and Mihas jumped to catch them before they escaped into the shadows forever.

"I can't—" I said, and ran for my room.

I forgot to grab a candle, and too soon I was running through passageways I could not see. I didn't stop running, though; I followed the wall by touch. There were no carpets to catch my feet, and the flagstones were smooth, so it was completely safe to pelt onward into the blackness—

I ran smack into a wall, hitting my nose so hard that blood flooded my face. The blow set me onto my bum, and I flopped backward too hard onto the floor, banging my head as well.

I'd missed the turn. I was supposed to turn left at the end of this passageway, and then my room was the sixth door on the right. But I'd forgotten that this hallway ended in a wall.

I cried then. I cried a lot. Usually when I cry, I remember that it's not helpful and get up and do something that is helpful instead, but this time, I just didn't see the point.

I realized pretty quickly that fast-flowing nose blood was seeping down my chin and neck onto my chemise, and of course, this just made me cry harder. I tried to tell myself that it didn't matter about the herbary, because Pa was going to rescue me, but I didn't believe it. There was no way Pa could rescue me. Dragos was a gigantic *zmeu* with obsidian claws, and *he could breathe fire.*

I'd been preparing myself to stay because I feared staying was inevitable.

And what a cold and lonely and dark place this was. No wonder Dragos wanted a wife.

I forced myself to my feet, even though I didn't bother to try to make myself stop crying, and staggered down to my room, counting doors by feel. When I thought I was at the right room, I opened the door—but it wasn't the right room. There was a fire lit, yes, but the room was enormous, and the curtainless bed was thrice the size of mine, and carved with dragons and wyrms, so intertwined that they looked like they were fighting.

There were books and a few papers scattered on an otherwise neat desk, with a chair suitable in size for a *zmeu.* There were maps on the walls, but no tapestries. Two swords hung crossed over the bed. A bough of plum blossoms rested in a vase on the mantel.

Dragos's room.

I backed out and closed the door. I'd counted wrong. I went down one more door, and there was my room, just as spartan as my betrothed's. More so.

I found my herb pouch and stuck bits of wool in my nostrils, then dosed myself with comfrey to rebuild the blood I'd lost and was still losing. I washed myself with water from the pitcher, figuring that even if it was the water of Lethe, it was probably safe to wash in.

Probably.

I didn't care right then.

I found the bread that I'd stowed in my herb pouch two nights before. I ate some of it, then crawled into my bed and vowed not to come out again.

CHAPTER 25

I don't know how long I hid under the covers before my sobs calmed and I fell into a deep sleep. I woke disoriented, feeling as though I'd slept for days. Time really was impossible to sort out here. The endless night didn't help, either.

The room was faintly lit by the embers in my hearth. When I slid from the bed, I took a deep breath, and no sob caught in my chest. My storm had passed, then; I'd never yet met a fate so gruesome that a good sleep didn't put a slightly better face on it. A bath and a meal would have helped even more, but . . .

There was a tap at the door, and when I opened it, Lord Dragos was on the other side. His ears widened in astonishment. "What happened to you?"

"What do you mean?"

"You have terrific bruises around your eyes, and your

chemise is stained with blood."

"Oh." I looked down and brushed ineffectually at the dried stains. "I ran into a wall in the dark."

His ears relaxed. "You should have taken a candle with you. Or a torch."

"Obviously," I muttered.

"I have brought your servants," he said, and snapped his dexterous fingers. From the dark of the hall emerged Mihas and several men and women, carrying all manner of things. They swarmed into my room, and in mere moments, the place was transformed—clothes were spread out, carpets were laid down. Several people started hanging bed curtains. Two men carried in a desk; more followed with crates, a chair, and an armload of fabric.

"These are eidolon servants," Dragos said.

"If eidolons are ghosts, how can they serve?" I asked.

"Eidolons are souls, and in the Underworld, they are as physical as I, or Mihas. But they cannot manifest in the World Above without a blood sacrifice."

"Oh," I said. I must have looked a little bit horrified.

"In any case, I used mortal servants while I could because we at least speak the same everyday language. It was more comfortable."

"How—?" My question was cut off by the noise of hammering. *Bang! Bang, bang, bang, bang!* Before I knew it, there were pegs nailed high on the walls, and servants were hoisting tapestries onto them.

One tapestry showed the same dragon kidnapping a maiden as outside the Princess Consort's solar. I squinted and found the mended snag on the maiden's cheek.

"Where did you get *that*?" I asked.

Dragos glanced at the tapestry with indifference. "It is usual for the rulers of a land to pay a tithe to the local lord of the Underworld," he said. "I hadn't collected for a while."

"Wait—does that mean Prince Vasile owes you tribute? Does he *know* he owes you tribute?"

Dragos gave a dragonly shrug with one wing. "Most rulers and priests know to leave treasures beside entrance points to the Underworld. Vasile's tithes had grown rather tokenish—a mediocre sword tossed once a year into the Little Well is hardly what Thonos deserves."

My eyes widened. "Is that why you cursed the princesses to dance with you?"

Dragos's cheek spines compressed. I decided this was his frown. "The princesses made their own luck. I would not punish children for their father's doings."

Speaking of the princesses . . . my eye was drawn to the pile of clothing now lying on my bed. "Did you collect those as well?" I asked, scanning the gowns for any signs of familiarity. They were the same style as the princesses', with silky underrobes and dark overgowns. I glanced at Lord Dragos. "You want me to dress like a princess?"

"I want you to dress like a queen," he replied, and went to adjust the angle of the second tapestry on my wall. This one was of a white unicorn resting in a dark garden. At first it seemed pretty, until I realized that the unicorn was trapped in a pen, a tiny, isolated figure in a vast darkness.

The feeling it evoked was a little too familiar.

The third tapestry was no less disturbing. On it, a dragon flamed across a night sky, and while this was truly beautiful, it was altogether too clear that the dragon was a *zmeu*.

"Now," Dragos said, "Zuste and Mihas will be your footmen—and your secretary is Skiare. Zuste and Skiare speak Greek, but they will learn our language—slowly, though. Eidolons are not fast learners."

"That's not necessary," I said in Greek, and greeted the two men, Zuste and Skiare, in that language. I merely nodded to Mihas.

Skiare had been unpacking boxes and arranging things in the pigeonholes of the desk. Lord Dragos trailed a finger over the items Skiare had lined up. "Pens, ink, sand, sealing wax . . ." He plucked a wooden box from the table and took off the lid, holding it out to me. "Your seal," he said, while I stared at the golden thing inside.

It was a ring carved with the silhouette of a dragon twined around a chalice.

"*My* seal?" I asked, intrigued.

"Our seal."

"Of course." I put the ring on my forefinger. I'd never owned any jewelry before. I studied the way the gold looked against my skin, amazed.

"And there is Phithophthethela, who will be your handmaiden," Dragos added, pointing to a woman in rather plain peasant's garb—no embroideries, but the shapes of the clothes were similar to mine.

He addressed her in a language that I did not understand one word in ten of, then said to me, "You can call her Thela."

The woman smiled widely and bowed. I gave her a dignified nod in return.

"Let her dress you," Dragos said. "It is time for dinner, and you are still covered in blood." That rather put my dignified nod in perspective. I blushed a little.

With a simple gesture, Dragos caught everyone's attention, and the men departed the room as quickly as they had come, leaving me alone with Thela.

I tried to give my new handmaiden a reassuring smile, but she wasn't interested in reassurance—she just wanted to get my bloody chemise off me. Since we did not share a common language, I started holding up objects and making inquisitive noises, then repeating whatever word she said. We got through *water, toweling, dress, fire, wood,* and *candles* before she grew impatient, took the brush I'd been showing her, and dragged it through my hair.

It was going to be a long time before we held a good conversation, I decided.

My stomach growled while Thela helped me into stockings, underrobe, and outer gown, and cinched it all with a stiff belt just below my bosom. The cloth felt very fine against my skin, and I liked it. Until I tried to walk across the room and nearly tripped.

I glanced back at Thela. She shrugged and mimed picking up her skirts. I grimaced.

I paused at the bedroom door. "Um, farewell," I said. But she was muttering to my bloody chemise in her ancient tongue and didn't seem to notice I'd spoken. I closed the door and went to face down dinner.

Chapter 26

I sat across from Dragos and nearly moaned as the scent of food filled my nose. My stomach rumbled to life. I dug my fingers into my thigh and kept my eyes off the food.

Mihas came in and spilled my soup across the table. Per our agreement, I shouldn't eat anything, then. I hadn't thought there'd be food for me yet, but I sighed anyway. I looked over at the bank of dark windows behind Dragos.

"Why are there so many windows, when it is always pitch-dark night outside?" I asked.

Dragos said, "Eventually, you will understand the answer to that question. But not until you eat."

I pointed at the soup spilled across the table. "How can I eat that?"

"This charade is unnecessary, Reveka. Not until you choose to eat the food of this realm will you truly be the Queen of Thonos."

"I thought I would be queen when we married."

"We could journey to the surface world and have a priest marry us tonight, but we would not be married in the eyes of the Underworld."

I was silent for a moment. "I see."

"When you choose to eat, Reveka, all my lands will bow to you."

I shivered at those words. They struck a memory in me, though of what I couldn't say for sure. I decided to change the topic from eating. "What is the extent of your land? Where are the borders?"

"If you come to a river in any direction, do not cross it, for you will no longer be in Thonos, and that would be dangerous for you. I have good relations with Rhadamanthus and Minos in the south, but elsewhere, there are Underworld lords who would do harm to you—or kidnap you."

"Harm me or *kidnap* me?"

"Brides are hard to come by in the Underworld," Dragos said. "Now, you would have to travel on foot many days to reach the borders of my realm—and of course it is impossible to map the World Above to the Underworld precisely, but roughly, I rule to the edges of the influence of the Turks, of Kiev, of Hungary, and to the seas. I am the ruler of the Underworld for what remains of the old Roman people who lived in these lands once."

So all the land beneath Sylvania, of course, but also from Bulgaria to Bessarabia—and more besides. I was astonished. I would be queen of all that, too, when I married him?

If I married him?

I stared down at a cluster of grapes on the table, thinking of how simple it would be to just pop a handful of them into my mouth. I could end this agony and be the queen of extensive lands, no matter how dark and damp.

It was the right thing to do, wasn't it? To live up to the promise I'd made when I stepped forward in the pavilion. But I *couldn't* eat the grapes—I couldn't make the irrevocable gesture that would bind me to this world, not when there was a World Above where Didina lived again, and I could have the dowry for breaking the curse, and—

Dragos was speaking. "We are bounded by Lethe on the south and west, and by Alethe on the north and east. As for upward, you can claim the protection of Thonos anywhere that you can travel without being seen by the yellow sun."

"But I met you in daylight!" I said. "More than once."

"Always in shadow."

I frowned. "So if you go to the surface at night, does that mean your realm extends throughout the surface world?"

"Not my realm, but my power, yes. Why do you think people fear the night so?" He smiled a toothy *zmeu* smile.

He was finished with his meal and I hadn't even made a pretense of eating mine. I rose and made some fumbling excuse, and he let me retire to my room, where I heated water from Alethe and made a thin soup of lovage from my herb pouch, with purslane for thickening, and a tisane of rose hips to drink. It was the most unconvincing meal on earth—or under it. I was reduced to eating the rest of the bread in my herb pouch to quiet my anxious stomach, which didn't stay quiet for long.

I hoped Pa would come tonight, but I wondered: What is "tonight" in a place where time flows differently than in the World Above? How would he and Mihas manage to meet?

I slept, but not well.

When I woke, I lay in bed thinking about the Darkness that had oppressed me the day before. I had something to be thankful for, and that was the fact that I hadn't awakened paralyzed and unable to breathe, right?

But when I thought about the Darkness, I realized I could still feel it there at the edges of the room. It kept its distance, but it was present.

I got up and rearranged my paper and writing supplies on the desk, until I grew restless. Was it even day or night right now? I couldn't tell. I guessed, by the fact that Thela remained absent, that it was night.

I sorted through my fine clothing, but since I couldn't

figure out how to get into a bodice on my own, I simply put on a new chemise, with my old apron and skirt over it. I also forwent the appalling princess shoes and donned my practical stockings, shoes, and leg wrappings. I gave my hair a good brushing, covered it with my old cowl, and opened my door.

Zuste, the footman, slumbered in the hall outside, slumped against the wall. I chose not to disturb him. Candle in hand, I set forth to investigate my new home.

Castle Thonos was filled with hundreds of unoccupied rooms, most indistinguishable from one another. I noted the location of an indoor privy with smooth wooden seats not far from my quarters, but most of the rooms were uninteresting, being devoid of much furniture or decoration. That which was small or useful, I collected to carry back to my room.

I took note of several things I liked that were too heavy for me to carry on my own: a stone bowl here, a nice long table there. It was only when I found a mortar and pestle high on a dusty shelf, and gleefully brought them back to my desk, that I realized that I was assembling an herbary.

Once I understood my purpose, I settled down with my scads of clean paper and wrote a list of the things I would need. I already had paper and pens, a mortar and pestle. I would need flasks, bowls, pots, drying racks, dirt, an amphora or two, wine, vinegar, water, sweet oil, a handful of good knives, a funnel, string, wax, extra candles, perhaps some lard. . . . I would need a collecting basket, and I would need to make some collection trips.

I couldn't bring myself to eat the food of Thonos and commit to being its queen. But I would have an herbary for as long as I remained in the Underworld.

CHAPTER 27

When Mihas next knocked to ask if I needed anything, I was prepared. I'd found a basket and I was
ready to go.

"Go where?" he asked.

"On a collecting expedition. My herbary is completely
bare."

He lowered his voice and ducked his head. "You're not
going to try to escape, are you? *He* can find you wherever
you go. It's unwise to run."

I found it interesting that Mihas thought I might be
considering such an action, so I played along. "But he
can't go anywhere that sunlight touches—"

"The sun *sets*," Mihas said bluntly.

Excellent point. "I have no intention of trying to
escape. I simply want to look for plants."

"Did you ask the King?"

"Do you think I need to ask the King?" My voice was rather unpleasant—not because I was mad at Mihas; rather, because I was scared that maybe I should have asked Dragos. But then I straightened my shoulders. If I was going to be Queen, I had to carry on with my own occupations.

"Don't make him angry," Mihas cautioned. "It's dangerous."

"Dangerous how? What's Dragos going to do to me?"

"I don't care what he does to you," Mihas said. "I care what he does to me."

I raised my eyebrows, amused by this display of temper.

"Fine," he said in answer to my wordless reaction. "But *I'm* going with you."

I raised my chin. "That was my plan all along. *You* are going to row the boat."

In the forest of the four seasons, I lifted my eyes gratefully to the dark spring sun. It was not true sunlight, and no one could ever mistake it for such, but it was better than the dim candles of the castle—better even than the pavilion lights.

On my first journeys through the forest, I'd barely noticed the tarnish and patina on the trees, and I had certainly not seen them as signs of illness in the plants. But the farther I strayed from the princesses' well-worn path—as Mihas diligently marked our way back with bits of ribbon I'd given him—the more I noted signs of sickness in the forest. Where trees had fallen, no seedlings took their place. Flowers withered on the stalk, fruits rotted on the vine.

I carried a large basket with me and collected everything of interest, samples from every plant I saw: shriveling tree buds and broken twigs; drying grass stems; even whole wilting flowers by the root. In the spring forest, I gathered crocus, narcissus, and hyacinth. In the summer forest, I found roses and irises. In the autumn forest, I collected the colored leaves of the trees, small white berries from a sort of wintergreen-looking plant, and even a few jeweled apples. And from the winter trees, I gathered silver twigs, mistletoe, holly berries, and snow-chilled wild grapes that shone like beads of glass.

Everything was a wonder, and every new discovery caused me delight that I couldn't always contain. But every single item I found was imperfect, touched by either blight or age, and I didn't understand *why*.

When we came out the other side of the forest, I felt puzzled—confused. Why was everything here dying? Why was nothing springing to new, vigorous life? You couldn't have a forest without constant renewal—unless it was truly a forest of ungrowing things, as the place had first appeared to me. But these things grew, I could see that, and they decayed—I could see that, too. It was not an unchanging place, not a tomb, as I would have expected of a forest in the Underworld.

We wandered around the perimeter of the winter forest while I looked for the princesses' recently abandoned path. I found it—and also found the staircase that led to their tower.

Completely destroyed.

Mihas and I stood side by side, staring. "What happened?" I asked.

"The earth shook, the first night you stayed here," Mihas said.

"I dreamed that it did," I whispered.

"It wasn't a dream."

Our mood had been far from chipper when we started out, but now we were distinctly depressed. I plunged deeper into the forest, looking for something, though I didn't know what. A sign of hope, a sign of rebirth—something. Anything.

I didn't find anything hopeful, but I did insist we circle back into the spring woods. Along the riverbank I discovered a patch of plants that I hadn't seen before—some sort of reed.

Mihas evidently found plant collecting wearying beyond reason, for he settled down against a tree and commenced snoring. I shrugged and started packing asphodel lilies into my basket, alongside willow branches and violets. I was kneeling to inspect a patch of narcissus for cankers when I felt the sensation of someone's regard on my back.

I expected to find Mihas staring at me while filling the air with fake snores, perhaps to lighten the mood. But Mihas still slept. Instead, a woman watched me from the shadows. She wore white robes in elegant draperies, and her hair in elaborate curls—but her feet were bare.

I scrambled to my feet as she stepped into the beams of the dark sun, which seemed to shine right through her. She cast no shadow. I shivered a little. Was she a dead soul? If so, she was far less substantial than Zuste and Thela.

She bent to touch a narcissus plant, and the drooping flower pulled itself upright. The slightly withered petals became smooth and vital once more, but the woman seemed, if anything, *more* transparent. "You're the new bride," she said, straightening to gaze at me with dark-eyed interest.

I stared at her. "I'm Reveka," I said.

She glanced around, from the forest floor to the treetops. "You have much to do to renew Thonos, you and the new King."

"*New* King? Hasn't Dragos been ruling here for, well, at least six years?"

She looked upward, as though calculating. "It's been fourteen summers, in fact, since he struck the bargain and came to the dark-walled world."

"Fourteen?" At my cry, Mihas jerked awake and stumbled upright. The woman waved her hand and he slumped down, banging his head on the tree trunk, and fell asleep once more. Or he was knocked unconscious. I couldn't say which.

I took a step backward, suddenly afraid. But the woman smiled.

"There is no reason to fear me, not you, nor anyone. Some, fearing death, once called me Dread, but I no more command death than any mortal does anymore." She bent to touch another narcissus. "Now, life, of course . . ." The brown petals of the flower turned white and glistened pale silver in the light. Again, she was a shade sheerer than before.

"Who are you?"

"Me?" She smiled into the heart of the flower. "Such questions always lead to riddles. For now you may know me as the nymph of the river Alethe."

"I . . . I . . ." A nymph? A minor goddess, like in the Greek myths? Flummoxed, I fell silent.

Taking no notice of my tongue-tied state, she stood straight again, twitching the folds of her robes into place. "What are you doing in the Queen's Forest, Reveka?"

"I am collecting samples for my herbary," I said. "I am an herbalist's apprentice."

"Of course!" She clapped her hands toget[her], folded them, a broad grin breaking across [her face. Of] course. An herbalist is perfect. Lovely. Drag[os made an] excellent choice."

"I don't know that there was a choice on his part," I said. "He was rather desperate, since the twelve princesses wouldn't have him for the past six years, and . . . I offered, to save my father."

"Your father? What does your father have to do with anything? Where was your mother?"

"My mother died when I was very young. My father is the gardener for Castle Sylvian, you see, and—"

She chopped a hand across my words. "No matter. All paths don't have to run the same to be worth walking. Of course, it would be *better* if you had a mother, but a queen is a queen, and better that Dragos has not left it *too* late. . . ." She frowned at me. "But you have not eaten!"

Mihas stirred, muttering, and again the woman waved at him and he puddled into sleep once more. She turned to me, her face etched with sympathy. "It is difficult, I know, for a gardener's daughter, for an herbalist, to dwell in the Sunless House."

"The sunless house?" I repeated.

"This whole land is the Sunless House. The Underworld, you perhaps call it? It is a vital place, a reservoir of life and death and magic, which exists in tandem with the World

.bove. Without a properly functioning Underworld, the World Above suffers—and vice versa, of course."

"Is the Underworld suffering?" I asked, though I suspected I knew the answer, had *seen* the answer, written in the blight in this forest.

"*Thonos* suffers. The rot you see around you is but a manifestation of the rot across the whole land. Trees fall and none take their place; you have seen this here. But elsewhere, worse occurs. Souls disappear on their journeys and gain neither the Heaven nor the rebirth they have earned. It will be your task, as Queen, to stop this, to heal the land." She glanced down at herself, at the light visible through her body. "Even I am not as strong as I once was. The river Alethe suffers, just like the souls, just like this forest. Heal us, Reveka."

"Er . . . *how* am I to heal Thonos?"

She smiled. "By simply being who—and what—you were meant to be: the Queen of Thonos. A queen will rebalance the land, spur life to awaken where now there is only gray death."

No wonder Dragos had tried so hard to get a wife; his land was dying, and he needed a queen to heal it. He'd said he didn't seek heirs. And he didn't seem to have such a burden of governing duties that splitting them with a wife was necessary.

The nymph was still talking. "When you are Queen,

the healing will be as breathing." Her smile faded. "But not until then. Never until then. I know; for there was a time I refused to eat, to give myself to the Underworld, too, and everyone suffered for it."

Mihas moaned, waggling his head like a turtle. I was prepared for her to put him to sleep again, but in the moment between when I looked at Mihas and when I looked back, she was gone. I strongly suspected an invisibility cap was in play—they seemed as common as dirt around here.

"Get up, Cowherd," I said sharply, irritated and not a little frightened by the nymph's visit. "It's time to go back."

Mihas struggled to his feet. "I'm not a cowherd, you know, so you can stop calling me that. My family raised sheep. We owned but the one cow."

I opened my mouth to retort, but no sharp words were forthcoming. Instead I said, "You're right. I don't know that I liked being called Cabbage Girl by the princesses all that much, either. I'm sorry. How's your head?"

"Fine," he said, but my apology must have stunned him to silence, and we followed the ribbons back to the boat without speaking another word.

Chapter 28

I did not know what to think about my conversation with the nymph, but my mind returned again and again to her words about the blight on the land: *It will be your task, as Queen, to stop this.*

If I could heal the land, Dragos wouldn't need a queen. If I could heal the land, I wouldn't have to become his wife and dwell in the "Sunless House," and potentially lose my soul by marrying a demon. If I could heal the land, I could go home to Pa, and the herbary, and Didina—to the dowry I'd earned by breaking the curse. I could take up the dream I'd despaired of.

The nymph seemed certain that my being an herbalist was a good sign. How so? I wondered. Was curing the ailment of Thonos, at its root, as simple as curing a body of a fever?

There was no time to waste in getting my tools in

order, if that was the case.

I decided quickly that my bedroom was not going to be an adequate herbary. Fortunately, the bedchamber next to mine was completely empty and seemed disinclined to dampness.

I had Mihas and Zuste move two long tables I liked into the room, and I added all the bits and bobs I'd collected around the castle. I had my servants hang drying racks for me, filched from the kitchens, while I unpacked my herb pouch and sorted my bounty from the forest. I sent Skiare out with the long list I'd made, after adding cheesecloth to it.

While my servants worked to obtain the rest of my materials, I began a careful assessment of the plants of the Underworld. I divided all the seeds I'd collected in half. The first half I planted in tiny pots of earth. The second half I studied closely. I wrote down all the observed characteristics of the seeds: their smell, their shape, and their color. Then I cut them and examined their inner layers, and finally I powdered them, and tasted each seed in tiny doses—noting flavor, of course, but also any effect, such as immediate tingling on my tongue.

After I finished with the seeds, I moved on to flowers, then roots, then bark, then finally leaves and stems. While there was not a one-to-one correspondence of properties between World Above plants and their Underworld counterparts, there were many similarities. Mistletoe grew the same way down here as above and showed all the signs of being a potent poison; roses still smelled sweet; and so forth.

All this activity served, for a time, to make me forget that I was starving; for though I drank mug after mug of tisanes made from the herbs I'd brought from the World Above, they did not fool my stomach into believing I'd eaten, even when I chewed the too-tart dregs of my teas.

I worked steadily throughout the day. Only when I heard a knock down the hall at my bedchamber door did I realize that I was going to have to make the case for my herbary sooner, not later. I yanked open the herbary door and poked my head out. Dragos turned, surprised.

"My lord." I beckoned him over, and he came in, ducking his head and folding in his wings to fit through the doorframe. He looked around at the chaos I'd made.

"An herbary," he said, though sounding more inquisitive than anything else. I launched into my defense anyway.

"Even in a land where people don't fall sick and die, there are baths and bath herbs. Or there could be. And clothes! Clothes need scenting. Aren't there mice or moths or spiders to keep out down here? Doesn't matter—I *like* the smells of southernwood and santolina. And cooking herbs! You must need cooking herbs. And yet you say there's no need for an herbary!"

Dragos's ears twitched. "I'm sorry. I spoke hastily. I should not have tried to deprive you of your few pleasures. It's just—"

"I know," I said. "It's silly, and a waste of my time."

"Not at all. You may find that there are other properties in the plants that grow down here. Healing is not a necessity, but—"

"Not a necessity? I learned today that your whole world is suffering! Thonos is ailing."

His ears flexed and tightened. "Yes," he said slowly. "Thonos *is* ailing. I hadn't thought of it in terms of needing an herbalist, but yes, we are ailing. Streams dry up, trees die. . . . Souls are disappearing, just slipping away into nothingness, sometimes before my very eyes."

Exactly as the nymph had said. "Like the cursed sleepers," I said, thinking of Didina's ma, slipping away before Adina's eyes.

"Pardon?"

"The men and women Princess Lacrimora and her sisters poisoned. They've lain for years in a sleep like death. Sometimes, they just . . . die. Decline. Slip right away."

"Poisoned," he said, the word a dull thud.

"Yes! They poisoned my friend Didina, just poured noxious wine down her throat. To protect their secret. Their dancing with you."

"Poisoned . . . I see."

"You did not know?" Somehow, this thought made me feel a little better—until I remembered what he did to the men who followed the princesses down into the Underworld. Instead of poisoning them, he'd enslaved them and made them drink the waters of Lethe, and put their immortal souls in danger.

In a way, I could see that perhaps Lacrimora's poison was a little bit—just a very tiny bit—more generous than the alternative. Broadly speaking.

"I didn't know." He seemed lost in contemplation for a moment, but then he stirred. "They had their reasons," he said. "As I had mine. I came to ask if you were going to dine with me tonight."

My head was shaking no before I even gave it permission to move. If he was going to ask, apparently I was going to tell him the truth.

"Sorry," I said pathetically. If I joined him at dinner, the temptation to eat might prove to be too much, and now that I knew Dragos didn't need a wife as much as he needed a healer, it seemed foolish to give in.

He was gracious. He did not press me.

∽∾

I crept back to my room not much later, too hungry to concentrate anymore. Mihas was standing outside my door, attentive, like a footman. I asked him to fetch me the Water of Life.

"The Water of Life?" Mihas's eyes widened. "Do you have some?"

"Obviously no, since I asked you to fetch it for me," I said, but I was too curious to be irritated. Was the water not freely available? I told Mihas to wait, and I trotted off to find Dragos, who was of course dining.

The *zmeu* seemed amused by my request. "The ordinary water around here will do you no harm," he said. "It is the same water that wells up through the ground and runs through the rivers of the World Above."

"I don't want to accidentally drink Lethe."

"You would have to drink from it daily, not just once."

I thought about the legends of the Underworld I knew, the Greek stories of Hades and Persephone. "I thought souls only drank once from Lethe and easily forgot everything."

His ears flared. "You are not an eidolon soul but a mortal girl, so it is different. It interests me, though, that you should know this about Lethe—do they tell these legends, or are you well-read, Reveka?"

I shrugged. "I've read every book of herb lore I have ever had the chance to, and all the pamphlets about Draculea, and the Gospels. When we lived in Moldavia,

I wasn't apprenticed, so I read everything King Stefan's librarian would let me, which was mostly Homer and herbals. I've read . . . about thirty books, I suppose?"

"So the answer is, for your age and station, you are well-read."

"I guess," I said. "If being well-read matters. Hades is supposed to be ruled by, um, Hades, and that doesn't seem to be the case anymore, so I can't vouch for any of the information I learned by reading."

Dragos rose to fill a silver pitcher from a stone amphora in the corner. "Hades the country broke apart two hundred fifty years ago, around the time that the Golden Horde swept into Europe. Hades the King, or Pluto, or Dis Pater—whatever you'd like to call him—is long gone."

"Thonos used to be part of Hades, then? Like Sylvania and Transylvania and Wallachia used to be part of the Roman Empire in the World Above?"

"Yes." He handed me the silver pitcher. "Thonos was a prized region of Hades, largely due to the fact that the sources of the rivers Lethe and Alethe are here."

"Ah. Well, thank you for the water." I stumbled through a curtsy, trying not to slosh, and scurried back to my bedchamber.

When I gave Mihas the pitcher, he guzzled the entire thing, then fell into one of the fireside chairs, eyes closed.

"Mihas?" I shook his shoulder.

He opened his eyes. "It's coming back. I didn't think it would."

"What's coming back?"

"My memory of the World Above."

When Mihas left, I lay down to rest just for a moment—and fell asleep.

When I woke again, Thela was in my room preparing my clothing. It was the only signal for morning that I could recognize in this dark world.

I wobbled to my feet and let her dress me. I couldn't focus my thoughts, and I felt that this did not bode well for a day of study in my herbary. While Thela combed out my hair, I sat still and considered the disappearing souls of Thonos, and how their fate mirrored the way the sleepers in the World Above sometimes slipped away from Adina's care.

My hunger-addled brain recalled bits of yesterday's conversation with the nymph—something about how whatever happened above was mirrored in the world below. And perhaps this was true—perhaps the Underworld was a shadow cast by the World Above. Or a reflection.

But the dying plants? The falling trees? The new life that would not take?

The new life that would not take . . . Vasile couldn't get an heir and hadn't had a child in years. He'd proven himself fertile many times, years ago, but no longer.

A terrible hunger pang gripped my belly, and the Darkness came back, springing shut around me like a bear trap, pressing me to the ground. Memories rolled over me: every half-recalled nightmare of Muma Pădurii, every hungry hour of my life, and every moment of fear I'd ever experienced, from the first time I'd been called a liar and received a beating from the Abbess to the first time I'd heard the distant thunder of the Turks' cannons to the moment when the princesses had poured poison down Didina's throat and I had been unable to save her.

When the Darkness finally moved off me, it seemed to be laughing.

I opened my eyes to Thela patting my cheek and calling what seemed to be my name through her thick accent. She pulled me to my feet and plopped me into a chair.

I would normally think I had fainted from hunger, but I'd fainted from hunger before, during the worst of the famine rations, and this was different.

I was terribly hungry, but the hunger wasn't as bad as the Darkness. The water of Alethe had kept the Darkness at bay for a little while, but that was all.

I would go to Dragos. I would eat. Because I had to admit that Pa wasn't coming. It had been days, and the steps from the princesses' tower were caved in. Pa wasn't coming.

While horrified by this realization, I was also relieved. The Darkness would leave me alone, and I wouldn't be hungry, true. But if I ate, if I became the Queen of Thonos, then the souls would stop disappearing and the Queen's Forest would grow again.

I hadn't realized how much I felt the burden of Thonos's illness until the decision was out of my hands.

I stood on reluctant, trembling legs and started toward the hall.

CHAPTER 29

A knock at the door arrested me. I swayed and sat back down while Thela admitted Mihas.

I smelled food, the warmth of bread and the sourness of cheese. For a brief, dizzying moment, I thought, *He knows what I've decided, and he's brought me the food of the Underworld. How could he, after all his talk of rescue?* My gaze narrowed on the basket over his arm, and steadiness returned. Mihas wouldn't do that.

"Send your handmaiden away," Mihas said. I waved at Thela and said, "Shoo!" but that was all I could manage for communication. She kept on making my bed. I shrugged at Mihas.

"If you're fine with her knowing," Mihas said, "then your father brought food."

"What?" Instantly, my resolve to dwell in the Underworld for the rest of my life withered. My stomach gurgled to life. "No! Pa came?"

"Yes. I met him at the edge of the forest, by the lake, when he signaled." Mihas went to my desk and began unpacking the basket. I tallied the breads, the cheeses, the apples, the plums, the thyme pies, the tartlets. It looked like a lot, but it wasn't actually very much. No more than two or three days' worth, at full ration.

I was starving. It wouldn't hurt anything if I ate a bite of cheese from above while I asked for the tidings from home. I lurched to my feet and crammed a wedge of cheese into my mouth. It was so good, salty on my tongue, and so sharp that my jaw tightened in shock.

"How did Pa get down here if the stairs to the princesses' tower are caved in?" I asked around the lump of cheese in my cheek.

"He has his own way in. He dug a tunnel."

"Oh." I chewed and swallowed. Food! Glorious, wonderful food! I ripped a chunk of bread next and felt my withered resolve shrivel further. "How is Didina?"

A muscle near Mihas's mouth twitched, and he avoided my eyes by staring at the tapestries on my walls. "What do you mean?"

"Well, Lacrimora woke the sleepers, right? So—how's Didina?"

Mihas met my eyes. "Lacrimora didn't wake the sleepers, Reveka."

"What?" I shrieked. Startled, Thela looked up. Not perceiving danger, but reading my face well enough, she started toward me. I waved her off. "Did Lacrimora *even try?*"

Mihas took a deep breath, fingers fidgeting with his sleeves. "Your papa says she tried, but it was no good—she doesn't have the cure." As I opened my mouth again, he said, "I don't know any more than that!"

"Did they try the water of the Little Well? The water in the Little Well mixes with the Water of Life, with Alethe!"

"I don't *know*, Reveka!" Mihas said. "I would think they tried. It's what the princesses drank when they came down here; they would know its properties."

I crumpled back into my chair, feeling smaller than a child. I'd come to the Underworld blindly assuming that Lacrimora would be able to reverse her poison, and had not considered that the end of one curse wasn't the promise of the end of the other.

There was no way I could eat the food of the Underworld now—not yet, anyway. Consign myself to the darkness when the sleepers needed me? I had so much to do, so little time, and . . .

"So little food," I whispered. "Why did he send so little?"

"Well, for one thing," Mihas said, "it's been only a day in the World Above since they returned."

"A day? But it's been . . . three or four days down here!"

"I know. Time is not the same, above and below."

"Yes, I know, but . . . " I stared at the food, my mind

calculating half rations, quarter rations. The time disparity was to my benefit, when it came to finding a cure for the sleeping death. I had far more than a scant two weeks to keep Didina's mother from death, to pull the Duke of Styria back from the edge, and to prevent a war.

But the time disparity worked against me with Pa sending so little food. If I didn't get enough to eat regularly, I'd be useless in the herbary. Pa's food was my only hope—well, *Sylvania's* only hope, and Didina's. I had to keep up my strength and keep my wits about me, if I had any chance of waking the sleepers. But I also had to make the food last. . . .

Unless I took the plunge and ate the food of the Underworld.

Not yet, I thought. I felt the burden of Thonos's illness on my shoulders, but I couldn't think about that now. I forced myself out of my chair. The mouthful of cheese and bread hadn't been enough, though, and my legs shivered. Mihas caught me before I could fall, and he and Thela moved me back to my chair.

"It'll be all right," Mihas said. "Your father will come for you." He put another chunk of bread into my hand.

There was a tap at my door. Thela opened it to reveal the hulking *zmeu* form of Lord Dragos, while Mihas and I froze. "Is everything all right in here?" Dragos asked.

I glanced at the bread I held. "Yes. Everything is fine."

We were silent while Dragos looked at the food from

the World Above half scattered across my floor and desk. For someone who didn't speak the language, Thela proved perceptive: She scooped up my dirty clothes from the day before and escaped down the hall.

Dragos drew in a great breath and let it out in a slow stream redolent of ash and almonds. "I brought you something, Reveka," he said, and pulled a large crate in from the hall. He carried it over and pried the lid from the crate easily with his claws. Mihas scurried around him to stow the food back in the basket, though I noticed that he tucked a plum and a thyme pie into a pigeonhole of my desk. He left with the basket, and Dragos let him.

"Books," I said in surprise. I stumbled to my feet and went to look. There were easily three dozen, all with wooden covers.

"Codices, really," Dragos said. "Handwritten texts, mostly in Greek or Latin. They are for you."

"For—all for me?" I stammered, surprised and not a little bit touched. I picked up one of the books and flipped it open: *Consolatio philosophiae*, "the consolation of philosophy." Another, in a language that didn't seem to be exactly Latin: *Le livre de la cité des dames*. I looked, but didn't see anything that might be an herbal or a book of medicine.

"Thank you," I said sincerely, for all that I regretted no book of herbs. I was too amazed to know how to show him my appreciation. I had never owned a real book before. "I look forward to reading these." *Someday.*

"Good," Dragos said. "I thought I would take you to collect herbs in some other areas of Thonos today. Places you might not be able to get to easily on your own." He flexed his wings a little.

"Yes, please," I said, feeling grim reality resettle on my shoulders. On one shoulder were the sleepers. On the other, all of Thonos. I couldn't know which problem to address first, but I also didn't know the plants of this world. If I could discover their properties, perhaps the priority would assert itself.

And perhaps there was something to the observation I'd made about the problems seeming mirrored. Maybe I'd solve both problems with one cure. I could dream, couldn't I?

"I'll leave you to dress," Dragos said, and departed.

When the door closed, I crammed the hunk of bread into my mouth and cast about me for something to wear. I knew I couldn't get into a fancy princess dress without Thela's help, so I laid out my old chemise, skirt, and apron—and devoured the thyme pie. I got dressed between bites of plum and sucked the pit free of the last threads of flesh as I bound my hair up in a scarf.

I spat out the pit and opened the door. Dragos was waiting. Mihas was nowhere in sight.

"You're going to wear *that*?" Dragos asked.

"Thela has disappeared, and I can't get dressed in *those* alone." I pointed at the shimmering gowns hanging across the room. "Does it matter?"

"You're to be a queen," Dragos said. "Do *you* think it matters?"

I weighed this in my mind for a bit. A queen was a queen regardless of clothing. But it was easier to command the respect one deserved if one looked—and acted—the part.

"I suppose it does," I said. "But there is no way that I can get into gowns such as those by myself. There are all these lacings and knots."

"We can wait for Thela. Though perhaps I will tell her to make herself a little more available in the mornings."

"Well, don't do *that*," I said. "She's probably got things to do—"

Thela came around the corner then and motioned me inside, where she divested me of my peasant clothes and shimmied me into a bodice, which she laced so tightly, I could only gasp at the end.

I mulled over the conversation with Dragos while Thela helped me into an underrobe, gown, and stockings.

Something didn't make sense. If I had to prove to the servants that I was a lady—well, no, a queen—I needed to dress like a queen. But I couldn't dress like a queen without help.

At some point, it began to seem as if the whole of royalty was simply a charade for the servants.

I supposed, technically, it was exactly that. *I can barely walk by myself,* the impractical gowns said. *But I can command people and send them on my errands.*

I might enjoy sending people on my errands. But I enjoyed not falling down when I walked, too.

When I was dressed, Thela stepped back and assessed her work. She smiled. Her eyes were as old as the mountains, but her face was as smooth as my own. I wished I could speak to her, discover her story.

If wishes were horses, beggars would ride, I reminded myself, and went to find Dragos.

CHAPTER 30

Thanks to Dragos's wings, we went from border to border of Thonos that day, landing here and there to look for likely herbs, while Dragos simultaneously educated me about his land.

Most of Thonos was as dark as the castle, but a few places—particularly near entrances to the World Above—were lighted areas like the Queen's Forest. In the Blessed Fields, where I plucked asphodel, a pale golden ball hung in the sky like a sun, shining on the souls of heroic men and women, the youngest of whom had fought the Romans. When we visited other places, there were more kinds of false suns and, occasionally, glorious moons and fields of stars.

Wherever there was light, I saw eidolon souls. Nearly everyone looked as normal as my servants Zuste and Thela—opaque, solid, real; aware of their surroundings and us, but not overly curious about anything. Some waved, but we were not, I could see, a normal, World Above king and queen to these people, to be touched and adored. I said as much to Dragos while we flew in darkness toward a starlit marsh. "It makes sense," I said, eyes closed and concentrating on something other than the fact that I couldn't see *anything*. "It's not as though they pay taxes and, in return, we distribute bread. Or do we? Do eidolons eat?"

"They *can* eat, but they don't need food to sustain them. But it is untrue that they do not receive anything from us. We protect them. And though there is no taxation, they would fight in my army if I asked them to."

"Who would you fight?" I asked, shivering. I had not truly thought that there was no war in the Underworld, but I had hoped.

"When the Golden Horde came through in the World Above, their gods tried to sweep through the Underworld as well. Or so I'm told. Right now, I do not worry overmuch about the Underworld lords linked with the Turks expanding into Thonos." He sounded unhappy. "That may change, of course, but the lords of the Turks' Underworld are djinn, and they are remote from the religious concerns of the Turks at present. Or *any* of their concerns."

I tried to imagine an army of souls, tried to imagine

a group of djinn ruling beneath the lands of the Sultan, but decided not to work too hard at it. I was more curious about the other direction.

"What of Corvinus?" I asked. "What is the Underworld region like where he rules?"

"That would be Hekat's land," he said. "She has all the German and Hungarian regions under her sway, having killed off most of their gods long ago."

I shivered. Killing gods was a strange and terrible thought, and one I didn't want to know more about. "She's not like Corvinus, is she? Trying to expand into Sylvania—or Thonos, I mean?"

"She is very much like Corvinus," Dragos said. "She's the one who sends the crows that spy for him."

Surprised, I tried to twist my head around to see Dragos's face, but it made my neck crick—and I couldn't see anything anyway. I faced forward again, feeling cold and scared, and suddenly glad to be in the overwarm embrace of Dragos. It was all I had in this moment that was familiar—the oddly comforting sound of his bellows breath telling me I wasn't alone in the dark. Strange, the things you can decide are normal once you get used to them, once other things seem stranger and more horrible.

"Is she going to invade Thonos?" I asked, past the lump of scaredness in my throat.

"No. Not now, anyway." This reassurance didn't still

my trembling, and Dragos went on. "She has made more trouble than she can handle by killing gods, and now everyone is on their guard against her. No one will deal with her, negotiate with her, even grant her an audience. So she moves in the World Above, trying to gain power there, and interferes with mortal lives and mortal kingdoms."

I thought about the crows sitting on the castle roofs, controlled by a sinister intelligence. I wondered how far Hekat's fingers extended, how deep her magics went. Could she be the cause of the blight on Thonos, in spite of Dragos's certainty that she moved only in the World Above?

I thought again about mirrors, reflections, and shadows. I'd exchanged one threat of warfare for another. In fact—

"If her puppet or whatever Corvinus is gains control in the World Above, does that give Hekat leverage for an invasion of Thonos?"

I thought perhaps Dragos would remind me I was a political novice at this point, and tell me to keep my theories to myself. Or maybe he would try to protect me from the truth with a well-timed lie.

But his words were as bare as a winter tree. "Yes. Hekat would be in a fair position to take over Thonos if Corvinus took Sylvania."

The promised marsh came into view, and even a starlit night seemed gloriously bright after the journey through darkness. Dragos landed and set me on my feet. I stumbled, trying to regain my sense of balance after the flight, and immediately found a patch of sweet reeds.

"Anything I can dig for you?" Dragos asked.

I pointed out a cluster of marsh marigolds and then white and yellow water lilies, floating on the water. I assumed they were white and yellow, anyway; those were the usual shades, though most color was leached by the faintness of the light.

"If you can reach those lilies, I'll take them," I said. My voice came out stronger here. When I spoke in dark places, it seemed the sound was flat, trapped, as though there wasn't enough air. Light seemed to allow my voice to travel farther.

Dragos decided he couldn't reach the lilies from shore, so he took wing and collected them from above. He hovered over the water, snatching lily plants from their pool.

Across the black, starlit water, eidolon souls gathered to watch Dragos's acrobatics. The dim light and the distance made it hard to observe their expressions, but I imagined they were impressed by their King.

One eidolon, a woman wearing a kerchief almost exactly as Thela wore hers, particularly caught my eye. At first, I couldn't figure out why I watched her. She was thin—not in the way of someone who hungers, but in the way of scraped parchment—and it seemed I could see reeds and bushes *through* her.

Dragos turned and tumbled in midair, dexterous for someone so large, and went back to collect another handful of lilies. The thin soul raised a hand toward her King, and the dark well of her mouth opened. Her body language bespoke an appeal, a plea—though I couldn't hear her voice over the sweep of Dragos's wings and the trickle of water flowing in the marsh.

And then the woman thinned out entirely. She disappeared. She was gone, as completely and as surely as if she had put an invisibility cap on her head.

I looked at the other souls and saw no further signs of thinness. The eidolons didn't seem to notice her disappearance, either, though I stood and stared at the spot where she had been, willing the woman to return, until Dragos landed beside me.

I hadn't even had a chance to call out to her, or to warn Dragos, or anything. She was just gone.

"Did you see her?" I asked Dragos.

"The soul that disappeared on the other side of the marsh? Yes, I saw her." His voice was neither gentle nor harsh, but sad. "Let's go."

"There was a woman," I said. "She visited me in the

four-seasons forest, the Queen's Forest; she said she was the nymph of the river Alethe. She told me about these . . . disappearances."

Dragos lifted me into the air. "I don't believe I've met this nymph Alethe."

I frowned, concentrating on that instead of my memory of the disappearing soul. "Oh? Well, she says you've been King for only a short time, so perhaps you've not had the chance yet."

"A short time," he said with a laugh. "I suppose someday it will seem like a short time."

"Fourteen years," I said. "As long as I've been alive. Actually, longer."

"Yes, well, I wouldn't have *chosen* a child bride, all things being equal."

I felt a little affronted by that, but I couldn't really argue with his sentiment. "I'm sure it would be easier if I weren't so young, but I doubt I would know my own mind any better." I didn't try to keep the asperity out of my voice.

Dragos replied, "I wouldn't even dream of doubting *that*." He spoke so lightly, and it was so easy to fill in Frumos as the speaker, and not Dragos, that I felt a pang.

And just like that, I was crying. The memory of the disappearing soul twined with the memory of Didina's still form lying beside her mother, and Adina's sorrow-lined face. I bit my knuckles, trying to keep from wailing out loud like a little child. But a sob escaped me.

Dragos's arms tightened around me gently—so very warm—and for a moment, I was comforted. Not because he could do anything, but because he was warm enough, and human enough, and he cared enough.

We landed again shortly, in a silver glade lit by moonlight almost as bright as the sun—sufficiently bright to cast shadows, in any case.

"Where are we now?" I asked, squeezing my voice out through my tears.

"This is a way station, a place of passage between Thonos and the World Above," Dragos said. "Or that tree is, anyway." He pointed to an oak trunk with a hollow space in the center of it.

"Why bring me here?" I asked.

"For a breath of fresh air," he said. "Go on through. I'll be right behind you."

I ducked into the passage and had little difficulty finding my way as the tunnel wound upward. I stepped out of the passage through another hollow oak tree, into gray light and warm air.

"I can see," I said, astonished.

Dragos grunted but sounded far away.

"Dragos?" I called, turning around to see if he followed. There was no hulking *zmeu* behind me. There was only a thin man with a clever mouth staring back at me.

Frumos.

I gasped. "You—you said you couldn't turn back into your human form."

"I said that I had no control over it. But in the surface world, I am human; in the other world, I am *zmeu*."

"Oh," I said, gaping like Mihas at his stupidest.

We stood together at the edge of a plum orchard—Castle Sylvian's plum orchard, the very place where Pa had ordered me to stay away from the curse. Dawn was lightening the World Above, enough that I could see colors around me: the deep green of the leaves, and even their vein patterns. I faced the outline of Castle Sylvian in the distance, a dark hulk against a blue-gray sky, with only a few lights flickering in the windows.

My eyes welled with tears again, though I managed to blink them back. I didn't look at Dragos until I had them under control, but when I faced him, I found that he was watching me.

His bright human eyes were just as penetrating in their way as when he was a dragon. I noted how his left eyebrow quirked a little more than his right, the faint freckles on his cheeks, and his blade of a nose. He was so very human. His *zmeu* form was so smooth, so symmetrical, so perfect and perfectly terrifying that it seemed unreal. I could not imagine Dragos's *zmeu* mother, hatching him

out of his egg. But the mother of this man, if such a creature existed, would have had the same lively eyes, the
same freckles. . . . His father was probably just as lean and
had just such an Adam's apple that bobbed in his throat
when he talked.

"Reveka?" he asked in his lighter, less thunderous
voice. "This was a mistake. I apologize."

"Mistake?"

"To bring you here, in sight of your home, which you
cannot visit."

"My home," I said, and my voice faltered. I hadn't
really considered Sylvania my home, but it was—had
become so. "I was raised in a convent in Transylvania, you
know."

"I didn't," Frumos—no, Dragos—said. "But you can
tell me about it."

So I did. I told him about my mother, and the convent,
and Pa; and the Abbess and Sister Anica, and the lying.

"But you aren't a liar?"

"I became one, for a time," I said. "But I don't really
think I started out as one, no matter what the Abbess said."

"You must have come to some accord with your father
on the subject, since you went to rather extraordinary
lengths to save him."

I frowned. "Did Pa and I ever come to an accord
about lying? I don't think so. He forced me to promise

to never lie to him. That's not an accord. But—you don't save people just because you get along with them. You save people because—well, it beats not saving them. And I saved more than just Pa, by coming to Thonos."

"Yes," Dragos said soberly. "Far more."

In the distance, a church bell tolled. Dragos stirred. "It's getting late. We should return."

I glanced around at the World Above, at the color and the brightness. I wanted to bolt for Castle Sylvian. Once the sun was up, Dragos wouldn't be able to follow me, would he? But then night would come again, and his power would swallow the world. It would be only a very temporary running away, and it wouldn't solve anything.

I nodded once, fiercely, strode back to the hollowed-out tree, and descended into the Underworld.

When I climbed out of the passage, I turned to wait for Dragos. What I saw made my scalp prickle.

As he stooped to come through the doorway into the Underworld, spines burst through Frumos's cheeks; his red velvet doublet smoothed and grew to cover his whole skin. His limbs grew longer, and his boots turned into hooves. I could make no sense of the transformation before it was over, and I would have said that I merely imagined the horror of it, save that I could not banish from my mind the bloody image of Frumos's cheeks sprouting spines.

Dragos was once more a *zmeu*.

And I would never, ever confuse Frumos and Dragos again. The image of the transformation was seared into my memory.

He must have seen my expression of horror, but he wordlessly lifted me in his arms and flew us back to Castle Thonos.

CHAPTER 31

The next two days in Thonos—though it remained hard to call them days with no sun to mark them—passed in a blur. I worried constantly about when Pa's next food delivery would arrive. Mihas went often to check for the signal from Pa, because not only did time not pass the same in the World Above and the Underworld, but the intervals could speed up or slow down randomly. I wondered how it was that the princesses had never been tripped up by this, but I didn't quite dare to ask Dragos.

I worked diligently in the herbary, trying to extrapolate magical properties of Underworld plants from what I knew of their World Above counterparts. I dismissed all the herbs known to induce sleep or calmness. Wakefulness was what the sleepers needed; I would go on the principle that wakefulness was what the Underworld also needed. It wasn't too hard a stretch, really. If no new life could begin in Thonos, that was a kind of lethargy, a sort of sleepiness. Life needed to be wakened in Thonos, vigor needed to be instilled in its disappearing souls, just as with the sleepers in the World Above.

With that logic behind me, I set aside narcissus, the flower Hades used to subdue Persephone; violet, which calms; and poppy, for poppies and sleep are synonymous.

I bottled potential remedy after potential remedy for the sleepers, intending that the next time Mihas met Pa, my possible cures and my notes on them would be delivered to Adina. That was my first plan, anyway; if I actually healed Thonos in the interim, I would concentrate my efforts on turning Thonos's remedy toward the sleepers.

How to heal Thonos, though? What was the heart of the land? I thought about the nymph Alethe. What had she said? She wanted me to heal the land, the souls, and also . . . herself. "I am not as strong as I once was," she'd said. "The river Alethe suffers, just like the souls, just like this forest."

My only other idea was to ask Dragos to bring a selection of thinning souls to me, so I could try the potions on them. I didn't think I could bear to watch another soul disappear in front of me. But I would pursue that course as well, once I had enough potions to make the testing worthwhile, and once I'd visited Alethe at her source.

When I wasn't in the herbary, I haunted the land around the castle looking for new plants.

I saw Dragos only intermittently, as we, of course, did not eat together and he had some sort of duties to attend to. Perhaps I should have been paying attention to what those duties were, but the need for healing this place was paramount, and if I could find a way to do it without learning the duties of the Queen of Thonos, well, I preferred that.

So I was surprised to smell Dragos's peculiar scent while I was digging rue outside the dancing pavilion.

"I know you're there," I said offhandedly over my shoulder. Dragos stepped within my circle of lamplight, hooves digging into the soft dirt. I bit my lip and looked away. Sometimes, the reminders of his *zmeu* nature made me ill.

When I looked up, he was staring into the darkness of the pavilion, not looking at me at all.

"Do you miss it?" I asked.

"Miss what?"

"The, er. Dancing, I guess?"

He considered. "It would be strange to miss it."

"You were not keen on dancing, then?"

"I danced more than I wanted to. Why, do you want to dance, Reveka?"

I blushed. I felt like a child who hints about sweets so overtly that the adult is forced to take pity on her and ask if she'd like one. I didn't *want* to dance. I didn't know *how* to dance. And it had looked horrible, the dancing, when I first saw it, with the half-fainting princesses and the blood in their shoes. . . . And yet . . .

You courted twelve princesses with dancing, and I didn't even get one turn around the floor, I thought, but I didn't know how to say it. It would come out either coquettish and coy or childish and whiny. And I was none of those things, or at least I didn't want to be any of them.

Dragos held his hand out to me. "Come along, then."

"Oh, no, I . . ."

He gestured impatiently, and I folded my arms. "No. It was a ridiculous thought. I don't want to be danced breathless and bloody."

"That's not how I always danced with them," he said. "In the beginning, it was all quite decorous and lovely. I'll show you." He clapped his hands sharply, and the pavilion glowed, softly at first, then brighter.

Reluctant, but intrigued, I let him guide me to the dance floor. When he clapped his hands again, the noise of tuning instruments swelled around us. The same insects that had made the place beautiful the first time I'd visited were waking up, not yet in full throat—or in full bum, in the case of the glowing bugs. It was like dawn. It was lovely, even if I hadn't been light starved.

Dragos bowed to me, and I curtsied to him, and we danced.

Which of course sounds much more elegant than it actually was, since I didn't know the steps. It was the same dance he'd performed with the princesses, and while parts of it looked familiar, I'd never had much chance to practice this skill in the convent or while traveling with Pa.

But Dragos taught me, very patiently, tracing the patterns tirelessly with me until I memorized them. Even though it was sort of like dancing with a tree given our size difference, it worked well enough.

Halfway through our first complete dance, I asked, "What's this called?"

"The *presoniera*," he said. "The 'prisoner's dance.'"

It was altogether too appropriate a name.

Not much later I asked, "Are you enjoying this?"

"More than I thought I would. It is novel, not to *force* someone to dance."

I was silent for a moment. "But surely you must have known after even the first *year* that it wasn't going to work. None of the princesses were going to marry you."

His voice was low, almost a growl. "I didn't have any

other choice," he said. "I had no other way to find a bride, so I had to hold them to their word and hope that one of them would give in before our agreement ended."

"I told you this when we first met! It's stupid to take the only choices offered, if they aren't any good."

He gave a huge-shouldered shrug. "I inherited a dying world. I thought I could bring it back on my own, but I—" His face held an expression I couldn't interpret, and I was angry, for a moment, that I wasn't looking at Frumos's face, which I had at least a chance of deciphering. "I tried, for the first years—I tried everything. But Thonos has to have a queen or the whole place will die, and everything and everyone in it will disappear."

"There's got to be a better way to get a bride!"

"How?" Dragos asked bitterly. "Hades got Persephone through kidnapping! And here am I, stuck as a *zmeu*—my choices came down to lying or extortion."

The vivid memory of the blood lining the princesses' shoes like red silk returned to me. "So that's what it was? Extortion?"

"Yes," Dragos said, his voice grim. "The first time one of them refused to dance, she would have had to marry me. I had to make it harder and harder to choose dancing."

The music crashed to its ending, and I slipped my hands from Dragos's and stepped back. I stared up at him. "I'm not sure that is better than kidnapping," I said.

His cheek spines bristled. I'd made him angry. "When you've been the monarch of a dying country for a few years," he said, "I'll let you judge me." He strode to the edge of the pavilion, spread his great crimson wings, and took flight.

My food ran out that night.

CHAPTER 32

A day later, I woke to the hollowest feeling in my midsection that I'd ever had, and to the taunting, crushing Darkness.

Thank goodness for Thela; she bustled in with a branch of candles, lit a fire, and gave me the Water of Life. The Darkness receded, even while my hunger clamped down like a vise.

As soon as Thela departed on some mysterious errand, I changed into my old, comfortable clothes—she had not been brazen enough to throw them out—and left to go somewhere, anywhere, else. If I stayed in the castle, I just might eat something.

Pa had to be coming today, I decided. He just had to be. I divided all my remedies in two, copied out duplicate notes, and put the notes and potions into a basket, then headed down to the lake.

I decided to row one of the boats to the Queen's Forest. I didn't get very far before I discovered I was raising blisters on my hands, but I pushed on. Halfway across, I got the bright idea to use my stockings as mittens, and that helped, though it did make me a smidge clumsy.

On the other side of the lake, I climbed a small, bare-looking hill and found, to my surprise, a succulent plant with jewellike, jagged leaves growing at the top. Burn plant, here in the Underworld? Brother Cosmin had a pot of it growing on a windowsill in his herbary, because it didn't like the cold winters very well.

I broke open a leaf of the plant, hoping there'd be a goopy juice inside like the burn plant I knew—and there was, though it shone like quicksilver. Hesitantly, I applied it to my blisters.

The effect was instant cooling, as if I'd plunged my hands into a snowbank. In the World Above, burn plant has a gentle soothingness for broken or burned skin— hence its name—but nothing like this. Astonished, I collected half the patch of the succulent and tucked it into my basket. This was too useful an herb not to know! Too bad I couldn't think of a way to apply its property to the problems of Thonos or Sylvania.

I settled to wait next to a tree in the very edge of the spring forest's morning sunlight. If Pa came, it would be to this spot, or very near it; from here, he would signal

Mihas—then Mihas would have to come all the way down the mountain and across the lake, giving me plenty of time to discuss things with Pa.

Hours passed. I collected moss, I took a nap, I wrote more details on my note to Adina. I began cataloging the kinds of blight I saw in the forest and considered the treatments I would try if the plants in my herb garden were ill like these.

It was a long time later—hours and hours—when a shadowy figure in a heavy cloak stole into the grove.

"Pa!" I cried.

The figure pushed back the hood of its cloak. It was not Pa. It was Lacrimora. I recoiled.

She held out a basket to me. I reached for it eagerly, but then hesitated.

"What?" she asked.

"You did poison my friend," I said. "And dozens of other people, too."

"Better asleep than a *zmeu*'s wife," she snapped.

"Oh, is that what you tell the dead-alive in the western tower?"

"I sleep at night, if that's what you're asking. None of them could free us from the curse, and serving in the Underworld seemed a fate worse than death. Perhaps it was—most of the men Dragos sent back don't remember anything about their lives before his service."

"You selfish, selfish princesses! *One* of you could have made the sacrifice. But not a single one of you would."

"And who among the rest of us could live with the shame and guilt of that, for the crime of sending a sister into the darkness forever?"

"Maricara could, I'm sure."

"We wouldn't give her the chance! Maricara was the one who got us into the mess in the first place. We never listened to Maricara once she sold us to Dragos for her own relative freedom. She was the one who stumbled into this realm and, like a fool, ate the food that was offered her. When Dragos claimed her, he asked for her hand in marriage, and she bartered for her parole instead—'Oh, Your Lordship, I have eleven sisters. Perhaps one will want to marry you!' And she sold us out. Brought us down here and tricked us into eating the food here all by herself! But the rest of us—we couldn't let any of the others go to this darkness. Not when there was a chance we could *all* go free."

"What chance?"

"If none of us gave in for twelve years, we would be released from the curse," Lacrimora said. "We were halfway there." I thought she might sneer at me then, but she held out the basket to me again and said, "We'll get you free, too, Reveka."

"Where's my father?" I asked, taking the basket. I rooted around inside it immediately and found a chunk of bread to pop into my mouth.

She reached up her sleeve and showed me the second invisibility cap, the one I hadn't had enough fronds for. I had wondered where that had ended up. It was starting to unravel. "There's only one of these," she said. "And I took it from your father. Dragos wouldn't hurt me if he found me here. But if he caught your father, Dragos wouldn't let him go. Not a second time."

I scowled. I was torn between admiring her for taking the risk out of my father's hands and being annoyed that she thought she knew Dragos so well. Did she really think that Dragos would kill *my* father and yet forgive *her* anything? Did my betrothal count less than all her stupid years of dancing?

"Tell yourself whatever you want," I said. "I appreciate the food. Next time, bring more."

"Hopefully, there won't be a next time," she said. "Your father *is* going to get you out of here, Reveka."

I snorted. "Except that I *promised* Dragos I'd marry him, in exchange for all your lives. And Pa is very insistent that I keep my promises." Of course, if I figured out how to heal Thonos, Dragos and I wouldn't have to marry. But Lacrimora didn't need to know that.

"It was a forced oath," Lacrimora said. "He was going to kill your father."

"Why does a forced oath mean less?" I asked, irritated at her casual dismissal of my sacrifice. If it was so easy to

· 273 ·

rescue me, what meaning did my action hold? "I had a choice! I made the bargain and gave my word."

Lacrimora rolled her eyes. "Look, you're what, four-teen years old?" she said. "You're a child. Your word is largely meaningless."

"I'm thirteen, and I'm old enough to be apprenticed, so my word is as good as yours. And I'm old enough to know that Pa needs to trust me. He can't fight Dragos!"

"Why not? He's a skilled soldier."

"There's a fair bit of distance between 'skilled soldier' and 'dragon-demon King of the Underworld!' Pa could die." *So could Dragos.* "Just. Tell Pa to please, please, *please* let me handle it. As long as I don't eat here, I can figure out how to leave." *All I have to do is stop the souls from dis-appearing. All I have to do is heal the land.*

"Don't worry," Lacrimora said. "I know how to kill a *zmeu.* I winkled it out of His Lordship during all those years of dancing."

"What?" All the air left my lungs. "Why would you kill Dragos?"

"It's the surest way to free you," Lacrimora said. There was a hard glint in her eyes. "He's a *zmeu.* You know what a *zmeu* is, Reveka! A dragon, a deceiver, a seducer, and a thief—"

"Dragos isn't like that—"

"Isn't he? He lured Maricara into the Underworld, he

tricked her into a duplicitous bargain, and he tortured us for six years. He *happily* took a child as his bride by threatening to kill her father, and—"

"Shut up!" I cried, nearly screaming with frustration. My voice rolled back to me, echoed by the trees, and I was embarrassed—by my voice, and by the angry tears that sprang to my eyes. I blinked them away. I didn't want Lacrimora to see me cry.

"I'm leaving," I choked out. "Take this basket—give all the flasks and the notes to Adina and tell her to try to wake the sleepers. Is this all the food you brought me?"

"That's all of it. We'll bring more soon."

"Soon! What does that even mean? You know that time doesn't run the same down here as it does up there, don't you?"

"I know."

"How was that never a problem, when you came down here every night?"

Lacrimora snorted. "Hasn't Dragos told you? He's the one who controls the pace of this world. He can make time stop or speed, whatever he likes."

I hated that she knew things about Dragos that I didn't. "Well, bring *lots* of food next time, in case Dragos is feeling capricious. As much as I can carry up the mountain. Maybe as much as Mihas and I can carry up the mountain together."

"The mountain?" Lacrimora asked.

"Yes, where the castle is," I said.

"There's a castle?"

"Of course," I said, suddenly feeling smug. I knew *something* about Dragos that Lacrimora didn't. "Where else would a king live?"

She didn't speak for a moment. "Reveka, do you *want* to marry the *zmeu*? Don't you care about your soul at all?"

"Of course I care about my soul! But is *my* soul any more important than all the souls in this realm?"

"The . . . souls in this realm?" she repeated.

I waved my hand at the Darkness around us. "This isn't an empty land, Princess! This is the Underworld." I found myself explaining, briefly, what I understood of the disappearing souls, which honestly wasn't much.

"Well," she said, dismissing them piously, "they aren't *Christian* souls."

"What does *that* matter? A soul is a soul. I wouldn't refuse to treat a *body* because it was a Turk! I'll do my best for these souls." I felt fierce and strong.

A light burst and faded on the mountainside—a door of the castle opening and closing. Mihas, playing lookout to see if my father would signal him? "I have to go," I said. "Tell my father—"

"If you're lucky, I won't tell him half the nonsense you've spouted tonight," Lacrimora said. "God bless your soul, Reveka! I hope he keeps you from foolishness."

Rather than argue with her further, I turned away. At the last moment, I remembered. "Lacrimora!" I called. "What was in your potion?" I rattled off the half dozen ingredients I had suspected, like the narcissus and sticklewort.

"You got all of those correct," she said. "Also, water from the lake. Scrapings from a gravestone. And a mushroom from this forest." She bit her lip. "Will that help you?" she asked. "Can you wake them, knowing that?"

It was the first time that she'd shown concern for the sleepers. I wondered: Did she *really* sleep at night?

"I don't know," I said. "What did the mushroom look like?"

She described it, nodded dismissively to me, and turned to leave.

I put my invisibility cap on as soon as her back was turned and followed her until she left the path to stride through the autumn forest. She came, in time, to a cliff face and wriggled through a narrow crack there. Pa's tunnel!

When she was truly gone, I turned back to the forest. I searched for Lacrimora's mushroom, nibbling bread as I went, until I found a few samples of fungus deep in the summer forest. I had no idea which was the one she had used, or if it was even important that she'd used a mushroom.

I was in a pretty little glade I didn't recognize; and

though I hadn't marked my path in or out, I wasn't worried about getting lost. It was a relatively small forest, and it was easily my favorite place in Thonos. I soaked in the weak, false sunlight. I wished the nymph would visit me again.

I took off my cap and lifted my face to the light. "O nymph Alethe!" I called. "It is I, Reveka, herbalist's apprentice, gardener's daughter, bride of Thonos, and I have questions for you!"

Nothing.

I chuckled at my brashness but waited just a moment longer in case she *had* heard. Still nothing.

I left the glade, and as I did so, I nearly stumbled. I saw something, something that I hadn't seen before. On a withered tree branch, tiny emerald leaf buds sprouted.

Perplexed, I stared at this for a long moment.

Surely this wasn't a sign of new growth. Surely it was not!

I looked for more evidence of this new life. Scattered here and there around the forest, green sprouts pushed from the crevices between stones and tarnish flaked from tree trunks, exposing bright silver underneath. These signs weren't everywhere—they weren't even to be seen in very many places—but there were changes in every season's woods.

How new was all of this? I hurried to the edge of the spring forest where I'd argued with Lacrimora. There,

I found the patch of dead dried moss I'd collected from while waiting for her. It was, without a doubt, much greener and springier than before.

I sat back on my heels.

Something had changed. But what?

I gathered my things and returned to the lakeshore.

I put my socks on my hands and clambered into my boat. Lacrimora's dark words returned to me: *I know how to kill a* zmeu.

I shivered and willed her never to return to Thonos again.

CHAPTER 33

I fell asleep that night with a full stomach and a sick heart. With regard to my stomach, even though I had vowed to portion the food out carefully so that it would last, I couldn't stop eating until sated. As for my heart, the thought of Didina and her dying mother lying still and silent in the western tower nearly broke it. And the thought of the disappearing souls—each soul was like a chain locked around my heart, holding it together.

And the thought of Pa fighting Dragos?

I rose as soon as I was rested and went to work.

My pace was frantic but not as fast as it could have been. I took careful notes as I went. I couldn't imagine anything worse than succeeding at waking *one* of the sleepers, or saving *one* of the souls, and being unable to replicate my success because I couldn't remember if I'd pulverized an herb or merely chopped it.

I lost track of the passage of time, and when Dragos came into the herbary, I blinked at him as though I hadn't seen him in ten years. His appearance caused my stomach to twist in knots of fear, but for a moment, I couldn't think why. Then I remembered: *Pa is coming to kill him*, and I was afraid for both of them.

Almost immediately, though, the fear was overcome by anger. "Why didn't you tell me you're the one who controls the passage of time?" I asked.

"That's not quite true," he said. "I *can* control whether this world follows the day and night cycle of the World Above, but it takes a great deal of concentration and attention. It is better for me and for Thonos to let it go along as it wills."

Oh. I was about to ask if controlling the time in Thonos meant controlling the time in all the Underworld when I realized then that he might now be curious to know how I'd learned as much as I had. I was an idiot! A double idiot, too, for being upset that Lacrimora knew something I didn't.

My hands shook as I held up a bowl of rose petals to the flickering candle, pretending to inspect them closely for mold and hoping that this action covered up the expression on my face.

"Why are you so upset?" Dragos asked.

I huffed. "I can't *see* very well in this candlelight. In the

World Above, we worked by sunlight for a reason. Mold is insidious."

The most astonishing thing happened then: Dragos hummed low in his throat, and a jeweled third eye opened high on his forehead. A beam of light shot forth, which he then directed at my bowl of petals.

There are a thousand stories of *zmei* in the world, and so many of them mention the third, blazing eye of the dragon that I had been a little surprised that Dragos did not seem to possess one. Now I was surprised that he *did* have one.

"Is this not bright enough?" he asked.

I nodded, too dry throated with wonder to attempt speech. When I had thoroughly determined that the roses contained no mold, he closed the eye, and his forehead became seamless once more. I wanted to touch his head and discover if I could feel the eyeball beneath his skin, but good manners kept me from asking.

Good manners—and a little fear.

"Is there anything else I can do for you?" Dragos asked.

I nodded. "I—" I fell silent, but his look was encouraging, so I tried again. "I have a few potions I want to test. On the river."

"Why?"

"When I met the nymph of Alethe, she told me that she was not as strong as she once was. She said she suffers—the river suffers—just like the souls."

Dragos was silent.

"Dragos?" I asked.

"I had thought—" He stopped, then said, "I had wondered if Alethe's waters were not as effective as they once were."

"Would you take me to the source of the Alethe?"

He wasted no time.

I knelt on the mossy bank where the river Alethe bubbled forth from the darkness beneath a half-ruined shrine. A cracked stone altar, dimpled with dead moss, was overlooked by a small statue of the nymph Alethe. The statue's paint had flaked away, and the face was worn to nothing.

I uncorked a potion I'd made of Underworld iris, rose, and mallow. I paused before pouring it into the water.

"This reminds me of when I first met you in the forest, except now I am the one casting things into the stream, not you," I said.

Dragos said nothing. He stared at the shrine and the statue of the nymph. I lowered the potion bottle to my lap, watching him.

"I guess you must have brought the plum blossoms from here," I said. "What were you doing, exactly?"

To my surprise, he answered. "I was honoring a memory."

"Whose memory?"

"Many years ago," he began, staring into the current as though looking into another world, "on exactly the day I met you, a woman. . . . No, not just 'a woman.' She was a sister to me. She threw herself into a river from a high place and drowned."

His stark words conjured a vivid picture. Too vivid. I also thought I had heard this story before. But the tale slipped away from my memory, like dawn's dreaming in the late afternoon.

"It was my fault," he added.

My mouth was dry. I licked my lips and looked away. I wanted to ask about his life before he became King of Thonos but didn't know how to begin.

I noticed the bottle in my hand and remembered what we had come here to do. I poured the remedy into the stream, where it was swallowed immediately.

I'm so very wrong about this, I thought. *If this is even the right tactic, a river and a whole land must need so much more than this tiny bottle to heal it.*

"Reveka?" Dragos asked. "Is there something I should be looking for?"

I wanted to cry out that I didn't know, that I had no idea what to look for, and why didn't he understand better what was going on with his own land? I almost threw the bottle into the stream but checked my motion at the last moment.

Chagrined, I stoppered the bottle and slid it back into the basket. I was throwing a tantrum, or nearly. Dragos *did* know what would save Thonos. It was I who stood in his way.

I got to my feet. "I need to rethink this. Let's try giving a remedy to a disappearing soul—if we can find one after it starts to thin but before it evaporates altogether?"

"We can but try," Dragos said.

On the flight back to the castle, I tapped his arm, which was wrapped securely around my waist. "I want to stop in the Queen's Forest," I said. "I want to gather more materials."

Wordlessly, he changed direction just a little, and moments later, he landed me in the spring forest.

And that's when I saw Didina.

She was standing on the path through the forest, running flat hands over the tops of the ferns, staring in minute concentration at the plants. She was dressed as always: short black and red striped skirt under a rectangular black apron; black leg wrappings over her stockings; leather shoes; and a white chemise embroidered by Adina.

I ran toward her, calling her name: "Didina! Didina, you're awake!"

But she didn't turn to me, didn't even look at me.

I stopped just short of touching her and stared. The light passed through her. She was a soul.

I screamed and clutched my head. "She's dead! Lacrimora has killed her! And now she's disappearing!"

"No." Dragos's voice was calm, matter-of-fact, as though I were not bawling like a newborn calf. "She's not dead. She's not one of mine at all—not even an eidolon."

"I— What?" I was jolted out of my tears and my rage and my wailing. "She's not . . . dead?"

"No." He waved his clawed hand in front of her, and she did not blink. She continued feeling the feathers of the ferns with her palms. "She's lost. But still very much attached to her body."

Now I was laughing with relief. "Oh, thank goodness. Thank God. She's fine, then. She's all right."

Dragos shook his head gravely. "Her body is alive, but she's trapped, wandering the Underworld. If she goes too far, the body will die."

I was silent for a long moment, absorbing this. Was this true of all the sleepers—were their souls in the Underworld? And the ones who slipped away from Adina's care, had they wandered too far?

I wiped my nose while Dragos politely watched Didina's face and not mine; he only turned to me when I said in a small voice, "Could you take me back to the castle, please?"

"I have a question," I said when Dragos set me down in the dark courtyard. "You said that your power does not extend where the sun shines. . . . Does that mean you cannot step into sunlight?"

"I cannot," Dragos said. "In a sense, I am a prisoner of my own kingdom, for I can never truly leave it. I cannot journey beyond the shadows at the edges of my land." Then, so low I almost didn't hear, "I miss the sun."

"You miss it?" I pounced on the phrase, turning my face up toward his voice. It was too dark to see him. "Were you ever able to go into the sun, then?"

"Yes."

"When? Why can't you now?"

"Before I became King here, I was freer."

"Then why become King at all?"

"It's a long story, Reveka," he said, leading me into the castle.

"Oh," I said meekly, as though that settled it. "Of course." Then I added, "I can see why you think I don't have time to hear it."

He gusted a sigh. "It was much like your decision to become my wife, Reveka; quickly made, to save another, and just as painful to me as your choice is to you."

I bit my lip to keep from saying something I'd regret.

I could make out the sounds of footsteps in the distance,

and then a light. Mihas emerged from the castle, bearing a lantern. I was grateful for the light and smiled widely at Mihas.

I glanced at Dragos, saw him watching me, watching Mihas. Puzzled, I tried to read his expression—and of course, that was when the Darkness returned and swallowed me whole. I didn't even have a chance to fight it. I fell into nightmares.

"Reveka," a voice said, cutting through the Darkness. There was a huge, warm hand holding mine, and another such hand across my forehead. I was being cradled in warmth. My nose was filled with the scents of ash and stone, almond and cherry bark.

I slit open an eye and saw Dragos's hand enveloping mine. My fingers were so slender and tiny in comparison to his. I closed my eyes and enjoyed that his skin felt warm and smooth and human.

We were not where I had fallen, in the courtyard. I had been moved. I lay on a thick carpet in front of the fire in Dragos's hall while he knelt beside me.

The Darkness seemed at bay for a moment, but I tasted the iron tang of blood on my lips. A nosebleed? Confirming my suspicion, Dragos dabbed a rag at my nostrils.

For a moment, I wondered what it would be like to

have Frumos here instead.

Frumos is Dragos, I corrected myself, quashing the dreamy girl within who kept trying to place the human face over the *zmeu*. *There is no Frumos. There never was.*

I sat up. Dragos left me the rag and retreated to his chair, where he watched me with shining dark eyes.

"I have patience," Dragos said, seemingly at random. "Or I thought I did."

"What?" I asked, standing up and holding the rag to my nose.

"You are reluctant. I am reluctant! You're barely more than a child, and— Anyway. I can see you are waiting— for escape, or for your father to come for you, or something. It doesn't matter." He spread his hands apart, bowed his head. He looked defeated. "Perhaps I should let you go."

"What?"

"Mere mortals cannot survive in this place for long, Reveka. If you do not become my bride, you will waste away down here and die under the strain of the Darkness. Alethe's waters alone cannot sustain you much longer. Do you see?"

"N-no. I don't see," I lied. I strode away from the fire, trying to buy myself time to think, to discover how to answer him. I checked to see if my nose had stopped bleeding. It had.

Dragos said, "You're blind, then."

I whirled to face him, as hurt and as angry as I'd ever been. Why was he doing this? He was the blind one! "Thonos *needs* a queen! So why don't you just force me to marry you? Or why didn't you force Lacrimora? Or Maricara, or any of the others?"

"I can't force it!" Dragos said. "I must have a *willing* bride. Do you think I would have danced around on my hooves for six years if I hadn't needed a *willing* bride?"

"The night I witnessed the dancing, the princesses didn't seem that willing!"

"Their father's stupid interference, with those iron shoes," he growled. "And if there had been *any other way*, don't you think I would have taken it?"

"Of course I do, Frumos!"

We both stopped then—stopped talking, stopped arguing. I stopped moving. The air between us filled with silence.

I'd called him Frumos.

"I am *not* Frumos," Dragos said, his voice so low I felt it more than heard it.

The tone of his voice made gooseflesh run up my arms. "Then you shouldn't have introduced yourself to me that way," I snapped. "It's your own fault, if you hate the name so much."

I thought I'd made him angrier, so I was surprised

when he started to laugh. I started to laugh, too.

I don't know what we might have said next, but then Mihas came in at a dead run. "They—the guards—they're bringing him!" Mihas panted.

"Who?" I asked.

Mihas's face was white, his eyes panicked. "Your father!"

CHAPTER 34

With a swirl of his cloak, Dragos left the room. My knees wobbled, and the Darkness that I had believed was defeated threatened to press me flat. But I hoisted my skirts and ran after Dragos, though I couldn't match his long stride. Mihas drew up the rear.

"Where are they taking him?" I gasped at Mihas.

"The throne room!"

I lost sight of Dragos in the dark, and had to let Mihas guide me with his torch.

The throne room was by far the most decorated place I'd seen in the castle. A variety of weaponry and armor hung on the walls, and a long trident with a stunted center prong was slotted upright into the arm of an ebonwood throne at the far end. Another, smaller throne sat beside the first. Between and behind the thrones rested a great iron scale.

By the time I entered the room, Dragos was already

seated on his throne, one hand resting on the shaft of his trident. The throne was large for a human but small for a *zmeu*. Dragos dominated the room and the throne, his hooves trailing halfway down the dais steps.

"Over here, Reveka," he said, patting the seat of the smaller throne. "He must see what you might become." Mihas tried to sidle into the room after me, but Dragos ordered him off with one word: "Go." The boy disappeared, and I felt bereft. I could have used a friendly face.

I climbed up the steps and settled myself on the edge of the seat, my stomach in knots. I felt the cold prickle of the Darkness catching up to me.

Lord Dragos inhaled deeply and sent a jet of flame out across the room. A thousand thousand candles lit, most so high above us that I hadn't known that they were there. The room blazed bright as day. No, *brighter*, for inset in the walls behind the candles were a myriad of faceted jewels. The Darkness should have skittered to unseen corners, but instead, it seemed to take up residence around my throat.

"Bring him in," Dragos called, his voice a low, rolling roar.

Doors opened at the far end of the room, and Pa was there, tiny and indistinct between two red-liveried guards, whose faces seemed made of bone.

The guards marched Pa to us at a slow pace. I nearly

twitched, so nerve-racking was this, but both Pa and Dragos appeared unmoved. When Pa was brought to a stop before us, I saw that his hands were bound. I shrieked and ran down the dais steps to him. I embraced him, then turned angrily to Dragos. "Unbind him!" I cried.

Dragos lifted one black claw, and a guard stepped forward and slashed Pa's bonds.

"Well?" Dragos said. "What will you offer me for her? Money? Jewels? As you can see"—he waved a set of claws at the jewels on the walls—"we are in no need of such here."

"I offer only myself," Pa said.

"What?" I cried. "That's no good, Pa! You can't be Queen of Thonos."

Dragos ignored me. So did Pa. Dragos leaned his spiny chin on one hand and regarded my father. "You come here armed only with that?"

"I was a soldier. A talented one, at that," Pa said. "I've fought for every prince in the land. I was in the Black Legion. I was field marshal for Vlad Ţepeş."

"If I need a general," Dragos said, "I have my own skills in that area."

Pa was silent for a moment, assessing. He glanced at me, then back at Dragos. "It's all I have to offer," he said quietly. "Please. She's just a child."

Well, that wasn't entirely true, but I didn't think I

should jump in to argue with Pa.

"When Demeter came to the Underworld to claim Persephone, she threatened the world with eternal winter if Hades did not comply," Dragos said. "That was a compelling argument. Yours is not."

"A threat to the world would move you?" Pa asked, furrowing his brow. "I can threaten the world. I could brush aside the names of Vlad and Attila and rain down hell on this earth if it meant freeing my daughter. I could make the Battle of Poienari look like a Christmas feast. I could tear open the throat of Corvinus's country and leave his blood for the Turks to drink. I could slash the flank of the Turkish Empire and lure in the Polish, and let them fight until Doomsday. I've always been a man who fought to create peace, but I could become a man who fights to create chaos. Tell me, Prince *Frumos*, is that what it would take?"

I stared at Pa. I'd never seen him like this. I'd never *imagined* him like this.

And why had Pa called my *zmeu* Prince Frumos?

Dragos leaned against the back of his throne. "I'd rather not see that," he said mildly. I almost thought he might be laughing at Pa, but his voice sounded serious. "I cannot take an unwilling bride, *Doamnule* Konstantin. I would not want one, and neither would my kingdom. She'll not take my food, so I'll not have her.

"Go now with my guards to my kitchens, and gather up that wretch Mihas, too. He has conspired to help her avoid eating my food, which is of course why I have no claim to her now. I want him gone with you when you two leave."

Pa didn't look triumphant. I didn't feel triumphant either, so at least we matched. Pa just gave a little bow, looked hard at me, and walked off with the guards. I watched them go, astonished.

When they were quit of the chamber, I turned to Dragos, who now stalked in circles around the throne room. He stopped beside a bowl of fruit and picked up a pomegranate, tossing it from hand to hand as he flopped back onto his throne.

"I don't understand!" I cried. "I promised to marry you to save him. To save all of them. How can you just let me go now?"

"It's as I said," Dragos replied. "I don't want an unwilling bride." He dug his claws into the pomegranate's tender flesh, splitting it open.

"So it has nothing to do with Pa's threat?"

"I egged him into that threat," Dragos said. "Even though I think he did mean it. Enough to try, and trying would be enough to make countries fall—Sylvania, at least." He ripped off a chunk of the pomegranate and tossed it down his gullet. The Darkness pressed against me, making it hard to think.

"No. No, it doesn't make sense. He knows something, and you know he knows it! I never told him about meeting you in the forest or beside the Little Well. I never once mentioned that I knew you as Prince Frumos. How did he know to call you that?"

"He has an invisibility cap; perhaps he overheard something."

"No, that's not *it*," I said, frustrated. He wasn't telling the truth! "It takes a liar to spot a liar, and you, Dragos, are lying." Annoyed with watching him nibble more pomegranate seeds, I picked up the fruit and threw it against the wall. It split into two parts. The Darkness hissed.

Dragos sighed. "I once lived in the world, Reveka. I was a prince once, and worshipped God, and walked in sunlight. Perhaps your father recognizes me."

I scowled, racking my brains for the name of a prince who'd passed from the world fourteen years before. "Ew. You're not Vlad Ţepeş, are you?"

He laughed bleakly. "No. It's part of that long story I've not told you, Reveka. And now there is no time to tell it."

"No. There's plenty of time. I'm not leaving." I climbed off my throne, intending to pace the chamber, but the Darkness pushed me down. I sank to the steps before my throne.

"You will leave," Dragos was saying. "I release you. Don't you understand?"

"No!" I said, struggling under the weight of the Darkness. "I don't understand anything! How can you release me? Think of Thonos, and the souls." *Think of yourself,* I wanted to add. *I can barely stand it here, with both you and Mihas. How can you stand it alone?*

He stared down at me. "I could force you to dance with me every night, too," he said at last. "But I found that sort of thing really wasn't to my taste, in the end."

I pounded my fist against my leg. "You're an idiot, then! A betrothal is a promise. Hold me to it! If I hadn't interfered, maybe you would have had a bride, in time, from among the twelve princesses."

He ignored that. "You're too young to marry. I was . . . overcome by the thought of the youth and life that you bring with you. And your love. Oh, not for me. But that you loved your father enough to give up your life for him. None of the princesses loved any of their sisters enough to do that."

"They were only half sisters to each other," I said, as if *that* were the important thing to consider. "And they would say that they loved each other too much to let any one of them sacrifice herself."

"Perhaps that's true. But *you* are not for this world."

I'm a little bit for this world, I thought, though I didn't know where the thought came from. I loved my herbary, rough and unsettled. I loved my forest, blighted but growing.

And really, in a way, I loved Dragos, too. Enough to

wish him a better life than the lonely stewardship of a dying and vulnerable kingdom.

I bit my lip. I glanced at the torn pomegranate lying against the wall, its juices trickling like blood. I thought of the sleepers in the World Above slipping away beneath Adina's watchful eye, of Didina's mother and the Duke of Styria dying in their towers, of the disappearing souls, of Didina, poisoned for trying to save her mother. I thought of the nymph Alethe, and how she had seemed so certain that an herbalist in Thonos would end the blight on the kingdom. How I'd come to hope for this myself.

Maybe in a thousand years I could save the sleepers, but I didn't know how right then. I had to choose: heal the land that I *knew* I could heal so simply, or stick like a leech to dwindling hope and lose both the sleepers and Thonos.

I plucked the seeping half pomegranate from the floor. A small piece of flesh dangled from it, five seeds attached to one other, shimmering darkly. I snagged them and tossed them into my mouth.

I closed my eyes. The juice burst on my tongue; the seeds crunched against my teeth. The Darkness drew back. I breathed deeply.

When I opened my eyes, Dragos was giving me *such* a look, and I realized that the Darkness was still there, still all around, all-encompassing—but that the Darkness was now nothing of the sort. I could *see*, not just within the circles of candlelight but far into the hallway and out the windows.

"It's daylight?" I asked, bewildered. I climbed to my feet to look outside.

"It is as it ever was," Dragos said. "The dead and the immortals have always seen it thus. And those who have eaten here."

"Even Mihas?" I asked, and even as I asked, I realized that he had never carried candles or lanterns except for my sake.

I stared outside. It was as if the world were lit by a thousand suns the size of dust motes, diffuse and tiny, by stars brighter than stars, bright enough to see color by. A wide valley spread below Castle Thonos; small figures roamed back and forth—distant souls.

I breathed in deeply, and it was as if I could smell the grass of the valley, all the way up here. I breathed in again and caught the mineral tang of the lake, and the scent of the brass trees in the Queen's Forest.

My forest.

The Darkness laughed, and there was no evil in it. It wrapped around me, and it was warm like a cloak, and I could breathe.

I felt like the whole world—the whole of the Under-world, that is—had accepted me, in that moment. Though one glance at Dragos dispelled that illusion.

He was angry.

"You haven't *won* the argument," Dragos said. "Eating

here merely puts you under my power, and I still wish you to leave."

I considered this. I didn't feel any impulse to obey him. In fact, I mostly felt hunger roaring to life. I bit into the fruit and scrutinized him as I chewed, and offered him the other half of the fractured pomegranate. He stared at it.

"I understand that you don't want to marry me," I said. "I mean, I don't know *why*, since I'm simply delightful to be around. But to each his own taste. It's just—for the good of your kingdom, I'd think you'd have me." I joggled the pomegranate at him.

"Don't you understand?" he growled. "I'm releasing you for your own *good*. Take your soul back to the sunlight and give it to God while you can."

I ignored that. I had to. If I condemned my soul by being Queen of Thonos, I had probably already done the deed. "I ate five seeds with my first bite," I told him.

"So?"

"So send me away for now. For a time. But then I'll return for good," I said. "In five years. One seed for each year."

"Five years," he whispered.

"I'll come back," I said. "I'll go with my father as you want today, but when I'm older, I'll come back."

He tilted his head slightly, thinking. "And then what?"

"I'll come back and marry you." I waggled the pomegranate at him some more. "Give Thonos her willing bride."

Reluctantly, he took the fruit from my hand.

"Now, say yes," I said.

I thought I had him. I didn't. "No," he said, crushing the fruit so the juice ran out between his fingers.

I thought about simply plopping down on the throne beside him and promising to stay, here and now. I thought about chaining myself to something.

My mind was in turmoil. Everything I thought I had wanted in the world—my own herbary, and the peace to practice my art—had paled when confronted by more simple needs, like sunlight and food. But now those barriers were gone, and the Underworld looked like a blessing. But . . . honestly, Dragos and Mihas and Thela were not enough company. I needed friendships. And a father. Could I really live in the dark-walled world, as the nymph had called it, when the sun-walled world was free to me?

And my obligation was at an end. Dragos had said so himself. I could want to heal Thonos, but in the end, could I force him to marry me? Thonos probably needed a willing groom as well as a willing bride.

And Dragos was most unwilling.

I couldn't talk around the lump of tears in my throat. I bobbed a pathetic curtsy and turned to leave.

Only I caught the flicker of something blue out of the corner of my eye as I turned. Before I even realized what it was, I shouted a wordless shout.

But Dragos was already in motion, pulling the gleaming trident from its notch on his throne and jabbing the butt of it into the blue flicker, then swinging his weapon around to strike from above.

The blue flicker became Armas, with the tatters of my frail second invisibility cap slithering off his head over his ears. He bore down grimly on Dragos with a sword, aiming for the center of Dragos's head, where the third eye resided.

I knew without a shadow of a doubt that Lacrimora had sent him to kill Dragos.

With one wave of his trident, Dragos disarmed Armas; with another, he slipped Armas's feet out from under him; another motion and Armas was on the floor, with the two long prongs of the trident around his neck and the short center prong pressed to his windpipe.

"I was letting her go," Dragos said.

"I was doing my duty to God, *zmeu*," Armas replied.

Without turning his head, Dragos said, "Reveka, leave."

I had been frozen in terror until then, but now a calm stole over me, and I walked forward and put my hand on the trident. "Mercy," I said.

"For him? Why?"

I shrugged. "Is there a reason good enough to spare one man over another, when simple mercy is requested? I could lie and say that he has two small children—"

"I do," Armas said.

"Hush. No, you don't." I was pretty sure. "I could say that it will hurt Otilia, and Sylvania, and me, if he dies. I could even suggest that you might fare better without the blight of his unnecessary death on your soul . . . but I simply cry mercy."

And I knew, then, that Dragos had to grant me the mercy I requested. I *knew* this, the same way that I knew I breathed—if I thought about it, I could count the breaths, but if I didn't think about it, I kept on breathing. It was part of what I had gained when I'd eaten the pomegranate.

Dragos's voice was harsh. "Go, call for the guards. We will bind him. Swear to me that you will leave him bound until he passes the borders of the Underworld; swear to me that you will never make him another invisibility cap, or let one fall into his possession."

"I swear, to all of those things," I said, almost laughing, exultant in my newfound power to grant mercy.

I dashed into the hall and called for the guards.

CHAPTER 35

We were an odd procession, entering the Queen's Forest: me in royal clothes but wearing peasant shoes and snacking on figs, Mihas looking dazed and carrying an armload of herbs from my herbary, and Pa nudging a bound Armas ahead of him.

I was gaping at the changes in the forest. Every step I took sent out a new wave of invigoration. Flowers unwilted at my passing, and tarnish vanished from tree trunks before my eyes. I was so enthralled, I didn't notice at first that no one was following me anymore. When I turned back, Mihas, Armas, and Pa were all standing stock-still on the path, staring straight ahead.

"What—?"

Then I saw her, the nymph Alethe, poised in the dappled shadows of the forest, looking much more substantial than when I first met her. She smiled and bowed, holding two chalices out to me: one plain, of dark iron; the other filigreed, and bright silver.

"Hail the Queen of Thonos," Alethe crowed.

"But I'm not the Queen of Thonos," I said. "Dragos doesn't intend to marry me. This is my escort out of the Underworld." I waved my hand in front of Pa's eyes, but he didn't blink.

"He can't hear you. I've . . . stilled him. All of them."

"Why?"

"To give you this." She held out the chalices, and unthinkingly, I took them. The cold of them made my arms ache to the elbows.

"What are these?" I gasped. From the iron cup, the scent of forest loam caught in my nose, making me want to sneeze. From the silver one, a waft of spring pollen almost finished the job. I held in the sneeze, though, by thinking of the word *cucumber*. It always works.

"You know the Water of Life, the Living Water, Alethe's gift. That is always carried in silver or stone. What you do not know is the Water of Death, which kills but also heals the wounds of the dead. Living Water brings the dead to life. Your sleepers upstairs, the ones whose souls wander this realm, are not dead. And since you cannot bring to life that which is not dead . . . So first, death; then life, to wake the unwakeable sleepers."

"You want me to *kill* them?"

The nymph tilted her head. "And bring them back to life."

"How did you know— No, wait. *Why* didn't you tell me this when we met?"

"I was not fully myself before," she said. "The Water of Life could not have restored life when you and I met. And I myself could not remember such simple things." She held up a hand, which looked as solid as my own. "With no queen in this realm, the powers of Alethe were fading."

"I told you," I said with some asperity. "I'm not going to be the queen."

"You already are," she said, completely unperturbed. "You did not eat just any fruit in this world—you ate the pomegranate, the fruit that makes indissoluble marriage, and the fruit that the dead consume in order to be reborn. You became the Intercessor of Souls in that moment, the true Queen of Thonos."

"I—" I paused. "I *did*? Does the *King* of Thonos know this?"

"I'm sure he'll figure it out." She waved a hand at the path. "Now. Go to work. You and you alone possess the power of rebirth in this country. There is no one better suited to the task of awakening those trapped between life and death."

"And . . . all because I ate a pomegranate, instead of . . . a fig?"

The nymph smiled. "If you choose to believe that, certainly; some would argue that it was your fate."

"Fate is for people too lazy to make choices," I said.

Her smile grew. "Maybe that's true. In another life, I made my choices and did not wait for fate—though that's not how they tell it in the stories."

"Wait—in another life? What other life?"

She laughed. "I will tell you the next time we meet. Safe journey to you, sister," she said, stepping backward into the trees.

"Wait! Who were you? Alethe!"

She was gone, and I had no notion of what to do now. My hands were full, and I was reluctant to let go of the chalices. Pa and the others stood still, staring into the middle distance. I contemplated them for a long moment and decided to try the obvious thing first. "Wake up!"

They came alert instantly. Pa stared at me and what I held. "Where did you go? And what are you carrying?"

"I have been given a gift," I said. "And it will wake the sleepers."

Princess Lacrimora waited at the tunnel entrance to greet us when we came up from the Underworld. Well, really, she was there to greet Pa, throwing her arms around him and giving him a big kiss, from which I averted my eyes.

Then she gave me a sort of perfunctory hug, too, which I returned stiffly. Armas she also embraced; Mihas she ignored, which suddenly made me irate. Mihas had been the one who gave up his freedom to come help me—Mihas had been the one to pass me food from the World Above, and now she acted like he didn't matter?

Soon after, Princess Otilia came at a run, heading straight into Armas's embrace. She untied his bonds and murmured to him in undertones by turns desperate and loving. It was clear that their courtship was no longer secret, nor troubled. They had probably used the time I was in the Underworld to their advantage.

Then Lacrimora and Otilia took Mihas and Armas off to who knows where. Lacrimora gave Pa a significant look on her way out, and said to me, "You must be hungry." She departed, leaving Pa and me alone.

"Well?" Pa asked in a quiet voice.

"Well what?" I asked.

"What do you think?"

"What does that matter? *You* have to live with her."

"And you, too. She'll be your mother."

"Stepmother," I hissed. Pa winced. "Oh, Pa! Why Lacrimora?"

"She saved your life—several times—you know," Pa said.

"She did not! And she poisoned Didina!"

Pa sighed. "Think back on it."

"I've thought back on it," I said. "I had days and days to think back on it. My conclusion is that any time she did me a favor, it had nothing to do with *me*."

"Well," Pa said, after a pause. "Maybe I won't marry her, then."

I rolled my eyes. I couldn't believe my father had snatched me from the bowels of the Underworld, that I was for all intents and purposes married to a dragon-demon, and I was even now a queen—and Pa and I were squabbling like this. And not over anything interesting, but rather over whether or not he was going to marry Lacrimora. "Marry her! She's a princess. You won't get another shot at a princess."

Pa said, "She's the one I want, Reveka, and I knew it as soon as I saw you didn't like her."

"Contrary, obstinate man," I grumbled.

"She poisoned Didina to save her soul—you do realize that?"

I did realize that, or realized that Lacrimora believed it. But that didn't mean I was going to start naming herbs after her. "Do what you want," I said. "I don't see how you can *love* her, but do what you want."

"Did I never explain to you about love, Reva?" Pa asked. I gave him a look, and he laughed uncomfortably. "I guess not. Let me put it in a way you'll understand. Love is like stinging nettles. Only they prick from the inside out, starting at your heart and bursting on around. It's worst when it gets here"—he rubbed the bridge of his nose—"then your vision goes a little strange. But eventually the nettles stop stinging—once she agrees to kiss you. But they start right back up again when she agrees to marry you—"

"Pa," I interrupted, "that's not love, that's fear."

Pa shook his head, looking off admiringly in the direction where Lacrimora had disappeared. "Same thing, in my case."

Pa wanted me to eat, sleep, bathe, and sleep again, in that order, but I could think only of the sleepers in the western tower. "I have to do this, Pa," I said, shaking off his guiding hand for the third time as he tried to divert me to the kitchens.

"Well, let me come with you, at least," Pa said, when he saw I couldn't be dissuaded.

When I entered the tower, Adina was overjoyed to see me, but I had a purpose. Reunions could wait.

I took a spoon and dipped it into the iron chalice. "What's that?" Adina asked, as I dripped the Water of Death into Didina's mouth. I didn't tell her. I could barely believe I was doing this.

I stroked Didina's throat gently, so that she swallowed. I waited for something dramatic, but nothing happened. I couldn't even tell if she stopped breathing. I took a breath of my own, then grabbed a clean spoon to avoid cross-contamination and dipped it into the Water of Life. I dripped several spoonfuls into her mouth and again massaged her throat.

Nothing happened. She didn't even swallow. I wondered how I was going to explain to Adina that I'd killed her granddaughter. I pushed despair back for a moment, calling, "Wake up, Didina," in a gentle voice. "You and I, we have much work to do. But you have to wake up."

She swallowed convulsively. Air rushed into her lungs.

Her brown eyes opened.

She struggled to sit up, but she was too weak to do so. She turned her head on her pillow. "Grandma?" she croaked, catching sight of Adina.

Adina froze, staring down at Didina; then her shriek of joy pierced my eardrums as the old woman got down on the floor with her granddaughter and held her and cried and whooped, while the poor girl stared around her in dazed shock. Pa, though, immediately drew me on to Didina's ma, and hovered over me while I gave first the Water of Death, and then the Water of Life, and urged the dying woman to wake.

And she did.

The following shrieks of joy were even louder, and I confess my own eyes clouded with tears when Didina saw her mother move and talk; but Pa and I had to ignore them. We had to move on, to Sfetnic, to Iulia, to all the rest.

And that's how we woke the sleeping dead of Castle Sylvian.

CHAPTER 36

Somehow, Pa got most of the public credit for breaking the curse.

Prince Vasile made him the count of some obscure hamlet in the hill country, and only reluctantly. Prince Vasile, I learned, was unconvinced that my father had done anything important toward breaking the curse. Vasile wanted to credit the iron shoes with the end of the dancing. But Pa was the one who was known to have gone down into the Underworld with an invisibility cap and to have come back up with twelve princesses and thirty lost men, so Pa got the credit and the right to marry one of Vasile's daughters. Even though all the princesses knew very well that it was my promise to marry Lord Dragos that had freed them.

I might have taken umbrage at this, but the fact that I could hear the worms crawling in the earth, and seeds growing, and that I could now read in the dark and smell the rain coming from miles away, and could put Mihas or anyone I liked to sleep with a wave of one hand—these things more than made up for credit. The secret of my new identity and my growing powers lay in my chest like a second heart, thumping slowly beneath my skin.

It wasn't as if I could have used the dowry to join a convent now anyway, not when I'd become, essentially, a pagan goddess.

Well, I didn't *know* if I was a goddess. I tried consulting with Brother Cosmin about the situation obliquely, but that sort of thing can't really get answered in the hypothetical. I tried not to let it keep me awake at night.

Becoming a count gave Pa an income and some land. It also made me a lady, which meant that I continued wearing stupid overlong dresses and padded slippers. Actually, things were worse than that: They plucked my forehead and made me wear a butterfly hennin, and the Princess Consort tried to teach me needlework. This was all supposed to be a thank-you for waking the sleepers—which I did get the credit for—and most especially for sending vials containing the Waters of Death and Life to the Duke of Styria and averting a Hungarian war, at least through that particular avenue.

I didn't see how plucking and needlework were

supposed to feel like *gratitude*.

The needlework I got out of by saying I was writing an herbal instead. This was fine; no one tried to consult me on silks if I scratched diligently enough at my vellums. The plucking—that I had to live with.

One of the only good things about ladyhood was that it meant that I had a lady's maid, and I used her to pass messages between me and Didina. Since I was a lady, I couldn't be Brother Cosmin's direct apprentice anymore, though I did still study with him daily. I just didn't have to do as much work.

Didina proved a good friend in the days that followed and became my faithful ally against Lacrimora, too—not that my stepmother was irredeemably wicked. But even if you poison people for their own good, you're still a poisoner. And maybe just a little bit wicked.

The other good thing was that I had enough rank to strong-arm Marjit into confessing that she'd been the one who'd told everything to Pa about my first invisibility cap, which was how Pa knew to come steal it. Unfortunately, since my rank in the surface world hung off Pa's, I did *not* have enough rank to take him to task for stealing my cap. So I just put him to sleep during a fancy dinner, so that he went facedown into the sour soup. Just the once. It eased my ire terrifically.

∽∾∾

Otilia married Armas, in spite of the fact that he'd gone into the Underworld when she had made him promise not to. Since he had given his promise when he was only seventeen or so, he didn't think he had to abide by it, and that's what they'd been fighting about, on and off, for years.

I wanted to be mad at Armas for trying to kill Dragos, but in the end, I couldn't stay angry. For one thing, he was grateful to me for saving him. For another, he was the one person who understood the most about what I had become in the Underworld—he'd overheard so much, and then I'd interceded for his soul. And for a third thing, I still had to match wits with Lacrimora, and I had no time to be angry at anyone else.

Lacrimora married Pa in a double ceremony, when Otilia married Armas. Only half of the princesses attended the wedding, since the other half were already on their way to marry various princes around the region. Including Maricara, who was finally packed off to the Duke of Styria, and Tereza, who went home with Iosif the Saxon, even though she protested that now that the curse was over, she could do better.

Too bad. I rather thought Lacrimora and Iosif deserved each other.

I enjoyed the marriage festivities well enough, all through the day of feasting and into the night, right until

Mihas asked me to dance with him. He'd been ridiculously calf-eyed toward me since our return, and I was smart enough to realize that he thought that we were going to end up married, just because Pa didn't seem to glower at him anymore.

And the problem with that was that Mihas had turned out to be a brave and stalwart fellow, and after what we'd been through together in the Underworld, I might have come around to his handsomeness. And while I couldn't lead him on, I couldn't tell him I was planning to go back to Thonos in five years, either, even though if anyone could understand what had *really* happened once Pa had left the throne room, it was probably Mihas.

But after he'd spent all that time helping me keep free of the Underworld, would he understand why I had eaten the pomegranate?

I turned Mihas down cold for the dance, and when he tried to follow me, I ducked behind a pillar and put on my invisibility cap, which I always carried with me lest someone else try to steal it. I sneaked out to the courtyard of the Little Well, where I leaned over the lip of the well, staining my dress with moss and dirt, and breathed in the sharp, stony scent of the river Alethe.

"I'd dance with you if you were here," I called down the well shaft.

I imagined his *zmeu* ears picking up the sound of

my voice in the darkness.

"Reveka?" Pa was calling. I slid the invisibility cap off my hennin so he could see me. My veil was now a wrinkled mess, no doubt, and I'd definitely bent the wires into some strange shape, but it had been worth it to escape Mihas. "You *could* give the cowherd a chance," Pa said. Pa appreciated what Mihas had done as much as I did.

"He's actually a sheepherder, Pa, and no, I couldn't," I said honestly.

He was silent for a moment, framing his next question. "Is it . . . is it that you . . . well. That devil didn't hurt you, did he? I know it took some time to free you. But I wasn't too late, was I?" Pa asked.

I stared down at the Little Well for a long moment, noticing the small patch of the Darkness that dwelled there. Sunlight never shone upon the well and never would. All through the day, the castle walls and towers would keep it in shadow.

He could visit me here anytime, if he wanted.

"Reveka?" Pa asked. "Was I too late?"

"No, Pa," I lied softly. "You weren't too late."

"Good," he said, relieved, and hugged me. I thought, *Fine time to start trusting my word, Pa,* but left it alone. I yearned to confess the full extent of what had happened in the Underworld, but there never was going to be a right time or a right way.

"I'm going to enjoy the night air a little longer," I said, and sent him inside to his new wife. Quickly. For I heard soft footsteps at the other end of the courtyard, and the swish of a cape. I turned.

Dragos was there, wearing his handsome, human face. "I heard you call to me," he said.

I couldn't hide my smile, though I tried by stroking the moss growing beside the Little Well. I was shy to see him, shy to ask if he had noticed yet that I was actually the Queen of Thonos.

"And you came," I said at last—and with that, we were easy with each other. Easier, anyway.

It had taken me a long time to see that he was cursed, as bad as Castle Sylvian or its princesses had been. He was an unhappy monarch, trapped in his *zmeu* shape in the Underworld, in his human shape in the World Above. A proper *zmeu* had control over these things, so clearly he was not a proper *zmeu*. His loneliness was palpable. His previous life must be the key to all of it. And I was sure the story didn't start with plum blossoms floating on a stream.

I wondered what mixture of lies and truth I might use to persuade him to tell me the story of who he was, of who he had been in his life before the Underworld.

"How is Thonos?" I asked.

"Waiting for you," he said.

"Oh? You noticed that, did you?"

"It was hard to miss. The souls have stopped disappearing, but the rest of it—the blight won't be entirely erased until you come and gaze upon it." He shook his head as though amazed. "But it can wait five years now."

I couldn't help the grin that stole over my face, and I hugged myself a little. "Five years till I return forever," I said. "But I never said I couldn't come visit." With that, the tiny Darkness around the well slunk and purred like a cat. "Five seeds. Five days? I could come to Thonos every five days, if Thonos needs me."

"Five seeds, five days . . . why not?" Dragos perched on the edge of the well, tracing the prisoners' inscription with his thin human fingertips.

"Why not?" I agreed. I was about to burst with hope and pleasure, so I changed the subject. "You know, the rumors about this well are very strange. That carving you're touching is supposed to be a curse from the Turkish prisoners who dug it."

"It's not a curse, it's a warning," he said. "It says that this is a gate to the land of the Lord of the Dead."

"I—oh, you can *read* that? Is it actually Turkish?"

He nodded. I tried to suppress a smile, but it slipped out. He couldn't keep his identity a secret forever, not if I was coming to visit every five days. Each time we spoke, I would grow closer to learning who he was.

And in five years? Well, five years was a very long time. Plenty of time to unlock his secret and break his curse.

Considering what I'd done for Sylvania in the course of a single summer, I figured it would be easy.

AUTHOR'S NOTE:

I f you look for Sylvania on a map of fifteenth-century eastern Europe, you won't find it. It's a fictitious region of Romania that I wedged between Maramureș, Bucovina, and Transylvania, created because all the regions of Romania have a clear and fixed history that seemed wrong to tamper with. I needed a place that could be cursed by a *zmeu*, menaced by Hungary, and resigned to twelve unmarriageable princesses. Since Transylvania means "the land beyond the forest," I thought, "Then let's make the land where the forest starts," and thus Sylvania was born.

My Castle Sylvian has a lot in common with the real-world Hunyad Castle (*Castelul Huniazilor* in Romanian) in Hunedoara, Transylvania. Both castles were built on Roman ruins, and each houses a deep well that was dug by Turkish prisoners. The well at Hunyad Castle doesn't have a warning about the Underworld, however, but rather a message that is rumored to say "You have water, but no soul" (but actually says something like "He who wrote this inscription is Hasan, who lives as slave of the Christians").

During the Middle Ages in Europe, medicine and herbalism were pretty much the same thing. After the fall of Rome, writings on medicine and herbs were preserved in monasteries, which became centers of official medical knowledge (Brother Cosmin, Sister Anica, and Reveka all studied in monasteries). However, the fall of Rome probably had little impact on folk medicine, as people also grew herb gardens and made observations about plants in the countryside (the way the herb-wife Adina worked).

A few notes on invisibility and herbs: Some medieval herbalists really did believe that fern seeds were invisible, and that the seeds also conferred invisibility. Fern seeds, of course, don't exist: ferns reproduce through spores, and have a strange life-cycle compared to other plants. If you've ever hung around any ferns (I spent a lot of time staring at them from underneath during ambushes when I used to play paintball), you know that they get funny, warty things on the undersides of their leaves. Few people would guess that those warts, or the fine-grained black dust they release, are the equivalent of seeds. Can't blame the medieval herbalists for being confused!

Even the great herbalist Hildegard of Bingen (1098–1179) had some magical ideas about ferns. She wrote in her *Physica* that ferns cured hearing loss by just being placed on the ear (but never *in* the ear—she's quite specific about it), and that demons would avoid a person who carried ferns with them. Hildegard is a fascinating historical figure, and besides being a master herbalist and a healer, she wrote music, plays, and poems. She founded and ran two abbeys, went on preaching tours, and corresponded with Popes and kings. Though she is widely referred to as Saint Hildegard (as Reveka thinks of her), she was never officially canonized. Hildegard was an amazing woman, and extremely worthy of Reveka's reverence.

ACKNOWLEDGMENTS

I want to thank my readers and critiquers. First, the Feral Writers: Julie Winningham, David Klecha, and honorary Feral Julie DeJong. Excelsior! group: Sarah Zettel, Lawrence Kapture, Jonathan Jarrard, Elizabeth Bartmess, Christine Pellar-Kosbar, Karen Everson, and Diane Rivis. The Hastings Point Workshoppers of 2009: Elizabeth Shack, Emily Kasja Herrstrom, Amy O. Lau, Stephen Buchheit, and Victoria Witt. And also Leah Bobet, Marissa K. Lingen, Jason Larke, Sunny Smith, and Kate Riley, and for more than just the reads. Thanks also to Sarah Prineas, Sherwood Smith, Jim C. Hines, Rachel Neumeier, and Stephanie Burgis for kindnesses rendered.

Thank you to my family—Kayla Fuller, Raluca Cook, Iulia Forro, Anne and Rick Fuller, and Bev Cook in particular for specific help on the book and giving me writing space and time, but thank you *all* for your support.

Thank you to my awesome coworkers at MLibrary at the University of Michigan: not only for the collections, the articles on Romanian folklore, and the OED, but for all the help and encouragement.

Thank you extremely very much no-more-than-that to my editor, Anne Hoppe, and my agent, Caitlin Blasdell, and everyone on their teams who helped this book along.

And thank you to Dann Fuller, who told me to go to Romania when I dithered and who made me write even when I didn't want to.